A Sense of Entitlement

A Sense of Entitlement

CHERYL MILDENHALL

Black Lace novels are sexual fantasies.
In real life, make sure you practise safe sex.

First published in 1996 by
Black Lace
332 Ladbroke Grove
London
W10 5AH

Copyright © Cheryl Mildenhall 1996

Typeset by CentraCet Limited, Cambridge
Printed and bound by Mackays of Chatham PLC

ISBN 0 352 33053 8

Chapter One

The vast lobby of the Sorbonne reverberated to the sound of Angelique's heels as they click-clacked determinedly across the smooth, white marble. The tone of her footsteps was clear and precise, echoing exactly the way she habitually moved and thought and reacted – even to the most shocking news. In her hand she held proof of that – a letter containing information of earthshattering proportions. And yet she was calm. Wasn't she? She had read it and yet hadn't gone completely to pieces. Had she? Her life wasn't about to change irrevocably and forever, was it? Oh, yes, it bloody well was!

Despite the fact that her name, appearance and inimitable sense of style were all undeniably French, Angelique was English. And even though she was living in Paris with her French mother and therefore duty-bound to speak French, she thought in English. It was almost an act of defiance but right at that moment she badly needed to swear and curse – she had a lot of anger to release – and unfortunately there didn't seem to be an English phrase crude enough to sum up her exact feelings. English was altogether too polite and restrained for her liking. What she needed were some good old Gallic oaths.

At the bottom of the wide flight of steps which led up to the main part of the university were several polished wood benches. Choosing one of them, she sat, crossed her legs primly at the ankle, folded her hands neatly in her lap and began to mutter a bilingual stream of obscenities under her breath.

To the innocent passer-by she looked like any other young French woman. A little more attractive than most perhaps. Her slight frame and delicate bone structure was amply covered with lightly tanned flesh and therefore gave her the appearance of someone who was just a bit too voluptuous to be fashionably thin. Yet she neither attempted to conceal nor flaunt her curves. Her body was kept neatly in check with expensive lingerie that fitted her measurements exactly – nothing squashed in or pushed up. And her outer clothing was well-tailored, understated and chic. Today it was a smart little navy skirt – plain and straight with a hem that finished just an inch above the knee – worn with a canary yellow cashmere jumper, opaque navy tights and matching court shoes with a two-inch heel. Even her long, silky brown hair, which could look wild and tousled if she let it, was kept under control and away from her high brow by a thin, navy head-band.

She looked stylish and self-possessed and not in the least bit dominated by the magnificence of her surroundings as she sat patiently and waited. But her hazel eyes glittered, her generous chest heaved and her full lips looked increasingly petulant as she mouthed each filthy syllable.

The minutes passed slowly, marked by the shifting of the shadows cast across the floor as sunlight streamed through each of half a dozen high windows. That was until, from behind her at the top of the wide marble

2

staircase, several pairs of mahogany doors burst open to release a heaving tide of the best France had to offer by way of its younger generation. The *crème de la crème* of the nation's educational successes.

They were eager, bright-eyed young things whose brains still whirled with the thoughts and ideas that had just been imparted to them and whose mouths repeated the wisdom of professors as easily as Angelique's now spouted the language of fishermen and whores.

A male voice interrupted her mutterings. 'Camus was a bastard! He has made my life hell this afternoon.'

Angelique was aware of the body flopping down beside her just an instant before the familiar voice spoke. She turned and smiled vacantly into the roguish face and simultaneously inhaled his overtly male odour.

'Is he one of your tutors?' she asked innocently.

Dark eyes creased at the corners with amusement. 'No, you idiot. Camus was a writer – very famous, very French. Even with your appalling English education you should know that.'

'Oh, yes. I suppose I should.' Angelique smiled apologetically and she felt her heart clench hard as she realised several things simultaneously. How close François was to her right at that moment. How exceptionally masculine he seemed and how she had come to depend on that. And how, very soon, she would have to leave him.

'Are we staying here indefinitely or do you want to go back to my place and fuck?' François said with a grin that was wolfish and full of promise.

Feeling uncommonly feminine and submissive in his dark presence, Angelique felt herself turning coy and positively dimpling as she replied. 'What do you think?' She regarded him flirtatiously from under long, dark lashes but didn't despise herself for her behaviour. On the contrary. He loved it and she got the best of his loving. It was a good arrangement.

As always, they took the most direct route to his

apartment building through her favourite part of the city, the lively, cosmopolitan Latin Quarter. Walking hand in hand along the Boulevard St-Michel – or the Boulevard St-Mich as François and his friends called it – they concentrated on dodging the inevitable little huddles of tourists who punctuated the pavement as they pored anxiously over maps of the city. For a while it prevented Angelique thinking about other things but she nevertheless breathed an inward sigh of relief when she and François veered off into the quiet sanctuary of the Jardin du Luxembourg. Skirting around the formally laid out flower-beds, which were just starting to burst forth with a profusion of colour, Angelique allowed herself to soak up the quiet dignity of the seventeenth-century gardens. Although it was late afternoon it was still warm and sunny and, as she gripped François' hand a little tighter, she felt the turmoil inside her dissipate to be replaced by a good-to-be-alive feeling.

In an instant her mood changed again. It was all very well enjoying her health and well-being but certain people couldn't do that any more. Certain people were lying six feet underground and pushing up the daisies in a pretty English churchyard. People like her father; or at least, the man she had always thought of as her father. That was until today. Until she had read the letter he had left for her. Tears sprang suddenly to her eyes and she pulled François over to a bench, the green paint flaking to show the metal underneath, tugged at his hand to make him sit beside her and thrust the crumpled envelope into his face.

'Read that,' she urged.

François gave her a startled gaze, noted her distraught expression and realised this would not be a good time to make one of his usual flippant remarks.

'Okay,' he said slowly. Taking the envelope from her he extracted two large sheets of embossed paper, the top one emblazoned with the logo and details of a firm of

London solicitors. He read the contents carefully. *'Merde!'* he exclaimed succinctly, when he had finished reading the whole thing.

'After two years at the Sorbonne, is "shit" the most intelligent thing you can find to come out with?' Angelique said, feeling quite superior to him for a change.

She instantly regretted her sarcasm. Although she felt like exploding with pent-up emotion she needed an ally and recognised that François was her best bet. Her mother didn't want to know. Her mother hadn't wanted to hear anything about Angelique's father since their divorce ten years earlier. *Father!* She spat the word out of her mind. There was no way she could call him that any more.

She tried to soften her expression as she continued to gaze at François. God, he was good-looking. Dark and rakish, with long, curly black hair and a small gold hoop earring in his left ear which made him look more like a Romany gypsy than a student of European Literature. She watched the way his lean body swayed toward hers invitingly as he shrugged.

'I am sorry, *chérie*. It was a shock, that's all,' he said, pursing full red lips then parting them to reveal brilliant white teeth.

Impulsively, Angelique leaned forward and kissed him on the mouth. 'I know. I'm the one who should be apologising. It's not your fault,' she murmured as she broke away. Her own lips curved into a smile. 'Now, never mind that. Didn't you mention something about a fuck?'

In common with a number of his fellow students, François had a very cheap, sparsely furnished attic flat in a back street in Montparnasse – an area where, he insisted, the ghostly legacies of Ernest Hemingway, Henry Miller, Jean-Paul Sartre and Simone de Beauvoir inspired him. Creative inspiration or no, having climbed about eight flights of stairs to get to his apartment, Angelique inwardly cursed his choice of residence and was relieved to flop down on his narrow bed, her chest heaving as she gasped to regain her breath.

'Don't stop breathing,' he said, smiling down at her.

'I had no intention of stopping.' Angelique returned his smile wanly and pouted a kiss at him.

'I meant breathing *heavily*,' he murmured as he kicked off his shoes. 'Your breasts look amazing the way they rise and fall like that. I can't wait to get that jumper off you.'

Feeling a certain familiar warmth rise within her, she giggled. 'Then don't wait.'

Having struggled into a sitting position, she sat as patiently as a child as he knelt beside her and gently removed every item of her clothing, pausing only to kiss each new portion of flesh as he exposed it.

'I'm going to miss you, Angelique,' he said eventually, sliding his naked body alongside hers and stroking a possessive hand across her torso.

Her eyelids flickered as she gazed at him. 'Miss me?'

His tongue darted out and lathed the nipple nearest to him. He smiled as she quivered in response. 'Yes. Miss you. When you go to England,' he said.

To her surprise Angelique felt her stomach clench hard. 'I hadn't decided whether I should go,' she murmured quietly, almost to herself. 'But I suppose I should, shouldn't I?'

François inclined his head, the ends of his hair tickling her breasts. 'Yes, you should. I don't know how you can think otherwise.'

They fell silent for a moment and then, as he started out on an interesting journey with his tongue, Angelique found her mind wandering over the contents of the letter from her father's solicitor.

Her father had left her a substantial inheritance, the letter said. And that full details should ideally be given

6

to her in person. It suggested that either she could go to England, or the solicitor – a Mr Kemp – would be happy to visit her in France. It was her choice. All of it from now on would be her choice. And the other part of the letter, of course, was about her parentage, or lack of it. Her father's death-bed confession she supposed.

'Are you with me here, *chérie*?' François asked softly, his words a chilling whisper across her torso which glistened wetly with trails of his saliva.

'Yes. Oh, yes. Oh, God! I'm sorry.' She clutched his head and tangled her fingers into his hair, pulling him up her body so that she could kiss him on the mouth.

He returned her kiss and their love-making moved up a gear into a familiar mode – a fine balance between the giving and receiving of pleasure that always managed to satisfy them both equally. His mastery of her clitoris was particularly exquisite and she cried out as he drummed his tongue against it and pushed her over the edge. It was a climax and beginning all in one, the start of a torrent of tears so great that she soaked his one and only pillow.

'God, I'm sorry,' she said, gulping and sniffing as she felt her sobs subside. 'I don't know what came over me.'

François pulled her into the comforting circle of his arms and held her against him, stroking a few damp tendrils of dark hair away from her face. 'Yes, you do. You just lost your father.'

Angelique shook her head. 'He died three months ago.'

Frangois continued to stroke her hair and whispered into it. 'No. For you he just died today. You have the written proof and, furthermore, a letter explaining that he was not the person you thought he was. It is a double bereavement.'

She stared at him. 'How come you got to be so wise?' she said, her voice catching on the thread of another string of sobs.

7

He shrugged. 'I didn't. Now, can I fuck you, or would you prefer me to make love to you instead?'

'No, don't make love to me,' Angelique begged, shaking her head. 'I don't think I could bear it. You're already being so nice. Just . . . Let's fuck. Let's really fuck!'

He was inside her in an instant. She face down, her hips thrust obscenely high into the air as he drove into her. Then he withdrew just as quickly, spun her over, dragged her down to the bottom of the bed by her ankles and thrust into her again. Each time he entered her it made her gasp with surprise and pleasure and his movements made her feel as though she could happily die from the effects of his love-making.

She felt so hot all of a sudden. Hot and desperate to stop thinking and lose herself in physical sensation instead. Life was precious, something to be enjoyed, to be celebrated and there was nothing that made her feel more alive than sex, especially really good sex, the kind she was getting now.

Winding her slender legs around François' waist, she ground her pelvis against him and delighted in the way his beautiful cock stroked her sensitive inner flesh. Shockwaves of erotic pleasure reverberated through her body, plunging her into a deep dark pit of desire.

Hearing Angelique's whimpers of lust, François increased the tempo, looking forward to the moment when she would abandon herself completely to carnal gratification. He loved to watch the changing expressions on her face and feel her delicious body squirming beneath him as she ascended to another plane, where only pleasure and erotic sensation resided.

'I love your cunt,' he growled, deliberately looking down at the place where their bodies were joined. 'You're so juicy.'

Angelique's whole body zinged with lust. 'Oh, God!'

she cried. 'That's terrible. I hate that word. Say it again. Tell me more . . .'

Looking back, she thought it was one of the best sessions they had ever enjoyed and was sad and yet grateful all at once that it might just sustain her through the ordeal that was to come. England was not just on the horizon, it was below her. A patchwork of green and yellow fields and then the sprawling grey mass of London. Staring down, she realised how strange the landscape seemed to her now. Even though she could easily pick out well-known landmarks such as Buckingham Palace, Hyde Park and the winding grey ribbon of the Thames, five years in Paris had succeeded in wiping out the comforting feeling of familiarity. That was the trouble with dual parentage. No, correction, dual *nationality*. She had to remember, she didn't know who her parents were any more.

Her mother had been no help and had ranted and raved when Angelique told her she was going to England. 'What about your studies?' she had argued. To which Angelique pointed out that she had just finished a cordon bleu catering course and wasn't about to embark on any further education. 'Then what about a job?' *maman* dearest had screamed, which only made Angelique laugh. Her father had been very wealthy. No doubt he had left her a fortune. Why worry about a job?

When the arguments ran out, Angelique tried to ask about her background, but her questions were obviously not welcome and answers were given sparingly. Angelique had already been a part of her father's life when he and her mother had first met, she discovered. And, of course, it was instantly assumed that Angelique's father was the natural parent – that he had been left holding the baby, so to speak. When her mother found out that he had adopted Angelique, her father begged his fiancée not to say a thing about it and she had kept her promise.

9

Even though she had ended up hating the bastard, her mother had added on a vitriolic note.

Angelique was doubly shocked. She had always assumed her mother was her real mother. Who wouldn't? She had no memories of an earlier life without her.

The final insult to her father had been delivered dramatically, her mother pressing the back of her hand against her brow, Hollywood-style, forcing Angelique to stifle both a sigh of irritation and any further questions. What was the point anyway? Her mother knew nothing and could be of no further help. Any answers that might exist lay across the Channel. She had no choice, she had to go to England to satisfy her curiosity if nothing else.

When she booked her plane ticket Angelique had made no other arrangements. Consequently, after collecting her luggage, she was met by no one. Walking out of the airport terminal into the chill London air, feeling more alone than she had ever felt in her life, she summoned a taxi to take her into the city centre. The taxi ride was expensive but the convenience was worth every penny. There was no doubt in her mind that by the end of the afternoon money would be the least of her worries. And as soon as she had dealt with the details of her inheritance she might have a clearer idea about what to do next.

The solicitors' offices were typically Dickensian – dark little rooms stuffed to the gills with heavy wood and leather furniture and overflowing with dusty law books and yellowing documents tied up with red ribbons. The dust made Angelique sneeze prompting the solicitor, Mr Kemp – a grey-toned man in a dark, fraying suit – to gallantly unearth a box of tissues which were hidden underneath an untidy heap of paperwork on his desk. With a dead-pan expression, he handed the box to her.

'Thanks,' she said, blowing her nose and then sniffing loudly. 'It's the dust.'

Mr Kemp nodded gravely. 'It is understandable that you would be feeling a little emotional at this sad time,' he intoned, ignoring her explanation.

Angelique fought down the urge to correct him. She had already said it was the dust but as he was obviously programmed to deal with weeping women, why disappoint him? She squeezed out a tear and in an instant he was leaning across the desk and patting her hand.

'I think the sum involved may cheer you up a little,' he said after a while.

A smile touched Angelique's lips but she blinked hard to keep her eyes moist. 'Really?' she gasped. 'How much?'

Mr Kemp let go of her hand and receded across his desk. Opening the top left-hand drawer he took out a large buff file which he proceeded to flick through.

'The exact details of your inheritance are all listed here,' he said, handing her several sheets of foolscap paper stapled together. 'Every block of shares, stocks and bonds is itemised and there are numerous bank accounts. Also, you'll find various direct investments into companies and of course, the hotel.'

The hotel! Angelique had allowed the existence of the hotel to slip her mind but now she realised how convenient such a partnership could prove. Particularly as she was a cordon bleu cook and had nowhere to stay. She glanced through the list Mr Kemp had given her and then read through it a second time but more carefully, her mind making rapid calculations as her eyes scanned the pages. In the end she gave up.

'How much does all this add up to?' she asked, gazing directly at the man opposite.

He picked up the buff folder, flicked through it again and took out another sheet of paper. 'At a rough estimate,' he said, his eyes wavering between the figures in front of him and her expectant face. 'Around a million. But,' he added quickly when he saw the way her eyes widened with shock, 'that is on paper, not actual cash. Most of it is tied up and some of the investments are unstable to say the least. You will need proper guidance – an accountant. I could suggest a few names.'

Angelique nodded dumbly.

She was left alone to absorb the information while Mr Kemp went off to organise some coffee for them both. By the time the solicitor returned to his office with a tray, Angelique had managed to compose herself again.

'About the hotel,' she said as soon as he sat down again.

'Yes.' Mr Kemp sipped his coffee, wincing when it scalded his tongue.

'How much say would I have in running the place?'

'Running the place?'

Angelique noticed a surprised look cross his face and watched the way his hand seemed to shake slightly as he put his cup and saucer back down hastily.

'I don't think that's a very – ' he began.

Angelique interrupted him with a sweet smile. 'And I don't think what I plan to do with my future is really up to you, do you, Mr Kemp?' She waited patiently as he cleared his throat and shuffled a few papers on his desk.

'As you can see from that list, your father owned thirty per cent,' he said carefully. 'Other investors total a further twenty-eight per cent, leaving Jordan Cavendish with the majority holding. But you would have a very important say in the running of the hotel if you didn't trust Mr Cavendish to continue managing the establishment single-handedly.'

'Oh, I never said I didn't trust him,' Angelique cut in quickly.

In all honesty, she felt certain her father would have trusted Jordan with his life. Their relationship had extended far beyond the realms of a mere business

12

partnership. They had been old and very dear friends. She tried to conjure up an image of Jordan Cavendish in her mind and almost failed. Then a fleeting memory swept the cobwebs away and filled her head with a picture so vivid that she felt as though she had been transported back in time.

It was the day her father had first introduced Jordan to her. At the time she had been a rather precocious ten-year-old and was thoroughly smitten by the young, blond-haired man who at twenty-five was a good few years younger than her father. She had liked the way he instantly squatted down in front of her and shook her hand, his generous mouth repeating her name and saying how delighted he was to meet her. His actions were thoughtful and his falsely solemn air made her giggle. And his grey-blue eyes had smiled straight into hers that day, making her fall immediately under his spell.

That summer her father had invested in a hotel. It was only in Buckinghamshire but to Angelique who was London born and bred it seemed as though the huge Elizabethan building was tucked away in the deepest countryside. Going there was like going on holiday only better because when they arrived it instantly felt like home. The property, Thornbury Court, belonged to Jordan, she learned, left to him by some aged aunt who had doted on him. But he had no idea what to do with it other than sell it or turn it into a hotel. He had the bricks and mortar, her father had the capital. The location was idyllic yet less than an hour away from the centre of London. Turning it into a hotel was the perfect solution.

What a wonderful memory it was: filled with sunlight, the scent of fresh summer meadows and cut flowers and the lingering flavour of strawberries and cream. She sighed with pleasure at the thought then, all of a sudden, Mr Kemp's undertaker tones cut through her dream.

'Do you wish to discuss the other thing, Miss Hemsley?' he asked.

'Other thing?' Angelique was still floating a little.

'The question of your true origins,' the solicitor said bluntly. 'I would imagine the news came as a bit of a shock.'

She stared at him, amazed at his capacity for understatement. 'A bit of a shock,' she repeated slowly. 'A bit of a shock. Yes. I would say it was a bit of a shock. No. Hang on. It was more like a fucking great bombshell, actually!' She felt the hysteria that she had been desperately trying to suppress ever since she had received the letter from him rise to the surface of her psyche, almost lifting her from her seat.

Mr Kemp looked alarmed and jumped to his feet. 'I didn't mean . . . I have nothing really useful to tell you.'

Angelique glanced at him, his reaction forcing her to remember that none of this was his fault, he was only doing his job. Taking a deep, calming breath she stood up straight, tugged at the hem of her navy jacket so that it sat neatly over her hips and picked up her matching shoulder bag.

'It's all right, Mr Kemp,' she said evenly. 'I'm not going to have hysterics and I apologise if I alarmed you.' She paused and smiled slightly. 'I would be grateful if you could do one last thing for me though.'

'Of course. If I can be of any further assistance, please do not hesitate . . .' he offered, his hackneyed words tailing off.

Deliberately ignoring his blandness, Angelique wandered across the room to stare out of the window at the street scene below. 'First of all I would be grateful if you could order me a minicab,' she said, 'and then perhaps you would be kind enough to phone the hotel to let Jordan Cavendish know that I am on my way. Tell him I intend staying at least until the end of the week. Do you think you could do that for me?'

14

The necessary phone calls were made in a matter of minutes. Then as she waited for her cab to arrive, she whiled away the time by gazing out of the window and forcing herself not to think too hard about the prospect of renewing her association with Jordan Cavendish.

It was unfortunate that her second taxi journey coincided with the rush hour – or rather rush three hours, being central London – forcing the minicab to remain almost stationary for long periods of time. The stop-start journey had its advantages at first, affording her the opportunity to become reacquainted with the city. But after what seemed like an age, the colourful street-life eventually ceased to entrance her. Instead of window shopping and watching the diverse medley of passers-by, she rested her head against the back of the seat, closed her eyes and concentrated on her memories instead.

Since the opening of the hotel her summer breaks from boarding school had been halcyon days spent wandering around its vast rooms and, indeed, the whole estate, which included a man-made lake. Picnics were enjoyed at the edge of the lake where ducks and swans vied for crumbs, while the tiny copse at the rear of the house played host to endless games of hide and seek.

Then disaster had struck. The first truly terrible thing to happen in her life. Her mother and father announced that they were getting a divorce. The news was a bombshell tempered only by the hasty offer for Angelique to stay with her father in England and continue her education. It was some consolation and she agreed readily. She didn't want to go and live with her mother in France just then, but by the time she was fourteen her summers at the hotel had become a thing of the past and she was tacitly expected to spend every holiday with her mother instead.

The arrangement worked out fine, although Angelique was slightly disappointed that she didn't get to see

15

Jordan any more. But there were enough distractions to take her mind off someone who was far too old to be anything but a kindly uncle-type figure. Male diversions of her own age, or thereabouts, abounded and at the age of fourteen Angelique had come to appreciate that she was more than a little attractive as far as the opposite sex was concerned.

By the time she was eighteen she had made the firm decision not to go back to England to university. She might have had a high opinion of herself but she wasn't too proud to admit in private that she wasn't what one would call an intellectual. By cramming hard she still only just scraped through her 'A' levels and the prospect of several more years' study appalled her.

Then there were other considerations to be taken into account, not least that she had really grown to love France by then and appreciated the myriad delights Paris had to offer an attractive young woman. Foraging through the second-hand bookshops and exploring the narrow streets of St-Germain, sitting outside pavement cafés simply watching the world go by, parading down the chic avenues of the Right Bank – always pausing to admire the gigantic carving of a winged foot that domi-nated the Hérmes window display – and sampling the diverse clubs and bars around Montmartre and Montpar-nasse had all become vital parts of her life. Eventually tiring of her mother's complaints about her indolent lifestyle, her natural inclinations toward good food and fine wines contributed to her decision to turn her back on academia and opt for an extended cordon bleu course instead.

Which brought her right up to date.

Opening her eyes she reached decisively for her hand-bag, took out her compact, flicked it open and studied her reflection for a moment. In that instant it surprised her to realise that she was no longer a gauche teenager with no prospects, but a pretty young woman of twenty-four, with a reasonably good figure, a diploma that would gain her entry to the kitchens of some of the finest hotels and restaurants worldwide, and a paper fortune of around one million pounds sterling. She had to admit that wasn't a bad state of affairs by anyone's estimation but her stomach still squirmed with anxiety and indecision. It was understandable, she supposed, given the events of the past couple of months. But she daren't let self-pity or depression get a hold of her. She had a lot to be thankful for.

The taxi began to pick up speed as it reached the A40 and she settled back in the seat again, trying to quell the excitement that was starting to churn inside her as she gazed at the vaguely familiar scenery which flashed past. Decisions would have to be made and questions answered. Two questions in particular occupied her thoughts during the remainder of the journey: what was she going to do to make her combined assets work to her best advantage? And who the hell were her real parents?

Chapter Two

'*A*ction stations everybody! Staff meeting. Jordan's on the war-path. Chop-chop!' Lesley Barker stuck her anxious head around the door to the staff sitting-room and glanced about, quickly. Out of the dozen or so occupants, only Betty Simmons looked up.

'What's up, Les?' she asked, already starting to heave her ample body out of the over-stuffed armchair. She too glanced around at the inert bodies, their heads still buried in newspapers and books. 'Come on you lot, you heard Lesley. Move yourselves.'

One by one the others got to their feet, grumbling and shuffling as they made their way down the polished wood corridor to Jordan's office. In a busy hotel time off was precious. Staff meetings were work and shouldn't infringe on their leisure periods. What the hell was the boss playing at?

Heedless of the possible consequences, Rod Bennet, the hotel's senior bell-boy, voiced everyone's grumble.

'This is an emergency, Rod. Stop complaining.' Jordan's voice sounded loud and clear, making them all jump visibly.

Lesley attempted a smile and pulled at the hem of her

black dress. Black and white were the order of the day for most members of staff and, even though she had recently been promoted from chamber-maid to house-keeper, her uniform was no more glamorous than that worn by anyone else.

'What is the problem?' she asked in her usual husky tone.

Jordan glanced in Lesley's direction and pushed his fingers distractedly through his hair. 'Sit down every-body and I'll tell you,' he said.

Everyone duly sat and Jordan glanced around the assembled group. What a collection of odd-bods they were, he thought to himself with a wry inner smile. Plump, middle-aged Betty Simmons looked to be just what she was – a good, plain cook. Rod Bennet was so tall and thin he reminded Jordan of a poplar tree blowing about in the wind. He looked far too fragile to hoist luggage about – sometimes carrying four or five cases a time along the seemingly endless corridors that bisected the enormous house.

The two waitresses, Liz and Polly, believed they were cute as kittens and tried to play on it – although they quickly found out that their blonde curls, blue eyes and dimples cut no ice with Jordan. Then there was Sandy Farndon the gardener, who had flaming red hair and a beard and temper to match, and his assistant, Fergus – Nordic-featured and rugged.

The new relief receptionist, whose name Jordan had temporarily forgotten, was there, and he couldn't help quickly noting how interesting her figure looked despite the severe cut of her plain black suit. Also present were several chamber-maids and other assorted members of staff. And last but not least there was Lesley.

Here he paused in his thoughts. Lesley was not like the others. Not by a long shot. Oh, she had a nice figure, attractive dark looks and a very pleasant disposition. And she was always willing to please, to do a little bit more and take that extra bit of care over everything. But she was treading a fine line every day of her life and Jordan knew the risks he was taking by employing her. Thank God that as transvestites went, Lesley was incredibly convincing as a woman. She had a host of very persuasive feminine traits, which, of course, helped a lot. And her figure was good, despite the bony knees and a worrying tendency to forget to depilate her body hair where it showed – little tufts of black hair appearing above the lace frill around the neckline of her dress could look a mite worrying to some of their guests. But on the whole she was pleasant, and most important of all in Jordan's book, she was very good at her job.

There were two key members of staff missing. He would bring them up to date as soon as they returned, one from entertaining a member of the local press and the other from a much deserved holiday in northern Spain.

'We're expecting a visitor at any moment,' Jordan said, reclining against the edge of his desk, in what he hoped looked to be a casual manner. He anticipated questions and put up a hand to close the mouths that immediately opened in response to his announcement. 'This is not just any visitor. We are soon to be visited by Harvey Hemsley's daughter, Angelique.'

'But she lives in France with her mother,' Betty exclaimed, managing to break through the invisible barrier put up by Jordan's hand.

'Lived,' Jordan said calmly. 'I think from now on the accent will be on the past tense.' He looked around and noticed how everyone's brow had creased to some extent. Even now some of them still had a little difficulty understanding the convoluted way he sometimes spoke.

'Are you trying to tell us that she's coming to live here?' Lesley asked, displaying her usual rapid grasp of the situation.

Jordan nodded, to which everyone groaned. 'According to Mr Hemsley's solicitor, she is considering a permanent residence here – perhaps even taking a hand in running things.'

'Shit!' Fergus blotted his copy-book in his usual forthright manner, but for once his boss treated him to a sympathetic smile instead of a glare.

'My sentiments exactly,' Jordan said. 'You know what I'm talking about when I say that we will have to play things by ear. Until I have managed to gauge her intentions and her disposition I don't think it will do any of us any good to apprise her of all the hotel's activities – if you know what I mean.'

Everyone nodded. Everyone present knew exactly what he meant.

Satisfied that he had imparted the news and his instructions with the minimum of fuss, Jordan glanced at his watch and then suggested that they all assemble outside to greet their new guest.

Angelique's first impression, as the minicab drove up the long gravel driveway towards the hotel, was of a building that had soaked up all but a few of the sun's rays and now reflected them itself. Throwing off a warm golden glow, the limestone walls of the sixteenth-century house seemed to beckon her to go nearer, to enter the inviting portals and bask in the cordial atmosphere of its interior.

Her enraptured gaze swept the length and height of the building, taking in the large mullioned windows to both the ground and the upper second floors. Diverse Gothic embellishments added a quirky touch to the otherwise traditional building. And the wide front entrance was bounded by another architectural detail: two stout columns which, like the walls, were covered with a blanket of lichen.

It was then that she noticed a sight which made her eyes widen. Her head came forward to check that her eyes were not deceiving her and her throat rumbled with unrestrained laughter. For out of the very same front entrance that she had just been admiring came a procession of people dressed in black and white. The unexpected sight made her feel for all the world as if she were taking part in an episode of the television series *Upstairs, Downstairs*, because now the group assembled outside, sorting themselves into a long line that ranged from the tallest to the shortest.

A moment later, as the taxi drew to a halt, a tall fair-haired figure emerged from the front doorway, stepped on to the threshold then descended the four flagged steps that led down to the semi-circular, in-out driveway. It was Jordan, Angelique realised, making the opposite of an 'entrance' but proving an arresting sight nevertheless.

He walked up to the car. As he came nearer she noticed how little he had changed in the ten years since she had last seen him. Then she had been fourteen and he twenty-nine – he a man and she a girl on the brink of woman-hood. Now they were equals – almost.

Jordan beat the taxi driver to the passenger door and opened it with a flourish. His smile twinkled at her as she alighted carefully, her high heels skittering on the gravel.

'Steady.' He caught her by the elbow and held her fast.

As though she were moving in slow-motion, Angelique turned her head to smile at him properly. But she found herself arrested by his eyes – the same blue-grey irises that she remembered from their first ever meeting, but now the twinkle in them had died to be replaced by something else. What was it she saw there?

Her stomach clenched tightly as she thought she recognised that particular expression, and yet she shook off the idea. How ridiculous, Jordan was her late father's oldest friend and business partner. Not only that, he was almost an uncle to her. He was just being charming and she was tired: it was easy to make mistakes when you hadn't slept properly for several days.

A tall, lanky man stepped forward out of the line-up when Jordan crooked his finger. As he approached the two of them he nodded curtly and then proceeded around to the back of the cab where he unloaded Angelique's two cases and a holdall.

'Take them into reception,' Jordan said, when the man glanced at him inquiringly. 'I presume you are planning to stay with us for a while?' He added, turning to glance innocently at Angelique.

'I ... I thought I would. If you don't mind,' she stammered, temporarily forgetting that she had asked the solicitor to phone Jordan to let him know she was coming. Then she remembered and wondered why she was being so pathetic. She had every right to stay there, and for as long as she liked.

Jordan's face creased into a relaxed smile as if he recognised her response to him. 'Of course, I don't mind. The hotel is as much yours as it is mine,' he said.

His relaxed attitude was infectious. Angelique immediately found the tension draining out of her and consequently her hunched up shoulders eased back and down, inadvertently thrusting her breasts out. Her heart missed a beat as Jordan's gaze wavered just for a moment and her cheeks filled with warmth. He wasn't afraid to show his interest in her, she realised. There was nothing covert about the way his eyes swept over her torso and then quickly appraised the rest of her. He even stepped back a little to do the job properly. A tingle started between her legs and she shifted uncomfortably from one foot to the other in the hope that certain of her body parts would rub together and quell the sudden urgency she felt to be touched and brought to orgasm.

She almost missed his next few words as he let go of her elbow and took her hand instead, leading her across the gravel to meet the assembled staff. Angelique forced herself to smile brightly at each person and tried to imprint their names on her memory. The problem was she was hopeless with names at the best of times, and as the line-up turned and began to file back into the hotel she found she had already forgotten most of them. Except Betty Simmons, Fergus and Lesley.

Betty was instantly likeable and there was no way Angelique could forget her. Fergus had an unusual name and a very horny appearance, making him equally memorable. And Lesley? Well, she couldn't exactly put her finger on it but there was something definitely out of the ordinary about Lesley.

Jordan was speaking again, she realised, and she turned to gaze at him. Her hand was still captured by his and it felt right, somehow. He held her hand the way her father used to hold it, firmly but gently all at the same time. It made her feel safe, protected from harm. And although she had a very independent streak she couldn't help basking in the luxury of allowing someone else to take control for a change.

The feeling lasted long after he had led her inside the hotel. As she stood in the middle of the vast entrance hall which, predictably, had been turned into the hotel's reception area, Jordan briefly left her while he checked that her suite was ready. Angelique hugged the word to her. *Suite.* That sounded inviting. Much more inviting than a mere bedroom. And much more permanent. She could live indefinitely in a suite, and for some unspoken reason she knew it meant he was happy for her to stay for as long as she wanted.

Soon tired of studying the impressive portraits of former residents of Thornbury Court that graced its walls, she turned her attention back to Jordan who was at the reception desk, several feet away from her. His tall, rangy figure looked well toned as he bent forward over the polished mahogany counter and rested on his

24

elbows to peruse a thick ledger which, she could only assume, was the guest registration book. His light-coloured trousers stretched tightly across firm buttocks, she noticed with a thrill of pleasure. Also, his stomach looked completely flat under his white polo shirt. She noticed how well-defined his thigh muscles were and the way they flexed and stretched the material of his trousers as he shifted his weight from one foot to the other.

Just at that moment he turned his head unexpectedly and caught her looking at him. She glanced quickly away but realised it was too late. Her cheeks flamed as she cast her eyes frantically around the high walls and pretended to study the portraits again. One, of a portly man in a grey wig holding a little white dog in his lap, was particularly fascinating.

'I was just admiring the portraits,' she explained as Jordan sauntered back to her.

An easy smile spread across his face, but she thought she detected a knowing glint in his eye. 'They are interesting, aren't they?' he said innocently. 'But then the human form is always a wonder to behold.'

He was teasing her and she knew it. She couldn't help laughing. 'I'm always curious about people. I'm sorry. I didn't mean to stare.'

'Oh, Christ! Don't apologise,' he insisted. 'Without curiosity we may as well all be dead.' He paused, suddenly looking guilty. 'Now it's my turn to apologise. That was a bit tactless under the circumstances.'

Angelique shook her head. 'I've stopped thinking about it. Honest,' she said, smiling. 'Plus the fact he wasn't really my father, was he?' She assumed he knew all about it.

'No,' Jordan said, shaking his head. 'Not biologically. But I hope you don't think that takes anything away from the way he felt about you, or your life together. He loved you to distraction, he really did.'

25

His words were so immediate and delivered with such honesty that she had to fight back the tears.

'Don't hold back,' he murmured. 'If you want to let it all out, do it. In fact . . .' He paused, took her hand again and began to lead her towards a door to their left. 'Come with me. We'll be more comfortable in my office.'

As soon as they were safely ensconced in the large, oak-panelled room, Angelique surprised herself by releasing a flood of tears. Between sobs she confessed her shock at receiving the letter from Mr Kemp, their subsequent meeting, her abortive conversation with her mother and finally her distress at having to leave her boyfriend behind in France.

'Have you known François for a long time?' Jordan asked, offering Angelique a handkerchief.

Feeling as though she were about five years old, Angelique took it and began to wipe at her tear-stained cheeks. 'Oh, God! I'm sorry,' she said, gazing in horror at the black streaks of mascara across the pristine white cotton.

Jordan shook his head. 'It's okay to cry,' he said, sympathetically.

'François and I have been seeing each other for about six months,' she added in answer to his question.

'And you have a sexual relationship?' he asked.

This very personal question sounded odd, and Angelique gazed at him dumbly for a few moments. Then she nodded. 'Of course, I am a grown woman.'

She realised she sounded defensive and wondered why. Had her father asked that question she would have felt less embarrassed than she did right at that moment. Perhaps it was because she had the feeling that Jordan was now imagining her naked and in bed with her lover. To her suprise the tingling sensation started again and a trickle of moisture soaked into the crotch of her knickers.

Forcing herself to gaze calmly back at Jordan she had the uncomfortable feeling that he was staring right into

26

her soul. Reclining in the brown leather chair behind his desk, he looked perfectly at ease, and yet she sensed a tenseness about him, as though he was a predator waiting for the perfect moment to pounce. Was she his prey? she wondered. Of course, who else would it be?

'I ... er ...' She cleared her throat, wondering what on earth she could say to break the spell between them. It was as though she was almost hypnotised, like a small, fluffy animal caught in the headlamps of a car. Stricken. Immobile. Suddenly she laughed at the image of herself, the indomitable, self-possessed Angelique as a fluffy animal, and the spell was broken.

'I'm glad you're feeling more cheerful now,' Jordan said, not bothering asking why she had burst out laughing. He got up abruptly, walked over to a tall mahogany cupboard and proceeded to pour them each a glass of Scotch. 'Drink up,' he ordered, 'then we'll go and check out your accommodation. I expect you could do with a nap before supper?'

Taking a sip of her whisky, Angelique allowed the warmth to trickle down her throat and spread into her stomach. 'I am a bit whacked,' she admitted.

A glance at the grandfather clock to the left of Jordan's desk told her it was already past six o'clock. Twelve hours since she had got up. That morning she had stared out of the window of her mother's Parisian apartment and watched the streams of traffic pass by several floors below. Now, as she gazed straight ahead out of the window behind Jordan's desk, all she saw was a profusion of flowers in well tended beds and a vast expanse of perfectly manicured lawn. Birds sang, squirrels frolicked and bees and butterflies swooped from bloom to bloom under the waning glow of an early June sun. It was all so idyllic that Angelique found herself sighing with pleasure and relaxing into the deep leather chair as she delighted in the way the amber liquid in her glass slipped so easily down her throat. It warmed its way right down to her toes. She sighed again.

'So beautiful.'

The words touched her ears but she couldn't tell where they came from, or if they had been spoken at all. Perhaps it was the sound of the early evening breeze.

'Did you say something, Jordan?' she ventured, turning her head to look at him. He stood a little way behind her, his gaze also directed at the vista she had just been admiring. Of course, he had been talking about the beauty of nature. Suddenly she felt foolish. Just for an instant she had thought he was referring to her.

He nodded and walked around the chair until he stood in front of her, his left knee just brushing her right. She shivered involuntarily as goose-pimples sprang to attention over her whole body.

'I couldn't help thinking what a beautiful woman you have become, Angelique,' he said softly. 'You always were a pretty little thing but now . . .' He broke off and allowed his gaze to travel all over her before coming to rest on her upturned face once more.

Her attempt at a smile failed. Her expression was frozen: eyes trapped by his, lips unable to move and to form a reply. As if a reply to such an unexpected compliment were possible.

An uncertain moment hung between them until they were disturbed by a knock at the door. It was the hotel receptionist, who introduced herself to Angelique as Susan.

'I just thought I'd let you know, Miss Hemsley's bags are in her suite,' she said, her attention now aimed at Jordan who nodded and then glanced at Angelique.

'Would you like Susan to show you the way?' he asked. 'This is a pretty big place. It's easy to get lost. In fact . . .' He broke off and glanced out of the window for just a moment. 'It's a shame it's so near to dinner time, otherwise I would have offered you a guided tour. As it is we'll have to leave it until tomorrow morning. Unless you have other plans, of course?'

Angelique shook her head, slightly disappointed that their little tête-à-tête was being cut short, just as it had started to get interesting. 'No, I have no other plans,' she said. 'A tour tomorrow would be lovely.' She got up and shook Jordan's hand. 'Thank you for the Scotch and the shoulder to cry on. Will I see you at supper?'

To her dismay Jordan shrugged. 'I can't say. Sometimes I don't get to eat until gone midnight. But we'll see. If the guests all behave themselves for once, I don't see any reason why we can't at least have a drink together later on.'

That satisfied Angelique, and she left him with just a fleeting smile as she followed Susan out of the room.

Her suite was everything she had hoped it would be and more. It was huge: two very large rooms, plus a small entrance lobby, and a modern bathroom complete with spa bath. The sitting-room and bedroom were both very cosy, despite their huge dimensions and the age of the house in general. Modern, squashy sofas and chairs covered in a bright yellow-and-blue-patterned chintz dominated the sitting-room and were featured in the bedroom as well. Thick, cream-coloured wool rugs covered the polished wood floors and pale blue velvet curtains framed the high windows – two to each room – which let in a lot of light. A built-in range of cupboards and bookcases lined one whole wall of the sitting-room from floor to ceiling, housing everything she could possibly need to make her stay comfortable. Books on a variety of subjects, a mini CD stack and selection of music, a few board games, packs of cards, backgammon and chess, and the latest copy of every single woman's interest magazine were among the items she found there.

Angelique was amazed at the thoughtfulness that had gone into equipping the room. She scanned through the

CDs, found one that featured a selection of soul music and put it on, with the volume quite low. Then she ran a finger along the spines of the books as she perused them. Hollywood blockbuster-type novels sat side-by-side with the classics. The Collins' sisters rubbed shoulders with Conan Doyle, and Pat Booth with Baudelaire. To look at the books on the higher shelves, she had to use the small set of library steps – but when she climbed up she was glad she had. Along the top shelf was ranked a collection of erotica – novels, collections of drawings, 'true' accounts – both old and new.

The sight of these books and the knowledge that most of them were totally unknown to her, excited Angelique. She wondered why anyone would presume to add erotica to the bookshelves of a guest suite. Might it not seem a little inappropriate, bad taste even? Not if this suite was normally reserved for honeymooners, she supposed. But then newlyweds would surely be more interested in the practical side of sex than the literary? The thought of a couple spending more time reading about sex than actually doing it made her laugh. She imagined the bride complaining of eye strain: 'Not tonight dear, I have a headache.' Oh, God! She was cracking up. She really was.

Picking up the latest copy of *Tatler*, Angelique wandered into the bedroom. Like the sitting-room it was bright and airy yet cosy all at the same time. The bed was a large, modern reproduction four-poster with draperies and bed cover in the same blue-and-yellow chintz as the rest of the soft furnishings. Under each of the two windows stood a comfortable armchair and between them a long walnut side table. And at the foot of the bed was a long, carved oak ottoman with a padded top covered in matching chintz, containing blankets and pillows. 'Just in case you need extra,' Susan had explained before she left Angelique to her own devices.

She felt she could stay there quite happily for the rest

of her life – and the way things were she might well do that. Perhaps. Maybe. Unless something better came along.

The main dining-room was very busy when Angelique ventured downstairs after a surprisingly deep sleep a couple of hours later. Considering its size and the number of guests the hotel could accommodate, she had been surprised not to see more people wandering around earlier. But now it looked as though they had all come out of the woodwork, so to speak, and were gathered together for supper.

As Angelique hovered in the doorway, the *maître d'* appeared and showed her to a little table that was not stuck in a corner out of the way – beware the embarrassment of lone diners – but placed by a window from where she could look out over the lawn as she ate, keeping her eyes peeled for foxes. This was a suggestion made to her by the cheeky-faced waitress who handed her a menu and reeled off a list of recommendations all at the same time.

'The trout's good and so is the lamb. Avoid the oysters like the plague, I didn't like the look of 'em when they arrived this morning. Oh, and the partridge is excellent, our cook does a very nice Madeira gravy to go with it. Now . . . Ooh, my God! Did you see that?'

Angelique followed the young woman's gaze as she craned her neck, her eyes sweeping back and forth across the lawn.

'That was a fox,' the waitress said, pausing to lick the tip of her pencil. 'They're absolutely rampant at the moment. Bonking everything in sight, even the squirrels. I tell you old Sandy our gardener is beside himself right now with 'em.'

'Why is that?' Angelique could tell by the young woman's expression that she was expected to contribute something. She had to force herself to keep a straight

31

face. She watched as the waitress's face creased up with laughter and tears bubbled at the corners of her eyes.

"Cos two of 'em had his little Jack Russell cornered yesterday. There it was, by all accounts, cowering and quivering the way they do.' She glanced to Angelique for a nod of affirmation before continuing. 'Pressed up against the side of the potting shed with a thistle up its bum and two of them buggers bearing down on it with a determined look on their faces. They had one thing on their minds and one thing only. Didn't matter that the poor little mutt wasn't one of them. They didn't give a damn. They just wanted to shag something.'

'Is there a point to this conversation, Polly, or are you just trying to bore Miss Hemsley to death before she dies of starvation?'

Neither of them had noticed Jordan walk up to the table and now both young women jumped as he spoke.

'Oh, God! Oh ... er, sorry Mast– ... Sir ... er ... I mean Mr Cavendish,' the waitress stammered, finding her voice. 'Sorry, Miss ... er ... What did you want to eat?' She turned to look at Angelique whose smile took in first Jordan and then the red-faced Polly.

'I think the partridge, as you suggested,' Angelique said pleasantly, 'and then the apple tart and cream, thank you.' She closed the menu and handed it back to the waitress who scuttled away. Then she turned her attention back to Jordan. 'Please don't be cross with her, I found her conversation quite ... er ... charming,' she said.

Smiling, Jordan pulled out the chair beside hers and sat down. Placing one elbow on the table, he rested his chin in the palm of his hand and regarded her, thoughtfully. 'We do have some business to discuss, you know,' he said after a while.

Angelique glanced down at the empty place in front of her, between her knife and fork, and then looked up at his face. 'I thought we would. But does it have to be now? I've just had the most wonderful couple of hours sleep that I've had in ages and am about to enjoy what I hope will be a very pleasant meal.'

Jordan laughed. 'Of course I didn't mean now.' He continued to gaze at her. 'You really have the most amazing mouth,' he said. 'Is it the same one you had before?'

'Naturally.' Angelique couldn't help giggling.

His eyes reassessed the full, insolent pout which made her look even more inviting. Just for an instant he imagined sliding his cock between those full red lips.

'Are we still on for that drink?' he asked, amazed at the way he managed to sound so calm when all the time he was aching to touch her. Christ! Why beat around the bush? He was aching to throw her across the table and ravish her in front of all the diners.

'Mmm, yes. Why not?' Angelique nodded and her pout disappeared into a smile.

Disappointed, but not with her reply, Jordan stood up abruptly. 'Good. I'll see you in the Piano Bar in an hour or so. *Bon appetit!*'

Chapter Three

*A*s the red Cavalier started to approach the junction for the M40, Geoff Wright flicked on the indicator. 'Soon be there now, Moira,' he said with a grin.

The blonde middle-aged woman seated next to him patted her heavily lacquered curls and nodded vigorously, her mind only on one thing. 'Oh, yes, my lad,' she said firmly, 'and you wait until tonight. I'll give you what for.'

Satisfied that she had given him due warning, she settled back in her seat, stared out of the window at the passing scenery and let her mind wander in its usual meandering fashion.

It was funny how things turned out, Moira O'Donnell thought, with a sigh of satisfaction. In the beginning there had been her and Ted, on their own at long last in their brand new semi in the Midlands for a few blissful years after his stint in the army ended. Then Jane came along. A bright, happy child but destined to be the only one for them.

More's the pity, she thought, as she often had in the past. She loved babies. She didn't like older kids much, but while Jane had been tiny and helpless, dependent on

34

her for everything, Moira had been in her element. Her thoughts wandered as they were wont to do these days and she decided it was a bit of a shame that Geoff wouldn't let her treat him like a baby. She had heard that some men liked to be dressed up in nappies and given bottles, the whole bit. But at least Geoff was what he was, and she was grateful for that.

She had married Ted, and at the ripe old age of twenty-one had given birth to Jane who grew up and married Geoff. Then out of the blue, Ted – the man whom she thought she knew inside and out – had upped and left her, just like that. And she supposed it was then she had started taking more notice of her son-in-law.

It had begun with her turning to him for help with the little things that went wrong around the house, especially anything involving the plumbing. Well, he is a plumber by trade – why keep a dog and bark yourself? she used to think. So, of course, she and Geoff, who up until then had just been the man her daughter had married and who hovered in the background during family get-togethers, started to talk to each other properly, as two individuals. Cups of tea were always more enjoyable when accompanied by a cosy chat and pretty soon the cups of tea led to glasses of beer, or Scotch. And then other things.

She mused for a while on the 'other things'.

It wasn't so much the promise of good sex that had drawn them together and kept them that way but an exchange of interests. Most people would be shocked if they knew about her and Geoff: older woman and younger man; worse still, mother-in-law and only daughter's husband; then – and this would be the ultimate perversion in a lot of people's eyes – dominatrix and submissive.

What a relief it was to put their relationship into proper terms at long last! It was something she had been trying to deny to herself for quite a while, almost four years in fact, telling herself that what she and Geoff enjoyed was just a bit of kinkiness. Now she'd finally had the courage to air it in her mind she felt as though a great weight had been lifted from her.

It was difficult to pinpoint exactly when significant changes had started taking place between her and Geoff. She supposed it must have been the day he came to her house to replace her old shower and had come across her latest copy of *Skin Two* magazine still lying on the kitchen table. She'd come across the publication quite by accident about six months earlier and, intrigued by the list of contents, had dared to buy a copy. Now she had a regular subscription and a resolve to try out some of the things that interested her the most.

'What's this?' Geoff had said, picking the magazine up and flicking through its glossy pages with an expression of detached interest, as if he was glancing through one of her copies of *Woman's Own*.

Not really knowing what to say in this case, she hadn't replied straight away but watched him covertly as his eyes widened and his mouth dropped open with shock – exactly the same way she had reacted the first time, too.

Without closing the magazine, Geoff had proceeded to pull out a chair, sit down and devour its contents from cover to cover while she made a pot of tea.

When the tea was brewed she set the fat, brown earthenware pot down on the table and made herself comfortable in the chair opposite him. Leaning forward on her elbows, her dimpled chin cupped in her hands, she stared at him until he was compelled to look up.

'What do you think, Geoff?' she said, her heart thumping as she waited for his reply.

There were several possibilities for his next move. He could come to the rapid conclusion that his mother-in-law was a dreadful pervert and refuse to have anything more to do with her. He could rush home and tell her daughter all about it and they would both have nothing more to do with her. He could pretend he had no thoughts about it one way or the other. Or he could show an interest.

Moira had held her breath.

'I didn't know this sort of thing existed,' he murmured, flicking through the magazine once again and stopping at a page which featured an advertisement for metal fetish wear on one side and the opening paragraphs of an article about masochism in literature on the other.

'It's still a bit underground,' Moira admitted, 'but lots of people like to indulge in the kinkier side of life these days.'

Geoff poured them each a mug of tea and flashed her a shrewd look. 'Freaks, you mean?'

Moira shook her head emphatically. 'No, not freaks, Geoff. Normal people. People like you and I.'

He snorted and had to put his mug down before he spilled his tea. 'You speak for yourself. This isn't my scene at all.'

'How do you know?' she countered quickly. 'You might enjoy it.' Moira threw him a challenging look across the table. 'Don't you and Jane ever – ?'

'No!' Geoff jumped to his feet. 'Jane and I – well, we . . .' His cheeks coloured a deep crimson as he broke off and sat down again.

Reaching across the table, Moira patted his hand. 'Come with me, Geoff,' she said. 'I want to show you something.'

Taking one of his huge hands in her own, she led him silently up the stairs to her bedroom where she proceeded to open cupboards and drawers and arrange certain items on the bed. She watched as Geoff glanced down. The innocent pink duvet had now become the background to a display of strange-looking instruments. A black leather crop, several different kinds of whip, various sex toys including some pretty scary-looking dildos, handcuffs and a black silk blindfold were among the display.

Moira walked around the bed and stood next to him. Picking up the crop, she cut the air with it a few times, smiling with satisfaction at the whistling sound it made. Then, on impulse, she flicked the tip across the slight bulge at the front of his jeans.

It was only intended as a playful gesture but to her amazement – and no doubt Geoff's, too – she noticed a distinct tumescence.

Moira regarded him carefully, thinking that she could possibly be right in her suspicions about her son-in-law's hidden desires. She flicked him with the crop again, only this time a little harder. Geoff groaned. The bulge grew and he sank to his knees, unzipping his fly as he went and literally begging her to chastise him properly.

Moira's lips curved into a smile as she flexed the crop between her hands. It was funny how life had its share of surprises.

That had been the first time for her and Geoff and after that it became a way of life to both of them. Geoff would come to her house once or twice a week on some pretext or other, and she would tie him to the bed, or the wardrobe door, and give him a good thrashing for which he was always piteously grateful. A fact which turned her on more than her ex-husband Ted ever had.

Gradually the punishment sessions began to include sex – firstly just for her pleasure and then the full-blown thing.

This was something they both had a little difficulty in justifying to themselves because neither of them wanted to hurt Jane in any way – she was the most important person in both their lives, apart from each other. But like every other aspect of their relationship, the sex just seemed right and natural. They desired each other a great deal and a frenzied bout of fucking and sucking always seemed to conclude the punishment sessions in a fitting and very satisfying way. Why not? she had reasoned after the first time. Despite her advancing years she was still a vital woman. Why shouldn't she enjoy a good sex life?

Geoff broke through Moira's lewd recollections by pointing out that they were just twenty minutes or so away from the hotel, to which she smiled and patted his knee. These long weekends were nothing short of little miracles and she thanked God that her own mother was still alive and dribbling away contentedly in an old folk's home near Windsor – she made the perfect alibi.

Moira's daughter hated travelling. In fact, Jane was a little bit agoraphobic and so she had been consumed with gratitude the first time Geoff had gallantly offered to drive her mother 'down south' to make a duty visit. Now the visits took place every six weeks or so.

As far as Jane knew, while her mother was visiting Grandma, Geoff was off enjoying a football match at one of the London grounds. And as everyone seemed so happy with the arrangement, it never occurred to her to wonder how her husband and mother entertained themselves during the rest of their stay.

Strong sunlight fell on Angelique as she drew back the curtains, almost blinding her for a moment. As she allowed herself to bask in its warmth she remembered where she was. With a quiver of anticipation she recalled that Jordan had offered to give her a guided tour. She was looking forward to exploring the old place again, but even more exciting was the prospect of spending time with a man whom she had spent half the night dreaming about. As arranged, Angelique had met Jordan in the Piano Bar where they shared wine and conversation until late. Throughout the evening, she had been aware of a special electricity passing between them and, if she wasn't mistaken, knew this could only be the spark of sexual attraction.

She shivered again, even though the warmth of the sun caressed her bare arms and reminded her that the morning was already well underway.

The night's dreams had started off quite pleasantly: romantic little vignettes in which she and Jordan shared a glass of wine, a pleasant meal and one or two tiny kisses. Deep, dreamless sleep intervened and then at some point – probably only an hour or so before she awoke – pure erotica took over where hearts and flowers had left off.

Suddenly she was confronted with the image of herself naked and pinned beneath Jordan's lean and powerful body. Or Jordan ordering her to strip and then having her in front of a room full of people. And then there was a terrifically arousing scene during which Jordan didn't touch her at all but merely watched while she was fucked by someone else, someone she knew.

Her mind wandered, tried to concentrate and then – oh, God! The other person had been that gardener, what was his name – Fergus? Angelique blushed and then sighed with relief that at least her dream had involved the young, good-looking gardener and not the red-haired, bearded one. Come to think of it, Fergus was *extremely* good-looking. No harm in turning that dream into reality if possible. Good gracious, what a difference a good night's sleep could make! She felt a hundred times more optimistic already.

Later she found Jordan, or rather Jordan found her, on the terrace outside the dining-room.

'Don't you want anything to eat?' he asked, indicating the empty table top. But Angelique shook her head.

'I drank a pot of coffee in between showering and getting dressed. I can't really face any more than that in the morning.'

A certain warmth spread over her as Jordan appraised her carefully. She had to admit she felt good, with or without his admiring glance. Feeling light and summery, she had chosen to wear a dress that reflected her mood exactly. With thin straps and a hem that just skimmed her ankles, the pale, floral-patterned dress managed to cover her up and yet reveal more of her body than her usual clothes. For one thing, there was no way she could wear a bra underneath it unless it was strapless and she hadn't packed a strapless one. Consequently, her full breasts and tight button nipples were clearly outlined by the fragile fabric. They tightened perceptibly under the impact of Jordan's gaze, and she had to force down her blushes.

'Where shall we start?' she asked. For some reason it seemed a loaded question and her stomach cramped almost painfully as soon as the words were out of her mouth.

Jordan didn't seem to notice her discomfort one way or the other but reached out and with a pleasant, totally neutral smile, took her hand and began to lead her across the terrace and away from the house.

'I thought we'd explore the grounds before it gets too hot,' he explained. 'I notice you're not wearing a hat, although with your colouring I expect you can stand quite a lot of sun?' His eyes flicked briefly over her face and throat again and this time Angelique couldn't stop her blushes in time. 'Do I make you feel nervous?' he added, a slight smile touching his lips.

Shaking her head vigorously, she forced herself to look squarely at him. 'No, but you sometimes look at me in a way that makes me feel funny,' she admitted candidly. 'I suppose I'm used to you being "Uncle" Jordan rather than just a man.'

Jordan laughed. 'Oh, so I'm just a man now, am I? What a pity. I thought I might mean more to you than that.'

Angelique felt uncomfortable. She glanced down at

their hands, where his still held hers in a light, non-threatening grip. She wondered whether she should pull away.

'I didn't mean that to sound like an insult,' she said. Her attention was suddenly diverted by first one magpie and then a second walking across the lawn in front of them. 'Two for joy!' A smile lit up her face as she remembered the old saying and Jordan laughed.

'I hope so. We could do with some of that around here,' he said.

'What? Joy?' Angelique's smile faltered a little.

Jordan nodded and ran his free hand through his hair in a familiar gesture that incited another little twinge in her stomach. 'I'm afraid to say everything in the garden is not as rosy as it looks,' he murmured, as though afraid of being overheard.

She glanced around, her gaze taking in the well-stocked flower-beds and the carefully striped croquet lawn to their left. They were just approaching a fountain and she led Jordan over to a small wooden bench that faced it. By unspoken agreement they sat down side by side.

'I take it by that you mean money troubles?' Angelique said, referring to his earlier remark. She looked down at their lightly clasped hands, noting how Jordan's slender fingers were enhanced by very pale, perfectly oval fingernails.

Jordan squeezed her hand lightly and covered it completely with his other hand. 'Mainly,' he replied with a slight nod. 'But there are other little niggles. I don't want to bore you with them though.'

'You won't bore me,' Angelique insisted earnestly. 'If I'm going to stay here I need to know what the state of play is. I'm not a little doll who needs protection from the big bad world, you know?'

He glanced quickly at her. 'Aren't you?' he said teasingly. 'I thought you were. That's what your father

42

always used to say to me. "Jordan," he'd say, "that daughter of mine is just a fragile little doll who needs protection from the big bad world." He was most emphatic about it.'

'Liar!' Angelique exclaimed, laughing. There was no way in a million years her father would have said anything of the kind.

'Actually, Harvey told me once that he thought he had created a monster,' Jordan said. To Angelique's surprise he brought her hand up to his mouth and kissed her knuckles lightly before continuing. 'It was just before the Easter break one year, when you insisted you didn't want to go on a trip with your mother but wanted to come here instead. He said you were so insistent about it he just had to back down in the end.'

Angelique laughed. 'Oh, yes. I remember that. It was the last Easter I spent here when I was fourteen. We had that big party with a marquee on the lawn, and jugglers and everything.' Her eyes sparkled as she recalled the event, and then she found her mind wandering further. That day had been wonderful but something else had happened. What was it?

Like a picture she had once seen of the parting of the Red Sea, a path seemed to clear through the mists of time that clouded her memory and her head became filled instead with the images of Jordan and a woman. His girlfriend of the time, she supposed. The woman had been pretty but very shy. And apparently her shyness made her clumsy because she kept dropping things: plates, food and finally a glass of wine. Jordan hadn't looked angry though and, as she recalled it, the woman seemed more excited than upset by her clumsiness.

After the wine incident, Jordan had ordered his girl-friend to go inside and clean herself up. A few minutes later he had followed her. About half an hour after that Angelique had gone inside to use the lavatory and had heard voices coming from Jordan's office. The door was slightly ajar and giving in to the temptation to peek inside, she had found herself rooted to the spot by the sight that met her eyes.

The woman was bent forward, spread-eagled face down across Jordan's desk and her skirt was hitched right up around her waist. She was not wearing any knickers, Angelique recalled with a tiny shudder. Jordan was lightly stroking her bare bottom. The woman was moaning quietly – Angelique supposed at the time it was with the awful shame of her predicament – and she kept calling Jordan, 'Master.'

Jordan was muttering things that Angelique couldn't hear, and then – and this was the worst part – he picked up a length of thin bamboo and began to strike his girlfriend with it across the backside. Instead of crying the woman began to moan louder and began to gasp, 'Yes. Yes. Oh, yes. Oh, please, yes!' And it was at that point Angelique found her feet and ran off down the corridor, putting as much space as possible between herself and the terrible scene in Jordan's office.

But the breathless, pleading voice of the woman stayed in her ears for a long time afterwards, and so did the image of Jordan's hand raising and lowering the cane.

As though the event had taken place that instant, and not ten years earlier, Angelique glanced up and gazed at Jordan in amazement. 'You – you whipped that woman. I remember now,' she gasped.

'Pardon?' Jordan's brow creased in confusion. 'I don't know what – ' He broke off as the realisation dawned on him. Hell! He hadn't realised at the time that Angelique had witnessed anything untoward. There had been a lot going on then, one way and another, but he thought she had been kept well and truly in the dark. 'You saw that?' he said, trying to sound a lot calmer than he felt.

Angelique let her head fall back and simply stared at

the cloudless blue sky for a moment. 'Yes. I saw it although I didn't understand what I was witnessing at the time.'

'And you do now?'

'Not really.' She glanced sideways at him again, then returned her gaze to the wide expanse of sky. 'I know a bit about sadism and that sort of thing. I read a bit of Marquis de Sade once.'

'But you didn't like it?'

Angelique shook her head slowly. 'I wouldn't say I didn't like it exactly. I didn't understand it. I didn't understand how men could derive pleasure from beating innocent young women day and night.'

Despite his discomfort, Jordan laughed. 'The Marquis de Sade is a bit extreme. You should read some of the books in your room instead.'

She turned her head, the nape of her neck still resting on the back of the bench. 'Do all the rooms have those books – or did you put them there especially for me?' she asked.

Jordan hesitated. 'Some of the rooms have similar bookshelves and some don't,' he said finally, deciding that partial honesty would be the best policy. 'We have a certain number of regular guests who appreciate that sort of thing.'

'Oh.' Angelique sat up straight. 'Do you provide them with anything else? Anything "special"?'

She noticed her perception seemed to surprise him but buried the urge to mention it.

'What makes you ask that?' he said.

She shrugged. 'Well, it stands to reason. If certain guests have particular requirements and you are able to meet those requirements as fully as possible, then they'll keep coming back to the hotel, won't they?' Her smile was guileless although her heart was beating nineteen to the dozen.

'That's about the size of it,' Jordan said, apparently

unwilling to expand on the subject. 'Oh, look,' he said, changing the subject hastily. 'Some new guests are arriving.'

They both turned to look as Geoff Wright and Moira O'Donnell swept around the driveway in a red Cavalier and disappeared out of sight.

'Don't you need to go and greet them?' Angelique asked.

Jordan shook his head and stood up, pulling her to her feet at the same time. 'Not yet. They know their way around. But you have forgotten, so shall we continue with our tour? We haven't got very far yet.'

Their walk took them around the perimeter of the house, through an abundantly-stocked kitchen garden and across a wide, pebbled courtyard. Angelique stared up at the house as it seemed to glow in the midday sun and Jordan pointed out a few architectural features.

'You might notice the building is a bit of an oddity in places,' he said.

Angelique laughed. 'I'm not that up on architecture, I'm afraid.'

Jordan swept the air with his hand. 'Look, there,' he said. 'Typical Elizabethan, but then . . .' He took her hand again and dragged her around to another part of the house. 'A hundred years after it was built the owner commissioned the famous Lancelot "Capability" Brown to widen the wings on the south front here. Even then the remodelling didn't stop. Nash added a new wing and finally, in the Victorian period, Nash's work was pulled down and all this heavy-handed Jacobean-style stuff was put in its place. Really and truly the house should be an absolute nightmare but it all works somehow.'

'Yes, it does. I love the place,' Angelique said, nodding. 'Turning it into a hotel was a good idea.'

Jordan shrugged. 'Oh, well. It wasn't strictly my concept. This house has been a hotel before, you know?'

'No. I didn't.' Angelique was surprised but then she supposed that people in bygone eras had needed hotels just as much as people did today. A thought occurred to her and she asked, 'Was it my childhood imagination or did this place have a veritable maze of secret passages?'

For a moment, Jordan hesitated. 'Yes, you remember correctly,' he said. 'But most of them are blocked off now.'

Angelique pouted. 'Oh, that's a shame. I used to love exploring. Dad even told me once that one of the passages led all the way underground to Thornbury village church.' She gazed around, still entranced by her surroundings, not quite able to believe that she was actually here again after such a long time.

The tour apparently concluded, she followed Jordan into the house and his office, where a pot of coffee and plate of tiny sandwiches miraculously awaited them.

'You realise I need to sort out this problem of my true parentage?' she said when she had eaten a couple of the sandwiches.

'I don't know if I can be of much help,' Jordan admitted, as he swung casually from side to side in his swivel chair. 'Harvey didn't tell me a thing until the eleventh hour and even then it was only as much as he told you in the letter.'

Angelique pursed her lips. 'It's so frustrating. I honestly don't know where to begin.' She ate another sandwich and stared out of the window. 'I suppose I could start by obtaining my proper birth certificate. At least it will have my mother's name on it and an address, although I expect she'll be long gone from wherever it was. She might even be dead for all I know.'

Strangely, the desire to find out who her biological mother had been was not as strong as her urge to know her true father. It was as though he would have to at

47

least match up to Harvey, who had been such a successful and charismatic man, otherwise she would feel less of a person herself. It was, after all, that man's genes in her make-up and not Harvey's.

'There's a lot more to a person's development than simply their genes,' Jordan said, as though he could read her mind.

Glancing up, Angelique smiled wanly. 'I know. But I have to find out. I just have to. Can you understand that?'

He nodded. 'I think so. I'm sure I would if I were you. So, are you going to try and get hold of a copy of your birth certificate?' He sat forward and rubbed his hands together as though the simple act would help galvanize her into action.

'Yes. But not today. I'm still finding my feet,' Angelique said. 'In fact, what I'd really like to do this afternoon is have a look at the kitchens and some of your sample menus. I have an idea that there's a bit of room for improvement there.'

Unbeknown to her, Jordan had to fight down an attack of panic. He knew Angelique had spent several years completing a cordon bleu course and had suspected that her interests would veer in that direction if she planned to stay at the hotel permanently. Betty wouldn't be too pleased at what she would regard as interference, but too bad. Angelique was entitled to go and do more or less whatever she wished.

'Of course, feel free. Just try to avoid the busy times,' he suggested. 'Betty can get a bit tetchy, if you know what I mean.'

'Trust me,' Angelique responded, with a smile. 'I don't intend to tread on anyone's toes, either literally or figuratively.'

Half an hour later Jordan watched her go. He wondered how long they could continue to keep her in the dark.

She had already touched on some very delicate subjects and it was only a matter of time before someone opened their mouth, or she stumbled across something she shouldn't. Perhaps he should just come clean now and let her make her own decision about whether she still wanted to stay. He nodded to himself. Yes, that was exactly what he would do. Tonight he would wine her and dine her and tell her everything.

Chapter Four

'You filthy little pervert!' Moira raised her foot and nudged the trussed figure under the ribs. 'Horrible little poof!'

Lesley groaned with delight and tried to wriggle into a more uncomfortable position. Oh, God, she adored Mrs O'Donnell! She would do anything for her: kiss her toes, suck the high, spiked heels of her black patent boots, even lick her hotel room clean from top to bottom. In fact, on one occasion Lesley had offered to do just that, but Jordan had refused to entertain the idea – it was not time-efficient, he had pointed out, forcing Lesley to agree. Jordan was very hot on efficiency.

Lesley looked forward to Mrs O'Donnell's visits with a passion. She was really heartless was Mrs O'Donnell, uncompromising and with an unerring ability to understand exactly what her submissives needed and when they needed it. Mostly, Lesley just needed to be tied up and left for as long as possible and the mere sight of a ball of string was enough to set her heart racing.

Of course, during the daytime Mrs O'Donnell was just like any other guest. She came and went, ate in the dining-room and slept in the bed that Lesley had turned down with her own fair hands. But when darkness fell, she took Lesley down the back staircase to the cellar where a secluded 'dungeon' awaited. And when she ordered Lesley to lie face down on the cellar floor with her hands clasping her ankles, the thin, eager 'woman' in the sober black dress couldn't abase herself quickly enough.

Throughout the careful tying-up procedure, Geoff would invariably look on from whichever contraption he was bound to. He neither envied the attention Lesley received from Moira nor resented the intrusion of a third party. Lesley's ritual humiliation gave an added dimension to his own pleasure. It meant he had to wait a little longer for chastisement – hanging in some unspeakable position until Moira was ready to attend to him, and until his arms and legs ached with the strain. But it all added to the enjoyment of their sessions. Having Moira's undivided attention was good, but being reduced to just a part of her 'harem' was even better. It reminded him how little he mattered to Moira's entertainment and how lucky he was to have her as his mistress.

Whatever perverse enjoyment Geoff might derive from this notion, it wasn't strictly true. Moira couldn't envisage a future that didn't include her son-in-law – but he wasn't to know that. It did him good to keep him dangling, she thought – in more ways than one.

Striding across the shadowy, cloistered room to inspect her other 'slave', Moira obtained an erotically-charged satisfaction from the proud way her body moved and the ominous sound of her heels clicking decisively on the stone floor. Tonight, Geoff was hanging spread-eagled on a frame, wearing only a simple version of a Roman legionnaire's outfit with nothing underneath, his long, thinning, mousy hair gathered in a high ponytail.

She herself had chosen to wear her new black leather corset and a short matching skirt. The skirt barely skimmed the top of her ample thighs, where the tops of her hold-up stockings hugged the white flesh just a little too snugly for comfort, and her breasts overflowed the corset's meagre cups. Despite the slight discomfort of wearing too-tight clothes, she felt good and knew she looked powerful. She was 'Moira the Magnificent'! A mental image which made her smile to herself as she smoothed her palms over her ample hips and buttocks with obvious relish.

Turning her attention to Geoff, she curled her upper lip in disdain. 'Well, well. And how are you feeling my fine, strong soldier?' she mocked.

Reaching for a tawse which hung on a rack on the wall with a selection of other whips and torturous-looking instruments, she used the tip to lift the front of Geoff's 'skirt' and regard his burgeoning erection. 'Naughty,' she admonished. For a moment she stroked his upper thighs with the whip before lashing him smartly across the stomach a couple of times.

Geoff winced but bore the strokes bravely and in silence – it hardly hurt at all and was only a taster of what was to come later.

Moira, satisfied that he had been duly forewarned, inspected him again.

From the corner, Lesley – still trussed like a Christmas turkey, perspiration marking trails in her thick pancake make-up which was intended to disguise the distasteful appearance of a five o'clock shadow – watched wide-eyed and groaned aloud when she saw how livid Geoff's engorged cock looked.

It was a moment to savour for all three of them, and each felt a distinct surge of arousal. There was no doubt about it, it was going to be a good night.

Angelique was surprised and flattered to be invited to dine with Jordan in his own apartment that evening, instead of in the hotel dining-room. He had instructed her to let herself in when she arrived, and as she pushed open the front door of the west wing her ears caught a slight whispering sound as the bottom of the door slid across the maroon carpet. Crossing the threshold, she immediately noticed a profusion of fat, creamy candles flickering in wall sconces and freestanding wrought iron candelabra as the draught she had created touched each tiny flame. And a moment later Jordan appeared, looking relaxed and casual in light-blue jeans and matching chambray shirt, wiping his hands on a tea-towel.

She glanced at the tea-towel and then up at his face. 'You look as though I caught you in the middle of something,' she said with a smile.

'You did. Supper,' he replied, stepping forward and pushing open a door to his right. 'If you'd like to make yourself comfortable in there, I'll be with you in about ten minutes.'

Walking into the elegant dining-cum-sitting-room, she wondered at the sort of man who would willingly cook supper for himself and a guest when all he had to do was pick up the telephone and order room service like anyone else at the hotel. All members of staff, she'd discovered during her visit to the kitchens that afternoon, were entitled to order their meals free of charge from either the daily or à la carte menus.

For a while she contented herself with wandering around the room, examining various *objets d'art* and the combination of oil paintings and watercolours that hung on the walls, or stroking an idle hand across the smooth patina of the antique walnut furniture. Only the large round dining table was covered, by a thick, white linen cloth that provided the perfect canvas for the eighteenth century blue-and-white porcelain dinner service, heavy silver cutlery and crystal glass that graced it. A delicate chandelier cast a pool of light over the table top and right in the very centre of the table sat an arrangement of freshly-cut flowers in varying shades of pink, mauve and blue.

The perfection of her surroundings entranced her so much that she missed the sound of Jordan's light tread until he was standing right behind her. Consequently the surprising touch of his hand upon her shoulder startled her.

'Oh, God! Jordan. You frightened the life out of me,' she gasped, holding a hand to her chest and feeling the rapid beat of her heart. Her eyes caught his gaze and held still. And held.

Finally, he was the one to break the spell. 'I just came to ask you which wine you would prefer,' he said.

Angelique felt her heartbeat gradually return to normal and shrugged with feigned nonchalance. 'It depends. What are we having?'

Delighted with the way she reacted to him and her attempts to conceal her feelings, Jordan smiled. 'Rabbit terrine to start. Followed by salmon steaks *en papillote* and if you can manage it, traditional sherry trifle for pudding.'

'Gosh.' Angelique was stunned. 'I thought I was the cookery expert around here. I suppose a Nuits-Saint-Georges or something similar, to go with the starter, and then a white wine, Chablis perhaps.' For a moment the professional side of her came to the fore, a fact which made Jordan's smile widen.

'I absolutely agree with both suggestions,' he said. 'But I must insist on a third wine with our pudding. I already have a good bottle of Dom Perignon on ice.'

'Perfect!' Angelique's eyes glittered in the candlelight and for a moment she felt tempted to reach up and plant a kiss on Jordan's mouth.

She had to remind herself he was probably just being kind, that his attentiveness and charming behaviour were no more and no less than he would show to any other close relative of a dear, departed friend. Suddenly, she realised he was speaking to her.

'I asked you if you felt hungry enough to eat now?' he repeated when she apologised. 'I could turn everything down if you'd rather wait a while.'

'Oh, no. Don't do that, it would spoil,' Angelique said quickly. 'If the food is ready so am I. All I've done today is pick at this and that. I haven't really eaten anything substantial.'

Jordan nodded. He'd had to fend off Betty's complaints earlier in the day about Angelique's inquisitiveness in *her* kitchen.

'Don't know who the little madam thinks she is,' the plump woman had grumbled, wringing the bottom of her apron between her hands. 'She even had the cheek to insinuate that the menus could be a bit more exciting – started suggesting all sorts of dishes with poncey French names. Well, I'm not having any of that, thank you very much.'

Jordan had sighed with barely disguised irritation, tried to placate Betty and when that failed, concluded by pointing out that, whether they liked it or not, Angelique was part-owner of the hotel and did know what she was talking about when it came to food. It was a tricky situation and he didn't relish the prospect of having to tread a fine diplomatic line between the two women.

As the evening progressed, he managed to push all thoughts of Betty and, indeed, the entire hotel from his mind. Angelique was charming and diverting company. He loved the way her eyes sparkled as she spoke and the manner in which the candlelight picked up the shades of red, copper and gold in her soft brown hair. And he derived an aesthetic pleasure from the stylish clothes she wore – tonight, a simple off-white dress, the pure silk virginal yet revealing, clinging to her sinuous form like a film of fresh cream.

Right now she was facing him, head slightly inclined to one side, the ends of her hair just brushing the table top, as she brought him up to date on the past few years of her life in Paris.

'I couldn't help noticing how over-populated and unstylish London seemed in comparison,' she said, sitting back in her chair and patting her stomach where she was sure a bulge had appeared from all the good food Jordan had 'forced' her to eat.

'You sound as though you're already homesick,' he observed as he reached across the table to top up her champagne flute for the third time.

'Careful, I'm going to be under the table in a minute,' she joked, not bothering to stop him from pouring despite her words. All at once her laughing expression seemed to cloud over a little. 'To be honest, I'm not in the least bit homesick. I know it sounds odd but since I arrived at Thornbury Court I've felt as though I have come home. Does that make any sense?' Her hazel eyes widened with questioning and Jordan nodded gently.

'Perfect sense,' he said. 'You feel your father here. So do I. He's all around us.' He paused as he noticed the way Angelique swallowed deeply. Glancing up at her face he noticed how her eyes misted over with unshed tears. 'Cry if you like,' he murmured.

To his surprise Angelique shook her head and brushed a stray tear away angrily, using the back of her hand. 'No. I'm not going to do any more crying,' she said defiantly. 'I came here tonight with the full intention of enjoying myself. Not blubbering all over you again.' She managed a watery but determined smile which broadened as he smiled back.

Rising to his feet abruptly, Jordan began to clear the table and stack the dishes on a trolley beside it. 'In that case, might I suggest you retire to the lounge.' He pronounced the word 'lange' in a pseudo upper-class accent which made Angelique giggle and forget her previous distress. 'That's better,' he said. 'I won't be a minute. I'll just dump these things in the dishwasher and make us some coffee. Feel free to put on some music if you want to and there are some magazines in that drawer.' He nodded in the direction of a walnut side table.

At that moment Angelique realised there was no television in the room.

'I hate TV,' Jordan said when she mentioned it. 'My own father always used to call it the moron's magnet and he was right, judging by the dross they seem to put on it these days.'

She nodded. 'I don't usually watch it much either, especially as French programming seems to be marginally worse than in this country, if that's at all possible.'

As soon as Jordan left the room she wandered over to the music console, put on a selection of Mozart and then opened the magazine drawer, prepared to flick through a couple of magazines until Jordan returned.

It seemed that her host had been gone a long time, Angelique thought after she had flicked through and discarded a third magazine. She paused before making her next selection and gazed at the door expectantly, willing it to open. It remained firmly shut and she could hear no sound of movement outside in the passage-way either. Oh, well. There were still plenty more magazines to go.

Rummaging through the pile she discovered that under the top layer of issues of *Country Life* and *Esquire*, there were a number of rather more interesting publications. Not for Jordan the standard 'girlie' mag, these were pure erotica – sepia-toned photographs of men and women engaged in various stages of love-making. And similarly, there were other more esoteric photographs where the models were bound and attached to a bewildering variety of contraptions. Angelique's eyes became wider as she thumbed through the entire pile of magazines.

Although nearly all of the photographs entranced her, there were a few to which she felt compelled to return for a second look. One, of a slender dark-haired woman dressed only in stockings, shoes and a pair of Victorian bloomers, particularly caught her imagination. It was erotic in its simplicity. The woman's face – the top half obscured by a dramatic feathered mask – bore an enigmatic smile as she sat with her legs splayed, the open-crotch bloomers exposing everything, every soft fold of her shaven sex. *La Giaconda* uncovered, Angelique thought as she gazed at it. Rude innocence.

A shiver ran down her spine as she reluctantly closed the magazine and put it down on the pile. Somewhere deep inside her she felt the tiniest flicker of arousal turn into a flame which spread and encompassed her whole body by the time Jordan finally reappeared.

As he set down a silver tray on the low coffee table in front of the sofa where Angelique sat, his eyes wandered over the collection of magazines strewn beside her. It amused him the way her cheeks coloured when she realised she had been caught out and he couldn't help wondering what she thought of them. To him the photographs were beautiful, a sensuous portrayal of the human body at its finest. It was no good, he couldn't resist asking her opinion.

'They are – interesting,' Angelique said hesitantly in reply to his casual inquiry. 'I rarely come across magazines of this quality. If anything, the continental ones that I have seen have been grossly explicit rather than sensuous like these.' François had a great stack of them in his wardrobe, she remembered.

'You surprise me,' Jordan said. 'I've always considered Paris to be the most erotic city in the world.'

Glancing at him, Angelique felt her desire grow. 'That's true,' she murmured, almost having to force herself to sound casual. 'I suppose what I'm saying is, I never really took much notice of such things. To me, porn has always been porn.'

'But you don't consider these to be pornographic?' Jordan persisted.

Angelique stared at him, her stomach clenching so tightly she wondered if it would ever unknot itself again. 'No, I told you. I think these are truly sensuous.'

She held up one of the magazines and, with the discriminating eye of an art critic, regarded a photograph of two women locked together in a very intimate embrace. Holding the picture away from her, she cocked her head first to one side and then the other as she considered the erotic tableau.

Unbeknown to her a small serpent seemed to uncurl in the pit of Jordan's stomach and slither through his belly to his loins. 'So, you like them?' he said.

'Oh, yes. Very much.' Angelique deliberately selected another magazine, flicked through it and stopped at a photograph of a young woman dressed only in a white corset, matching stockings and bride's veil, who was being whipped by the leather-clad 'groom'. 'Look at this. Isn't it just wonderful?' she added, her eyes sparkling as she glanced from the photograph to his face.

It was too much for Jordan. Her expression. The way her mouth pouted and curved into a cat-like smile and the undulating movements of her body beneath the thin white dress all served to heighten his desire to an unbearable degree. Without considering the possible consequences he dropped to his knees in front of her, clasped her face gently between his hands and kissed her.

For a moment, Angelique was stunned by Jordan's action, then she felt herself responding. Her body acted almost of its own volition as her lips opened slightly under the pressure of his mouth and she felt the tip of her tongue investigate tentatively before beginning an earnest thrust and parry with his. A heady mix of emotions surged through her as he moved his hands down her body and clasped her tighter to him, pulling her right to the edge of the sofa. She felt helpless, like a rag doll. All she wanted right at that moment was for the kiss to go on indefinitely and for Jordan to hold her as tightly as he possibly could.

Ridiculous phrases kept darting through her mind as though she were the powerless heroine of an old Hollywood movie. Take me, take me! Make me yours! she thought. Perhaps she was so desperate to find a replacement for her father's love and devotion that she was pinning her hopes on Jordan. It was a sobering thought.

As if he sensed her change of mood, he broke away abruptly and gave her a searching look. 'What's troubling you, Angelique?' he asked softly. 'I can see pain in your eyes and your body has tensed up.'

She shook her head. 'I'm sorry, Jordan,' she said. 'I can't help it. Sometimes I just start thinking. Well, you know. I thought I knew who I was and where I was going. Now I feel kind of shipwrecked.' Her eyelids fluttered as she struggled to express herself succinctly without bursting into yet more tears.

To her relief he simply nodded his understanding and urged her head against the solid wall of his chest, his hand stroking her hair, calming her. 'I shouldn't have kissed you,' he said at last. 'I'm sorry.'

'No. Don't be.' Pulling away from his embrace, she looked up quickly. 'I can't explain it but it feels very right when you kiss me and touch me . . .' Her words trailed away as she glanced down, suddenly feeling embarrassed. Right at that moment her feelings for him definitely weren't those of a woman looking for a father substitute.

Jordan caught her chin with the tips of his fingers and tilted her face up to look at him again. 'I would like to make love to you, Angelique,' he said softly.

Her eyes widened and she darted wild glances around the room as though seeking either a means of escape, or the answer to her dilemma. Forcing herself to concentrate on Jordan's face, a mass of conflicting emotions surged through her, each of them jostling to take precedence. Her first thought was that she couldn't have sex with him. It would almost be like incest. And yet her body was already betraying her mind. The flame of desire still burned inside her more insistently than ever. It had been ignited by the photographs but now it blazed and grew for Jordan. She wanted him. She wanted him fervently and with a depth of longing she didn't think she had ever felt before.

'I think I want you too,' she said quietly, deliberately making her reply an understatement, scared of revealing too much too soon. Moving forward on the seat she stroked a heavy lock of blond hair away from his forehead and gazed deeply into his eyes. Suddenly, she felt overwhelmed by the strength of her feelings for him. 'No. I don't think it,' she amended. 'I know it. I do want you. I do.'

For a moment Jordan simply stared back at her as though he couldn't believe her words. And then he acted swiftly and decisively, standing up, then bending forward to scoop her into his arms.

Her own arms wound about his neck as he lifted her and carried her from the room and down the narrow passage-way to his bedroom. Sighing with pleasure, she pressed her lips into the dip at the base of his throat. He smelt of musk and autumn leaves where his top button was undone, his skin as soft and downy as a baby's. Putting out her tongue she licked him, from the point where the edges of his shirt met, right up to the underside of his jaw. There the skin was much rougher, like sandpaper, and she nuzzled against him instead, her mouth emitting another small sigh.

At that moment she felt so safe and protected and yet

the instant he laid her down on the rich brocade that covered his high, four-poster bed, she felt her innocence desert her. In its place the fire within her raged anew, the flames lapping at her nipples until they hardened and chafed against the fragile fabric of her dress, while hot tongues licked insistently between her legs. The desire she felt made her whole body feel tingly and alive and she couldn't ignore the sensation of her sex blossoming and moistening. Soon, very soon, Jordan would see the proof of her arousal for himself and the thought excited her even more, readying her body for their eventual union.

Moving across the room to the window, he drew the heavy drapes against the outside world, then returned to stand by the side of the bed. His eyes refused to leave hers as he undressed quickly, then bent forward to slide the thin straps of Angelique's dress over her shoulders and down her arms, exposing her high, firm breasts.

Her breath caught as he touched her. His fingers were so gentle they whispered across her skin, inciting goosebumps wherever they travelled. In moments he had removed her dress and the skimpy pair of white silk knickers she wore underneath.

'You are so beautiful, Angelique,' he murmured, his warm breath another soft caress upon her straining breasts. 'I can't believe how perfect you are.'

His compliments excited her as much as his hands as they mounded her breasts, stroking and squeezing in an assessing, controlled way that made her desperate to feel his touch on every part of her body. Added to her frustration was the fact that he wouldn't let her touch him. Every time she put out a tentative hand he moved it and admonished her gently. 'No. Just relax and enjoy yourself.'

So she had to content herself with caressing him visually, her gaze taking in every part of his lean, lightly tanned body which glowed with the lustre of burnished gold in the soft candlelight. Somewhere along the line her modest desire for him had been usurped by a raging passion and she groaned aloud as she felt him put his lips to her breast. Running the risk of being reprimanded for her boldness, she took his fair head between her hands and guided his mouth to the taut, berry-like nipples which craved his attention so much she thought she would scream.

Her heart pounded as his tactile exploration of her body was eagerly duplicated by his mouth which he moved slowly over her, his lips sucking at tiny portions of her flesh as his mouth travelled back and forth across her torso.

Apparently oblivious to Angelique's pleas to take her quickly, he gradually delved further and further until his chin grazed the soft curls that hid her burgeoning sex.

'Be patient. We have all night,' he said softly when she ground her pelvis urgently against him.

'But – I can't stand it!' Angelique gasped. 'I want you so much. I want to feel you. Feel you inside me.'

Jordan chuckled softly. 'All in good time. Now open up for me, darling, and let me explore you properly.' His fingertips nudged her thighs, which she parted obediently, then they spread apart her swollen sex lips with insolent determination.

'Oh, God!' A powerful surge of heat overtook her as she felt Jordan's breath caress her swollen clitoris, to be followed in the next instant by the tip of his tongue.

'Mmm, thick cream. My favourite,' he murmured wickedly a moment later as his tongue slid over the slick folds of her inner labia and delved inside her vagina, probing and exciting the sensitive flesh like a tiny cock.

She bucked wildly, hardly able to bear the myriad sensations which swept through her and threatened to drive her insane with pleasure. 'Jordan, please!' Frantic with lust her words were little more than an anguished gasp.

'Please what? Please stop?' he teased, laughing when she shook her head wildly from side to side.

'You know that's not what I meant,' she said, sounding as though she were in pain.

Jordan glanced up and, taking advantage of the fact that she had diverted his attention for a moment, she suddenly wriggled out from under him and pushed him over on to his back. Before he could protest she straddled his torso, her back to his face, her hands enclosing the rigid shaft of his cock. Lowering her head, she wet her lips then slid them over his glans. It looked as plump and succulently purple as a plum and she began sucking and licking it with true relish.

She winced as Jordan's fingers suddenly gripped her buttocks. Beneath her own fingers she could feel his excitement mounting – a certain surging sensation just below the tautly stretched skin covering his stem. Sliding her lips lower she endeavoured to take as much of him in her mouth as possible. He was moments away from coming, she could sense it and despite her yearning to take him inside her body all she wanted right at that moment was the victory of feeling him cede to the pleasure of her mouth. As he said, they had all night. Plenty of time to start all over again.

It took Jordan by surprise when Angelique suddenly turned the tables on him. But he was not complaining by any means. In fact, at that moment he thought he was as close to heaven as he was ever likely to get. The sight of her naked body – as brown as a berry with just the lightest covering of down, like a peach – sitting astride him, her lean thighs gripping his sides, her buttocks inches away from his face, was almost too much for him to bear.

But no. He was not yet in heaven. Perfect bliss was

when she leaned forward and took him in her mouth. It was a moment to savour: feeling the soft ends of her hair brushing his legs, watching her pouting sex moisten tantalisingly before his very eyes, and best of all, knowing that her soft, sulky mouth encompassed the most sensitive part of his body. His only regret was that she was not facing him so that he could see the way her lips caressed his erection.

He prided himself on his self-control, but in this instance there was no question of holding back. A deep, guttural explosion of pleasure broke from his lips as the warm salty fluid jetted from him and was swallowed instantly by Angelique.

'Christ! Oh, yes. Oh, God!' In the throes of passion he didn't have the words to express the way he felt. Instead he felt himself gripping the taut buttocks that swayed in front of him, his fingers spreading them apart and probing the puckered flesh thus exposed.

Wave after wave of delicious eroticism swept through Angelique as she tasted Jordan's semen and sucked him dry. As though she were coming back to earth she felt an unexpected rush of shame as she realised how wantonly she had behaved and how the man she had always looked up to was now probing the most intimate parts of her body. All at once she felt horribly exposed and tried to twist away from his clutches but he held her fast, his fingers relentlessly opening her up to his inspection.

'Oh, no. Please, not there,' she moaned as Jordan spread her buttocks even wider apart and began to press a thumb against the tight opening of her anus.

Somehow he manoeuvred himself out from under her and applied just the slightest pressure between her shoulder blades, forcing her cheek against the coverlet and her back to arch so that her bottom was thrust into the air even more lewdly than before. Then she felt his fingers opening her vagina and skimming the very edge of it.

'God, you're wet,' he said, his actions and words making her stomach cramp with a mixture of renewed shame and arousal.

Gathering some of her creamy juices with the tip of his index finger, he held it to her lips. She sucked obediently, her tastebuds delighting in the sweet, musky flavour of herself. When the fingertip was clean she licked her lips and sighed. By now she felt totally helpless, as though her body was his to do with whatever he wished. She craved the sensation of his cock inside her even more strongly than ever and yet she also felt strangely calm. All good things come to those who wait, and he would fuck her eventually. She had no doubt of that. In fact she trusted that by the time they had finished making love he would know her better than she knew herself.

Much later, Angelique made her way back to her own suite. She felt good, in fact better than good. For the first time in months her body felt totally relaxed and she barely noticed the floor beneath her feet as she retraced her steps down the passage-way towards the main part of the house.

At the end of the passage she stopped. If she remembered rightly there was a much shorter route back to the wing that housed her suite – now which way should she go? Trying a couple of doors to her left, the direction she thought she should take, she found to her dismay that they were locked, but the next door along still held a key in the lock. Turning it she found a passage-way beyond shrouded in darkness. Feeling around on the wall beside her, her fingers finally connected with a light switch. In a moment the passage was filled with dim light.

Guided by her rusty memory and natural sense of direction, she followed a route along the maze of corridors. Suddenly she reached what seemed to be a dead-end. Glancing back the way she had come, she realised there was no point in turning back until she had investigated the possibilities of the wall in front of her. She seemed to remember that some of the passage-ways were so well hidden that only by discovering a certain pressure point on the wall could she hope to reveal a hidden doorway.

Childish feelings of excitement welled up inside her. This was what she had always loved most about the old place. Not the vast gardens, or the architectural splendour of the building itself, but its mysteries, the myriad little secrets that it housed. Pressing her palms against the wall, she marked out a route from the floor to the highest point she could reach. Just when she thought she must be mistaken and had come across a genuinely blocked passage, she felt the wall give slightly beneath her hands. In the next instant her body lurched forward as the wall opened in front of her.

On the other side it was dark again, and just for an instant she wondered if she should go back. She wasn't that keen about being in the dark at the best of times, but further on she thought she could detect a glimmer of light. Making her way towards it she found herself at a sort of T-junction. By her estimation she needed to turn right, and so she did. Now the passage-way was lit again and glancing left and right she noticed the walls were punctuated by a series of low, heavy oak doors. She tried the handle of one, and was surprised when the door opened.

Chapter Five

Whatever Angelique had been expecting, an empty, dusty room, or a wine cellar perhaps, it certainly wasn't the sight that met her eyes. Leaning weakly against the wall, her hand resting protectively at her throat, she gasped for breath as she took in the scene that confronted her.

On the far wall, manacled to some sort of wooden frame was a man. He was in his early-thirties, she supposed, and had long mousy hair which was gathered into a high ponytail. He stared balefully back at her as her sweeping gaze took in his 'costume' – a sort of leather jerkin and short skirt made from strips of leather. He wore nothing on his feet, which were strapped to the frame a few inches from the floor by leather ankle cuffs and all things considered, her first impression was that she had inadvertently stepped into a scene from *Ben Hur*.

It was then she noticed the other one. A pathetic bundle, wearing a black dress and stockings, again no shoes, and trussed up in the corner. As its head came up to see who the interloper was, she realised with a second gasp of shock that the woman was Lesley, the house-keeper she had met earlier.

Before she had a chance to speak, breathe properly, or do anything at all, a door to her right opened and through it stepped the most amazing sight of all.

Moira had just been to the lavatory – her growing excitement proving too much of a strain on her bladder – and was returning with true wickedness in mind. She was going to give Geoff the beating she had promised him, the thin whippy cane in her right hand the instrument she had selected as most appropriate for what she had in store for him. It would stripe him neatly but the marks would fade by the time he got back home. Heaven forbid that Geoff should go back to Jane covered in tell-tale stripes. How ever would he explain that?

Intent on what she was about to do she almost missed the vision of the young woman dressed in white, her slender body pressed against the wall so hard she looked as though she were trying to melt into it. Thoughts of vestal virgins skittered through Moira's head and just for a brief instant she wondered if her dream of chastising another woman was about to come true at long last. Perhaps Jordan Cavendish had sent her by way of a token for being a regular customer.

Marching across the stone-flagged floor on perilously high heels, Moira pointed the end of the cane at Angelique.

'Did Jordan tell you to come?' she asked sternly.

Angelique heard the words, which were delivered in a slight northern accent and shook her head dumbly. What the hell was going on here? Who was this woman, clad from head to toe in black and looking like an overweight Barbarella?

She realised in the same instant, this was some kind of kinky sado-masochism scene – a grotesque reproduction of some of photographs in the magazines she had been looking at earlier that evening in Jordan's flat. The question, or rather two questions that sprang to mind were: why was all this taking place in Thornbury Court,

69

of all places? And did Jordan know about it? Then she realised that of course he must. The woman even had the nerve to ask if Jordan had sent her down there.

Dumbly, Angelique shook her head.

'Where's your tongue, girl?' the woman rapped out as she advanced menacingly. 'Don't you know your manners? Speak when spoken to.'

Feeling rather faint, Angelique nevertheless rediscovered her voice with a vengeance. 'Don't you raise your voice to me – who the hell are you?' she countered.

Now it was the other woman's turn to look slightly off balance. 'I – er . . ., Moira O'Donnell,' she said.

Angelique straightened up. 'Well, Moira O'Donnell. Perhaps you can tell me just what you think you're doing?'

Moira stared back at Angelique for a moment and then realised that one of the 'normal' guests must have inadvertently stumbled upon Thornbury Court's little secret. Turning to glance firstly at Geoff, who seemed happy enough, although his mouth strained around the thick leather gag as though he were trying to contribute something to the encounter, and then at Lesley who was wide-eyed but looking quite docile, she motioned to her unexpected guest to follow her over to a couple of chairs.

Sitting down, she tried and failed to cross her plump legs and instead put the cane down on the floor and folded her arms. 'Well, young lady,' she said, her tone of voice now more motherly than menacing, 'I think perhaps it's time I extended your education.'

Jordan was already in a deep sleep when he was roused by the sound of frantic hammering on the front door and a persistent buzzing of the doorbell. Stumbling from the bed, he lurched down the hallway, dragging on a bathrobe as he went.

'What in heaven's name . . .?' he began, flinging open the front door.

To his surprise he encountered Angelique. Or rather a version of Angelique. This one bore no resemblance to the delightful young woman who had graced his bed for the past few hours.

'You – you ...!' She advanced across the threshold, her eyes glittering with anger and indignation, her lithe body thrusting towards him like a weapon. Pointing a finger, she stabbed him with her fingernail in the middle of his chest. 'Bastard!' she hissed. 'Filthy, perverted, scheming bastard!'

Despite her agitation, he couldn't help being flippant. It was so often his way, although he had been forced to regret his levity in the past. 'Has something upset you, Angelique?'

Glaring at him in silence for a moment, she opened her mouth to speak. Then the fight seemed to go out of her, and she wavered like a leaf in the wind, before crumbling completely. Slowly she sank to the floor and pulled her knees up to her chest. Hugging them against her, she lowered her forehead to her knees and began to cry with harsh, strangled sobs.

Feeling genuinely worried, Jordan squatted down in front of her and attempted to put his arms around her shuddering body.

'Get off!' she snapped, shrugging him away. 'Take your filthy hands off me.'

'Angelique, I ...' He reached out to her again, wondering what on earth could be the matter with her but to his surprise she put out a hand and pushed hard against his chest with so much force that he rocked on the balls of his feet and went tumbling backwards.

'Get the fuck away from me!' she screamed. 'I hate you. I hate this house.' She paused, then glanced around contemptuously. 'And first thing in the morning I'm leaving. I don't know why I ever came here in the first place.'

Jordan opened his mouth to speak, but she silenced him with a glare.

'Don't say anything,' she warned. 'I've just about had it up to here.' Smacking her palm dramatically against her forehead she suddenly said, 'Ouch!' and to his surprise began to laugh instead of cry.

Straightening up he watched in silence as she sat, still hugging her knees, her head bent forward so that the ends of her hair trailed on the carpet, and shook with mirth.

Long minutes passed until the trembling of her shoulders gradually subsided. Finally, she raised her head and stared straight at him. 'I found out about your little secret,' she said, still sounding angry but no longer hysterical. 'I decided to take a short cut through the secret passages and came across a very bizarre scene – very bizarre indeed.' For a moment her memory flicked back to the sight of Lesley and Geoff, both bound and gagged.

Releasing her knees, Angelique straightened her legs out in front of her and allowed her arms to take her weight as she reclined slightly, her palms flat against the floor. All of a sudden she realised how tired she was and she felt her elbows sag a little.

Jordan sat up and crossed his long legs, his hands resting lightly on his knees. 'Are you okay?' he asked, looking genuinely worried.

For a moment Angelique stared back at him, then she gave a huge sigh that released some of the tension inside her. 'I think so, now,' she said, attempting a wry smile.

Jordan smiled back. 'I take it from your outburst that you've just found out about Thornbury Court's extra-curricular activities?'

'Apparently.'

'And you're shocked?'

'What do you expect?'

He shrugged, and she added, 'For some reason I can't honestly say I'm surprised. When I think about it a lot of things start to make sense.'

'Such as?'

'Well – the books. The magazines we were looking at tonight. That time I saw you cane your girlfriend. Each of them little things individually, but now they all add up.'

'And what conclusion have you reached?'

Now it was her turn to shrug. 'I'm not sure,' she said hesitantly. 'On the one hand, if people want to behave in a certain way, who am I to judge them?'

Jordan nodded but didn't try to interject.

'Yet on the other,' she continued, 'I can't help feeling as though I've been duped somehow. What with finding out that my parents aren't my real parents after all and then this – well . . .'

Nodding to show that he understood, Jordan stood up and put out a helping hand.

She hesitated for a moment before taking it and then got unsteadily to her feet. 'We will have to discuss this, Jordan,' she said calmly as she smoothed the creases from her dress with her free hand. 'Properly, I mean. I want to know everything.'

'Of course,' he agreed. 'That is your right after all.'

Gazing at him thoughtfully for a moment, it suddenly struck her that, like it or not, she was now a party to all the hotel's activities. An interested party. She shook her head slightly, trying to clear her mind. All that she had seen tonight: the photographs and then the reality – in the flesh, so to speak – had filled her with conflicting emotions.

Speaking to Moira had helped her to understand the motives of the three people in the tiny dungeon-like room but she hadn't felt the slightest inclination to become involved, even though the woman had made a veiled offer of sorts. However, she had to admit the

73

photographs had turned her on and when she looked into Jordan's eyes and saw the fear and expectancy that lurked there, almost hand in hand, she couldn't help acknowledging a faint glimmer of lust inside herself.

With Jordan she could expect more than just straightforward sex, she realised, although she instinctively felt that he would never try to push her in any particular direction. But the promise that lurked below the surface of their newly aroused relationship lingered inside her with all the fervent anticipation that she had felt as a child waiting for her birthday, or Christmas, to arrive.

'Shall I take you back to your room, or would you rather stay here? You look totally exhausted,' he said softly.

Pondering his offer for a moment, she decided that although the prospect of spending the rest of the night with him was tempting, she needed her own space. Space to think. To be herself without the added distraction of Jordan's presence.

'No. It's okay,' she said, letting go of his hand at long last. 'I can find my own way back.' She paused and laughed drily. 'But I think I'll stick to the main route this time. God knows what I might come across otherwise.'

Jordan smiled. There were no other guests using the playrooms that night other than Moira and Geoff, and he said as much.

Nevertheless, Angelique insisted that she would be fine going back on her own. 'Shall I see you sometime tomorrow?' she asked.

He nodded. 'Yes, of course. I've got rather a lot to do but I'll make time and come and find you, wherever you are.'

They kissed briefly, just the merest brush of lips upon lips, before she turned and opened the door. 'Night, night,' she said softly, remembering an old saying that her father used to use, 'don't let the bed-bugs bite.'

* * *

74

It was almost lunchtime before Jordan tracked Angelique down as she wandered around the hotel grounds. Taking her back to the terrace where a jug of iced Pimms awaited them, he proceeded to tell her about all the hotel's activities – the secret passage-ways and back staircases that led down to a series of themed rooms in the cellar. And the A-list of regular guests who were also devotees of all things erotic.

When there was nothing left to tell he went on to open up about himself. He told her that he much preferred the female sex and that, apart from being far nicer to look at across a dining table, their conversation and wit were infinitely more entertaining than the male variety. And of course, he loved to make love to them. Eventually he admitted – a little bit hesitantly, she thought, as well as a mite late in the day – that he actively enjoyed taking an overtly dominant role.

She knew exactly what he meant but, feeling wicked and not wanting to let him off the hook at all lightly, she forced him to be more explicit.

'I could never enjoy inflicting real hurt,' he said quickly, when he saw her expression cloud over and doubt creep into her eyes. 'To me, S&M is all about pleasure-pain, with the accent on pleasure.'

Angelique shook her head. 'I don't understand it,' she admitted bluntly. 'And I think if you are hoping to enjoy that kind of relationship with me, I suggest you look elsewhere. I'm not interested.' In the cold light of day, she had managed to conveniently forget how aroused she had felt the night before.

It annoyed her that Jordan laughed. 'I have no need to dominate you, my darling Angelique,' he said. 'Unless I can persuade you to change your mind, that is. I already have a number of female – er, friends – who enjoy being chastised on a regular basis.'

'Oh!' Angelique felt as though the wind had been taken out of her sails. 'Well, who are these women? Why haven't they been here since I arrived – what did you do, warn them off?'

Jordan sighed. He hated seeing Angelique get so upset again and yet he had to bring this out into the open now. It was too much of an important part of his life to keep hidden from her.

'A couple of them work here,' he said, wincing inside as he wondered how Angelique would respond to his admission, 'and the others are guests. Women who come here regularly with the express intention of being dominated – usually by me.'

'Really?' Angelique snapped, feeling almost beside herself with renewed anger. What a fool she had been to think that Jordan really liked her. God! Just once or twice during the course of the morning it had actually crossed her mind that they might be able to extend their burgeoning relationship. Perhaps build a whole future together, working side by side in the hotel during the day and fucking like crazy at night. Now she berated herself for being such a romantic fool. When would she ever learn not to trust any man?

Jordan reached out to her, shrugging helplessly when she brushed him aside. 'I wanted to be honest with you, Angelique,' he said. 'The hotel has two distinct facets and whether you like it or not, it is our A-list clientele who keep this place solvent.'

'I take it you mean the perverts?' she threw back at him, nastily. 'I suppose you'd better show me *all* of the hotel. Let me make up my own mind about this at least, before I decide whether to grin and bear it, or leave altogether.' Another thought occurred to her. 'I suppose my father knew all about this?'

As he nodded, Jordan felt horribly guilty and angry with himself for betraying his own and a lot of other people's natural inclination to a less widely acceptable source of erotic pleasure. 'He was also – ' he began, but Angelique interrupted him.

'I'm not interested in my father's sexual proclivities, thank you very much,' she said as scathingly as she could. 'In fact...' she paused to utter a bitter laugh, '... I sincerely thank God I haven't inherited his genes after all.'

On that final remark she turned on her heel and left a bewildered Jordan standing in the middle of the court-yard garden.

From an upstairs window, a young red-haired woman witnessed the heated exchange between Jordan and Angelique with mixed feelings. Deborah had yet to meet Harvey's esteemed daughter but she had heard enough about her during the five years she had been employed as assistant manager of Thornbury Court to form her own opinion. And in her view Angelique Hemsley was a spoilt little bitch who could do with a good thrashing. Despite her normally sanguine personality, Deborah felt her blood boil and a certain moisture gather and seep into the crotch of her seventy-quid Janet Reager's at the thought.

Hurrying downstairs to her office, she had just begun to sort through the day's mail when a pixie-like face peeped around the open door and inquired if Deborah would like a pot of coffee.

The red-head allowed the merest flicker of a smile to cross her face. 'Thanks, but no thanks, Christina. You can get your pretty little arse in here instead.'

The pixie face was framed by white blonde hair cut in a short, gamin style. She had a slender body with a narrow waist; small, firm breasts and hips which seemed surprisingly generous in comparison with the rest of her slight frame.

'What do you want, Deborah?' Christina asked, her hesitant voice giving away her excitement.

The red-head's emerald eyes glittered. 'What do you think, little slut? Get those knickers off and bend over

77

that desk. Now!' She waited until the young woman began to comply before walking over to a tall cupboard which contained, among other more mundane things, a small selection of crops, whips and paddles.

Christina's bottom seemed extraordinarily pale, framed by the black gabardine skirt which was now hitched up around her waist. Pausing only to close and lock the door to her office, Deborah walked over to Christina and tapped her inner thighs with the end of a leather riding crop.

'Wider,' she ordered tersely, watching with interest at the way trickles of moisture oozed from the other woman's vagina and ran down her legs. 'What a naughty little girl you are, Christina. I didn't say you could get excited yet.'

Christina's gasp turned into a moan as Deborah smacked the crop smartly across her buttocks. 'I can't help it,' she said, moaning over and over as the crop repeatedly stung her tender flesh.

Passing by the door to Deborah's office, Jordan heard the familiar swish and crack of the crop, followed by Christina's moans. All were sounds which made him smile to himself despite his concern about Angelique's reaction to his disclosure. Normally he would continue on to his own office and leave his two attractive employees to it, but today he felt in need of some friendly female company. Added to which the diversion of watching Deborah chastise Christina would not be unwelcome either.

His light knock on the door was answered instantly. They had a code, a way of knocking which he knew Deborah would recognise instantly. Smiling fleetingly at the beautiful red-head, Jordan's gaze skittered across her face to land on the sight of Christina's exposed and very reddened bottom. Moving closer he saw that Deborah had striped her very neatly.

A glow of pride swept over the dominatrix as she recognised Jordan's appreciation of her expertise. Although of the opposite sex, she and Jordan were very alike – both were very appreciative of women and both took enormous pride in their mastery of the unique skills necessary to be a true dominant.

Bowing to his higher status she offered him the crop without hesitation. 'Would you like to take over, Master?' she asked. 'This girl deserves a much more severe beating than the one I have given her.'

Jordan took the crop and cut the air with it a few times. 'Why, what is her "crime"?' he asked, amusement showing in his tone.

Deborah raised her eyebrows and pretended to think hard. 'Give me a moment and I'm sure I can think of something,' she said at long last. Then she squatted down and looked at Christina, who stared back with a pleading expression. 'Perhaps you know what you have done to deserve such treatment,' she added, giving the young woman a chance to double her punishment and receive a thrashing by the master of masters.

Christina thought for a moment, her voice wavering as she replied. 'I ... er ... yesterday I dropped a Waterford crystal bowl on the floor in reception and chipped a piece off it,' she said. 'And Lesley had to reprimand me for mislaying a whole box of chocolates and not having enough to put on all the pillows last night.'

'Well, well. A reprimand by Lesley.' Jordan looked as though he had to force himself to keep a straight face. 'What an experience. Did you learn your lesson by it?'

Christina raised her head and shook it earnestly. 'Oh, no, Master. I am so bad I couldn't possibly feel properly contrite after only a verbal warning.'

Jordan nodded. Their exchange was carefully executed, almost as though they were working to a script. And yet he knew that despite the apparently calm exchange everyone in the room felt desperately aroused. If he was in any doubt he only had to breath in the air that surrounded them, the rose petal fragrance of pot-pourri heavily overshadowed by the distinctive musky aroma of sex.

He flexed the crop in his hands, held it to Christina's lips for her to plant a kiss upon it and waited for her request for him to punish her. It was a rule of Thornbury Court that no one, whether employee or guest, administered chastisement without first being invited to do so.

Christina groaned with pleasure as the first of Jordan's strokes striped her flesh. It was difficult to differentiate between his method and Deborah's. Both were skilled dominants and she was sure that if she were blind-folded she would not be able to tell one from the other. Perhaps Jordan's strokes were just a little harder than Deborah's. And he did have a tendency to stripe first one buttock and then the other, whereas her mistress was more inclined to intersperse individual strokes with a lash that spanned both buttocks.

She could feel herself getting wetter and wetter, her sex swelling and blossoming in full view of her master and mistress. The punishment was nothing in compari-son with her shame, and her shame equally unimportant compared with the hunger that consumed her body. Shuffling her feet wider apart she thrust her bottom out more and silently wished that one of them would touch her. Her clitoris felt hugely swollen, almost screaming with the desire for release and her vagina, she knew, was wide open and soaking wet. She could feel the moisture trickling from her and drying in the slight breeze that Jordan created as he whipped her with the crop.

Only the lower half of her body was uncovered and yet she felt her breasts thrusting against the hard wood of the desk, her nipples hard and swollen, chafing against the scratchy lace of her bra. Moving her head slightly she was able to gaze out of the window, hoping that the view of the gardens would help to take her mind off her urgent need to be touched.

Just at that moment the familiar, brawny figure of Fergus came into view. Stripped to the waist, he was pushing a wheelbarrow full of grass cuttings. She watched Deborah's gaze drift to the same sight and instantly Christina knew what was likely to happen next. As the red-head walked over to the open window, Christina felt her stomach contract with the delicious prospect of further humiliation.

'Fergus, just put that down for a minute, would you, and come here!' Deborah's voice was so superbly author-itarian that both Jordan and Christina were forced to smother gasps of admiration.

Summoned by the lovely Deborah, Fergus was across the lawn like a shot. 'Yes, Miss Ford,' he said, being one of the few employees who did not refer to her as 'mistress'.

Fergus was strictly hetero, overtly macho and not at all interested in S&M, although he had no problem getting involved in some of the fun and games that went on at the hotel when duty called. His gaze flickered to the sight of the lovely little Christina naked from the waist down, bent forward over Miss Ford's desk. He found it easy to get a hard-on at any time, but right now his cock was threatening to explode right through his Levi's.

The window was tall and not very high off the ground, almost like a french window. When Deborah opened it fully, Fergus was able to easily climb inside the room. Immediately, his eyes travelled back to the beguiling sight of Christina's naked bottom and sex. He hoped he was going to get to play with her. His prayers were answered in the next instant as Jordan put down the crop and Deborah walked over to Christina and began to stroke her bottom and sex in a thoughtful manner.

'As you can see, Fergus,' she said calmly, 'Christina has just received a little light punishment and is now feeling somewhat aroused.' She paused as the young man nodded eagerly.

In her mind's eye Deborah could see his fingers itching to touch the impatient Christina. What a lovely picture they would make. Both of them so blond and beautiful. 'If it would not be too much trouble, Jordan and I would like you to fuck her,' she continued. 'Do you think you could do that for us?'

Fergus' fingers were already fumbling with the buttons on his fly. 'Christ, yes!' he gasped.

Christina groaned with longing as Deborah stroked her sex and then pushed a couple of fingers inside her. 'I'll just keep you wet for Fergus, darling,' the red-head murmured in her ear. 'You know something? I can't wait to watch him fuck you.'

Stimulated by the words as much as the relentless probing inside her, Christina's vagina contracted around Deborah's fingers in continuous orgasmic spasms until they were replaced by the thick hardness of Fergus' cock.

It didn't take Angelique very long to calm down after her exchange with Jordan, which surprised her. Usually she managed to keep up a sulky disposition long enough for the other party to come chasing after her and beg her forgiveness. François especially had never been able to bear her frosty silences and would have done anything to win her around again. A fact which she almost felt ashamed to admit, she had frequently used to her advantage.

Now she felt conscience-stricken about her behaviour. Poor François. He was so happy-go-lucky all the time and without a vindictive bone in his body. He hadn't deserved such appalling treatment. She would write to him later and apologise for being such a bitch. And she also needed to let him know that she wasn't planning to go back to France just yet.

Her thoughts returned to the hotel and Jordan, particularly the things he had told her. Of course she had been shocked. Who wouldn't be? And yet she had been staying at Thornbury Court for only a couple of days. How could she possibly expect Jordan not to have a life that didn't revolve exclusively around her? And just because she didn't like the idea of being tied up and whipped didn't mean that she had the right to spoil other people's fun. Especially if that particular side of the hotel's activities was as lucrative as Jordan had suggested. First and foremost she was a pragmatist. Silly romantic notions didn't come into the equation when there was a bottom line to consider. Suddenly, the silliness of her unintentional pun struck her and she began to giggle uncontrollably.

The sun blazed down on Fergus' naked torso as he strode across the south lawn in the direction of the greenhouses. Summer was well and truly underway now, he observed thoughtfully, casting a critical eye over the flower-beds as he walked. He would need to get the sprinklers out and all these beds would have to be watered twice a day if he and Sandy were going to keep the blooms in tip-top condition.

Glancing back over his shoulder, he noticed with a rush of affection how Thornbury Court seemed to bask in the noon-day sun – how the rays seemed to catch the pale yellow stone of the south front and cloak the solid structure with a veil of shimmering gold. Life felt good. Very good. He had his youth, his health, his looks and most important of all he had a job he loved, working with the best people in the world. What more could he ask?

His thoughts turned to his recent encounter with Christina which immediately set his cock stirring again.

Christ, she was a good fuck. She had been so eager he hardly had to do a thing – just grip her hips and hang on for dear life while she bucked and ground against him. In some ways he felt a little regretful. She had been so vigorous, her vagina contracting so tightly and rhythmically around him as she orgasmed that he couldn't contain himself and had come within minutes. Slipping his hand down the front of his jeans he tried to adjust his burgeoning erection which was becoming increasingly uncomfortable. It was no good, as soon as he was safely inside the greenhouse he would have to take himself in hand properly. It wouldn't take long. All he'd have to do was think of Christina.

The beauty of nature took many forms, Angelique mused to herself as she watched the young gardener stride purposefully across the lawn. She couldn't help noticing, even from a distance, how well developed his muscles were and how they seemed to ripple under his deeply tanned skin as he moved. Even the lower half of his body which was disguised by a pair of pale blue jeans seemed to undulate with a feline grace. Indeed his whole appearance was leonine. With his pale, shoulder-length hair and broad, golden body, he looked for all the world like the king of the jungle. Or at least, the king of Thornbury Court gardens.

Angelique allowed a flicker of a smile to cross her face as she continued to watch him covertly from the seclusion of a small white gazebo. Seeing Fergus reminded her that there were plenty of men out there in the big wide world. She didn't need Jordan or anyone else for that matter. The only person she had to learn to depend on was herself.

Jordan was surprised when Angelique unexpectedly waylaid him in the wine cellar. He was just checking the hotel's stock of vintage wines against the most recent inventory and had been totally absorbed in what he was doing. Consequently, Angelique's sudden appearance from behind a rack of claret made him take a step back and drop his pen. Cursing under his breath, he watched it roll across the stone floor and disappear under another wine rack.

'Sorry. I didn't mean to startle you,' Angelique said lightly. Dropping to her knees, she began sweeping the floor under the rack with her hand. 'Ugh!' She pulled her hand out quickly and regarded her cobweb-covered fingers with disgust. 'Bloody hell, I could have touched a spider then!'

She looked so horrified that Jordan couldn't help laughing. 'I should think any spiders that might be lurking under there would probably be more frightened by the sight of your hand rampaging about in their little world.'

'No. I don't think so,' she insisted as she shook her head. 'I'm petrified of the things.'

'Well, you've chosen the wrong place to visit if you don't like spiders,' Jordan said. He put down his clipboard and crossed his arms. 'What can I do for you?'

His tone and demeanour were both deliberately cool and business-like. A fact which made Angelique glance at him in dismay. 'You're still angry with me,' she said flatly.

'No.' He picked up the clipboard again and searched his pockets for another pen. Eventually he found a biro in the inside pocket of his taupe linen jacket. 'It's not up to me to be angry with you,' he added, resuming the stock-check. 'You have a right to your opinion. If you really don't like the way the hotel is being run you could always sell me your share. Or sell it to someone else.'

Angelique selected a bottle of Graves, blew the dust off it and pretended to study the label intently. 'I don't want to sell my share,' she said after a moment or two. 'In fact I have made up my mind to stay. At least until the end of the summer season.' She glanced up at him to note his reaction, disappointment sweeping through her when his expression remained inscrutable. If that was the way he wanted to play it, she would take another tack. 'May I taste this wine?'

Jordan fought back a smile. Despite the fact that Harvey had only been her adoptive father, Angelique was his daughter through and through. Stubborn, wily and totally unpredictable. Taking the bottle of wine from her, he walked over to a wooden bench where a corkscrew and a selection of clean glasses were arranged, covered by a cloth.

'You made an excellent choice, I must say,' he murmured, pulling the cork from the bottle. 'Nineteen-eighty-six was a very good year.'

'I know,' Angelique responded dryly.

She picked up a glass and twirled the stem between her fingers. Then she held it out to Jordan and waited until he had poured out about a third of a glassful. Tilting the glass to release the aroma she held it up to the light, casually bemoaning the fact that the gloomy cellar was only lit by dim, forty-watt bulbs. The wine was a nice bright red, lightening in colour quite close to the glass which meant it was fairly young but nicely concentrated.

Jordan copied her actions. Eyeing the colour and clarity of the wine, tilting the glass this way and that and swirling the wine around the glass to release more of the delicious aroma. At an unspoken signal, each of them dipped their heads, making sure their noses were as close to the wine as possible before taking a good, deep sniff.

'Ah!' The simultaneous exclamation echoed around the bare stone walls of the cellar, making both of them smile – firstly just at the sound and then at each other.

'Taste it,' Jordan urged. 'I think you'll be pleasantly surprised.'

With a slight nod of agreement, Angelique held the glass to her lips and tipped it slightly. Taking a moderate-sized sip she swirled the wine around between her tongue and the roof of her mouth, giving her palate the maximum possible exposure to the wine. It tasted full-bodied and slightly chocolatey. She swallowed, took another large sip, swallowed again and then licked her lips with relish.

'Good?' Jordan asked with a smile.

Angelique grinned back, already feeling slightly tipsy just on two mouthfuls of the stuff. 'Very,' she said. 'It has a lot of smell.'

He sniffed the air around them, the mustiness of the cellar lifted by the floral overtones of her perfume. 'So do you.' His smile widened.

'And it has a lot of depth,' she added, pretending to ignore his previous remark.

'So do you.'

'It's fresh,' she ventured.

'So are you.'

'And fruity.'

Jordan raised an eyebrow which made her giggle despite her earlier annoyance with him.

'And voluptuous,' she added. 'Yes, definitely voluptuous.'

'Christ, so are you!' Jordan crossed the small space that divided them in a couple of strides, took her in his arms and gave her a long, searching kiss.

Chapter Six

Despite their verbal jousting, Jordan's actions took Angelique by surprise and she felt suddenly weak and helpless again. Struggling feebly in the grip of his passion, she let the glass slip from her fingers. Even the sound of it shattering on the hard stone floor did not make Jordan falter.

Angelique returned his kiss with all the passion she could muster. He was such an aggravating man and yet she couldn't resist him. Deep inside she felt the familiar stirring of arousal – like a nest of vipers coming awake, slowly moving and uncoiling, slithering through her entire body to set her alight with fiery, flickering tongues.

She was wearing another summery, button-through dress, this time in a blue-and-white polka dot with a low-scooped neckline. And as the fire inside her grew, she felt Jordan's grip slacken a little, and then his fingers plucking at her buttons. She only wore a tiny, navy lace g-string underneath the dress and in moments he had exposed her unfettered breasts.

'Mmm, I adore these,' he murmured darkly, as he stepped back from her a little and cupped her breasts in his hands.

Her eyelids felt heavy as she watched his thumbs play with her nipples, rubbing and teasing them until she thought they would burst. Pushing back her shoulders, she thrust herself eagerly into his hands.

'Suck them,' she moaned. 'Please, Jordan. Please suck them before I explode.'

He grinned wickedly, then to her total amazement slapped each breast smartly. 'Punishment before pleasure,' he said, slapping them again.

She felt sure her nipples couldn't get any harder. They responded to his harsh treatment as though he had treated them to the tenderest of caresses. What did he think he was playing at, slapping her like that?

'You know I don't like that sort of thing,' she said, trying desperately not to feel so thoroughly hungry for his hands and cock.

'I don't know anything of the kind. And neither do you,' he said. Taking her nipples between his fingers, he tugged at them thoughtfully. 'You just assume that you wouldn't enjoy it.'

Groaning with desire, Angelique shook her head determinedly. 'I wouldn't like it. I know I wouldn't.' She couldn't take much more of his torment. Why didn't he just rip her knickers off and fuck her like any normal man?

It was then she realised that she was attracted to Jordan because he was not like other men – 'normal' or otherwise.

Ignoring her pleas, Jordan continued to unbutton her dress. Then he slipped it from her shoulders. For a moment he was content to simply look at her. Despite the shadowy interior of the cellar he couldn't mistake her beauty, the way her body curved as sinuously as an hour-glass: full breasts and hips, a tiny waist, taut, slender thighs. There was no doubt she was as near to womanly perfection as he could envisage.

'You are so beautiful, Angelique,' he said. 'I would

never hurt you. I want you to trust me. I want you to let me spank you.'

'No!' Despite her arousal she was shocked by his request. 'Can't you just be content with making love? That's all I want.'

Jordan was already shaking his head before she had even finished. 'I don't believe it is. I really don't. Otherwise I wouldn't try to push you.' He stepped forward and smoothed his hands across her shoulders and down her arms, which she held stiffly by her sides. 'There is so much more to pleasure than you already know,' he murmured beguilingly. 'Just let me show you. Let me teach you. Please, Angelique. I promise you will enjoy it. I promise it will be the best, most erotic experience you have ever had.'

'No. Please don't keep on about it, Jordan. I don't think . . .' Even as she spoke he could sense that she was weakening.

'You don't know,' he insisted. 'Where's your spirit, Angelique? Where is your sense of adventure, of conquering uncharted territory?' If she was anything at all like Harvey, he knew she would be unable to resist the challenge he posed.

He smiled inside as her defiant expression began to crumble. 'Would you promise to stop if I really didn't like it?' she asked hesitantly.

Jordan nodded. 'Of course. I promise.'

Angelique sighed as though her mind was already made up. 'Okay. But not now. Tonight. In one of the proper rooms. Like the guests,' she said. 'Now I just want you to make love to me.'

Going down in front of her on bended knee, Jordan hooked his fingers under the elasticated band around the top of her g-string and pulled until the tiny scrap of lace framed her ankles. Directly in front of his face the soft fleece of her chestnut curls tantalised him, and as

90

she moved to step out of the g-string he caught a glimpse of glistening pink flesh.

'I hope you won't be too disappointed, Angelique,' he said, picking her up and sitting her on the top of the wooden bench. 'But I really don't think I can bring myself to make love to you just now.' Disregarding her bewildered expression, he pulled her to the edge of the bench, forcing her legs apart as he did so. 'What I want to do is fuck you. Is that clear? Not make love. Fuck. Okay?'

Angelique felt her sex moisten and her buttocks clench hard against the rough wood as she watched him undo his fly. Her eyes widened as his cock sprang free, looking even more rampant than it had the night before. She fought the urge to comment and instead reached out and took it lovingly between her hands, guiding the swollen glans to the part of her body that craved him the most.

With a single fierce lunge he was inside her, filling her to the hilt as she wrapped her legs around his waist and urged him deeper still. She felt as though she couldn't get enough of him. Tightening the grip of her legs, she pulled him into her and released him, moving her body rhythmically against his. God, his cock felt big! She could feel the tip of it nudging her cervix and instead of trying to take more of him, she ground herself against him.

The delicate membranes of her sex responded to her vigorous actions, her clitoris swelling and pulsing as the flesh around it was rubbed and stimulated. As her desire mounted to fever pitch, primeval urges overtook her – to enclose, to seize her own gratification and to conquer the male inside her. It didn't matter that she was being fucked senseless in a grim wine cellar, her juices seeping through the cracks in an old wooden bench and her perspiring skin becoming streaked with grey dust. Nor did it matter that there was no prospect of a permanent relationship with Jordan. He was never going to walk up the aisle with her, or become the father of her children –

but he did care about her. What was more, he was there now, thrusting away inside her, proving what a good fuck he was, and right at that very moment that was all that mattered.

Arching her back, Angelique clutched handfuls of his hair and bucked against him desperately. Her body seemed to burn, it craved him so much. And when she came she cried out, the anguished sound reverberating around the damp stone walls of the cellar, making the bottles shudder in their racks.

Jordan felt his own orgasm explode a moment later, as Angelique's strong vaginal muscles milked him. Afterwards he held her close, stroking her hair until their rapid breathing subsided and returned to normal. He hoped – believed – that she would not renege on her agreement to let him widen her sexual horizons that evening. Taking the chance, he murmured into her hair.

'Tonight, Angelique. Don't forget, tonight.'

Dropping her head back she smiled faintly. 'I won't forget,' she said, wondering if she would later regret her own bravado. 'I never go back on a promise.'

Following their interlude in the wine cellar and then a very late lunch, Angelique asked Jordan if her father had kept any old documents at the hotel.

She told him that Mr Kemp, the solicitor, had informed her that nothing of interest had turned up at her father's Knightsbridge offices or at his home. Both properties were now completely cleared out and up for sale, following Angelique's own instructions. Therefore, the only other place to look was the hotel itself. It was then Jordan had suggested she went through Harvey's papers in the hotel's archive. The late Harvey Hemsley's collection of private papers filled three six-feet-high stacks of buff cardboard storage boxes.

'How on earth am I ever going to find what I'm

looking for among this lot?' she wailed, gesturing toward the boxes. 'I don't know where to start.'

Jordan took down the top box from a stack and opened it. 'At the risk of sounding boring, I would suggest you start at the beginning. But do you even know what you are looking for?' he asked, flicking through the papers before glancing up at her.

Pursing her lips ruefully, she came to stand by his side, picked up a handful of papers and dropped them again. 'Not really. I suppose a big part of me hoped that there would be a neat little file containing all the details of my origins,' she admitted. 'A birth certificate, adoption papers and so forth. Maybe even photographs.'

'It is possible, I suppose,' Jordan said slowly.

'But not very likely,' she finished for him. 'I know. I'm not that naïve.'

Glancing around the nondescript room which housed the hotel's records, he realised how inhospitable it was. 'I don't suppose you want to spend all your time in here,' he said. 'If you like you can have your own office. You said you want to stay for a while anyway. And if you stay, you work.' He paused to smile warmly at her. 'I'll get someone to bring you a few boxes at a time. Then you can go through them at your leisure.'

'Thanks.' Angelique picked up the box they had already opened. 'I think I'll take this one up to my room and make a start, if that's okay with you?'

Thornbury Court was always a haven of peace and tranquillity. A genteel hush pervaded each one of its tastefully appointed rooms, the only sounds were the occasional sombre chimes of a grandfather clock, the click of high heels on solid wood floors, or the muted whisper of voices.

On summer days doors were left wide open to let in as much air and light as possible, while huge bowls and vases filled with freshly-cut flowers occupied every available surface, scenting the rooms. It was as though the gardens were brought inside – a ploy which filled staff and guests alike with a powerful optimism, as well as an appreciation of the simple things in life that lingered in the soul long after they and the summer months had departed.

In the sun-filled reception area a crystal vase filled with early lupins in shades of pink and purple took pride of place in the centre of a nineteenth-century mahogany library table, its round, gleaming top strewn with a selection of magazines. Opposite the wide-open front door a broad flight of stairs led to the upper floors. To the left of the door groups of leather sofas and chairs – all comfortably 'broken in' – encouraged guests to linger. It was a place where they could rest for a while and read, or simply contemplate the view of the land-scaped gardens through the large mullioned windows that graced the front of the house.

It was one of Deborah's favourite parts of the hotel. Ordinarily just the fact that she was there would be enough to put a smile on her face. But her mind was, for once, on other things, and as she passed by the reception desk to the left of the staircase she suddenly stopped in her tracks.

'How is it going?' she asked, glancing first at the large, leather-bound register which lay open on the polished wood counter and then at Christina who was manning reception.

The smart young woman, dressed in a severe, black gabardine suit, bore little resemblance to the panting voluptuary who had been sprawled half-naked across Deborah's desk earlier that morning. Shrugging her shoulders, Christina turned the book around so that her colleague could see for herself.

'Less than half full,' she said. 'Nowhere near as many as this time last year, and we're only expecting one more guest this week.

'A-list?' Deborah murmured, finding it small compensation that her question was greeted with a nod.

Deborah's next stop was Jordan's office where she found him pouring over a pile of bills and bank statements. Perching on the edge of his desk she forced a cheery smile.

'I thought that was the accountant's job,' she said lightly.

He glanced up and looked at her with an expression that showed his mind was really elsewhere. 'I have to keep on top of things,' he muttered. 'We're running close to the edge as it is and now the bank – ' He broke off as though he realised that he had almost fallen into the trap of voicing his fears.

Leaning across the desk, Deborah smoothed back a heavy lock of fair hair that had flopped over his forehead. 'The bank what?'

'Nothing. It's just me being a pessimist.'

'But you're not a pessimist, Jordan. You're the man who makes the rest of us feel sick with your unremitting cheerfulness.'

'Gee. Thanks.' Placing the palms of his hands against the edge of the desk, he pushed himself away from it a little and reclined in his chair in what, he hoped, appeared to be a nonchalant manner.

'You know what I mean,' Deborah said, attempting another smile which, she was concerned to note, was not returned. 'Is it really that bad?'

For a moment or two Jordan didn't reply, then he let out a long sigh. 'Yes. No. Oh, I don't know. Ask me tomorrow. Or next week.'

Jumping to her feet impulsively, Deborah crossed the room and opened Jordan's drinks cupboard.

'I'm gasping,' she said with false gaiety. Dropping a few ice cubes into a squat, cut-glass tumbler, she poured a generous measure of gin before adding just a splash of tonic water. 'Do you want anything?'

Jordan paused for a moment before nodding. 'Oh, why the hell not?' He had been about to refuse, preferring to keep a clear head so that he could continue to fret over the hotel's accounts for a little while longer. Then he realised that life was too short and, like it or not, the bills would still be there the next day. 'We could do with a fairy godmother to come and wave her magic wand over this lot,' he said as Deborah handed him a glass of neat Scotch.

'You started to mention the bank,' she reminded him.

Jordan's smile faltered. 'Oh, yes. Them.' He took a large swig of whisky and swivelled from side to side in his chair for a moment or two before continuing. 'Basically, Pete Dales, the District Manager, is being unfairly influenced by those on high to put pressure on us. He told me quite bluntly that there's every chance we won't be able to renew our overdraft in October. He even hinted that somebody is angling to call in our loan as well.'

'Christ almighty!' Deborah, swung around to stare at him wide-eyed. 'If that's true it could be disastrous.'

'I know. You don't have to tell me.' Jordan stared into the depths of his Scotch. 'I wish I knew who was behind all this and why they are doing it. I can't think of one single reason why the bank would want to see Thornbury Court go under.'

'Neither can I,' Deborah said. Walking across the room to stare out of the window, she pondered the situation for a moment. Just a few feet from the window a deep border had been planted with a rich mix of peach, cream and orange herbaceous plants which seemed to be a magnet for bees, butterflies and a host of other flying insects. Watching two dragonflies thrust and parry like sword fighters, she formed a question in her mind which she hesitated to put into words. 'What about Harvey's daughter?' she asked carefully. 'Can't she put some more money into the hotel? He must have left her a small fortune.'

Jordan made a bridge with his fingertips and pressed them to pursed lips. 'Don't think I haven't considered asking for Angelique's help,' he admitted candidly. 'But in all honesty I don't think now is quite the right time. Her mind is in too much turmoil at the moment to make big decisions.'

'You really like her, don't you?'

He considered his colleague's question carefully before nodding. 'Yes. But you know me. I'm hardly a one woman man – and I think she would expect me to be. At the moment we're just getting to know each other. If I can, I'll keep it light for the time being.' He didn't add that he was intending to take Angelique down to the 'dungeon' that evening.

'Do you think she plans to stay?' Deborah asked, taking more notice of what Jordan *hadn't* said, a skill which she had acquired during their long association.

'Yes. For the time being.' He stood up, walked over to the drinks cupboard and replenished his glass of Scotch. Then he picked up the bottle of gin. 'Are you having another?'

With a brief nod, she turned away from the window and moved to stand by his side, thanking him as he poured her the perfect G&T.

'I told her about the A-list,' he said.

She glanced at him in surprise as he volunteered this piece of information. 'And what did she have to say about it?'

Despite his depression, Jordan grinned ruefully. 'Quite a lot as a matter of fact. She hadn't suspected anything at all and had no idea about Harvey's inclinations.'

Deborah sipped her drink. 'It must have come as quite a shock then.'

'Well, yes and no,' he said. 'Angelique refused to listen to anything I had to say about her father.'

'And she thanked God that she was only Harvey's adopted daughter, right?'

As usual, Deborah was spot on. She knew all about Angelique's discovery, the fact that she was not Harvey's blood daughter. Other than that she had no more idea about Angelique's true parentage than the young woman had herself.

Upstairs in the sitting-room of her suite, Angelique was feeling miserable and frustrated. She had gone through every scrap of paper in the box, perusing each one carefully in case it held some kind of clue before coming to the conclusion that she had completely wasted her time. Stuffing all the papers haphazardly back into the box, she replaced the lid, and on impulse decided to reread the letter that her father had left for her. It was very crumpled now, having been read so many times, yet she smoothed it out almost reverently and carefully digested the words as if it were the first time she had seen them.

To Angelique, the letter represented the last link with the man she had believed to be her father. She could almost hear his voice, low and throaty from smoking too many cigars, as her eyes scanned each line.

. . . From the moment you were born I felt responsible for your care and your future. . .

Now what did he mean by 'responsible'? Why should anyone feel responsible for another person's child?

Feeling bewildered, she read on.

. . . Your mother never really agreed with my decision to keep the truth from you . . .

. . . We always loved you as if you were our own . . .

. . . Promise me you will always follow your heart, Angelique. Discover the real you and at all times act on your true desires . . .

. . . There is a key to solving every mystery . . .

. . . Please, don't feel bitter, my darling. Don't hate me for what I've done. It was all for the best . . .

Tears ran unchecked down her cheeks as she read the last few lines. The truth was, despite everything she didn't hate him. She couldn't. Oh, she had felt angry with him for dying and leaving her but she couldn't hate him, not now, not ever.

Jordan's knock at the door of Angelique's suite later that evening was exactly on time. Feeling very nervous she rushed to answer it, placing a false smile firmly on her face before opening the door wide and inviting him in.

'I am ready, I just need to put on some lipstick,' she explained, backing away from him. For some reason he seemed a little menacing, although his face bore a smile – a warm one – and he had made no move toward her.

Jordan smiled even more broadly, wondering what Angelique was expecting from their evening. She was dressed in a quite formal long dress – red, halter-necked, with a long slit up each side – and her hair was piled up on top of her head in a loose topknot. To the casual observer it would looked as though she and Jordan were about to go to the theatre, or to a party, not down to the cellar where a bewildering selection of 'toys' and new experiences awaited her.

She was gone for only a minute and when she returned she stopped in the middle of the room and twirled around gaily. 'How do I look?' she asked, clearly expecting a compliment.

Jordan didn't disappoint her. 'You look beautiful, Angelique. But then surely you must know that.' Ignoring the slight shake of her head he added, 'I am flattered that you have taken so much trouble on my account.'

Twin dimples appeared in Angelique's cheeks. 'I didn't know how to dress for our – our date,' she said hesitantly, eyeing his simple outfit of black silk trousers and matching shirt. 'To be honest I thought you might laugh at me. I probably look ridiculously over-dressed.'

She was right about being over-dressed, but Jordan didn't think 'ridiculous' was the word he would have chosen. Offering her his arm in a deliberately formal gesture, he led her across the sitting-room to a door in the corner which she had not noticed before.

'How odd,' she murmured. 'I never realised this door was here.' She smiled up at him as he took out a key and unlocked it. 'You know me. I'm so inquisitive I would have been badgering you about it straight away if I had.'

'That screen was across it before,' Jordan said, pointing to a folding black-lacquered screen, decorated with orchids, lilies and other exotic flowers. 'I just moved it.'

He turned the handle and the heavy door swung back to reveal a narrow, undecorated passage. His searching hand found a light switch. Even with the lights on, the passage was still very gloomy and Angelique found herself stumbling time after time on the uneven flagstones.

'You should have warned me. I wouldn't have worn these shoes,' she grumbled, glancing down at the strappy pair of red leather sandals that graced her feet.

Suddenly, she realised how inappropriately dressed she was and how ridiculously nervous she felt about the whole evening. 'Are you sure this is a good idea, Jordan?'

His sideways glance showed his surprise. 'We did talk about it,' he said, referring to their brief discussion in the wine cellar. 'I thought you were quite happy about all this.'

Angelique pursed her lips and clung on to his arm as she almost stumbled again. 'I am curious,' she admitted. 'I don't know about being happy.'

Stopping them in their tracks, Jordan turned to her, took her face in his hands and kissed her lightly on the lips, the tip of her nose and the centre of her forehead.

'I'm not going to do anything that you won't enjoy, Angelique. I think you trust me. Don't you?'

She nodded, and Jordan continued. 'Trust is imperative but you will also decide on a code word that will exist only between us. Whenever you use it I will stop whatever I am doing instantly.'

Feeling a little more reassured, Angelique nodded again. 'I think our code word will have to be "flagstones",' she said, 'because they are the things that are likely to cause me the most harm tonight.' As if to add credence to her claim, she stumbled again and winced. 'See what I mean?'

In all honesty, Angelique had such mixed feelings about the forthcoming experience that she could hardly bring herself to think about it. In some ways it seemed too preposterous even to contemplate. The idea that in a short while she would give herself over to Jordan – for him to do with her whatever he wished – was bordering on the fantastic. And the thought of willingly accepting bondage and physical chastisement, well that was for people who were a little odd, wasn't it? It wasn't the sort of thing rational, independent young women such as herself indulged in, let alone enjoyed.

Nevertheless, despite all her preconceptions, Jordan's attempts to put the subject on a 'normal' footing and her agreement to go along with it, she felt as though her consent had been rash. But it was nothing she couldn't back out of gracefully once she and Jordan had fooled around with it for a little while. That way he would be appeased and she would not appear too straight-laced and unadventurous. To be able to turn around to Jordan and say, 'Look, I tried it but it didn't work for me,' should be enough to keep her credibility intact, she reasoned.

The passage led into another, and as they walked, Angelique was dimly aware that the narrow stone corridors had a downward slope. Eventually they arrived at a circular staircase. It was narrow with bare stone steps that were uneven and slippery. Jordan held her arm firmly as they descended, she just in front of him. When they reached the bottom he indicated yet another passage.

'Nearly there now,' he said, his light tone seeming to accentuate her nervousness.

She turned her head and flashed a brief smile at him over her right shoulder as he squeezed around her, taking her hand again to lead the way to a heavy oak door at the very end of the corridor. Like all the best dungeons she had ever seen in films, it had substantial iron hinges and a complicated series of locks. Jordan opened them using a selection of keys that were grouped, incongruously it seemed, on a key-ring bearing a crimson, heart-shaped pendant.

'One of the guests left it behind,' he explained when he noticed her interested glance.

Turning back to the locks, he used two more keys and then turned the round, wrought-iron handle. The door creaked ominously as it swung open into the room. Striding over the threshold, Jordan took a gold cigarette lighter out of his trouser pocket and began to light a collection of squat, beeswax candles which sat in black metal candlesticks of varying heights.

Angelique stepped cautiously inside the gradually brightening room and looked around, fearfully. There was no doubt it really was a dungeon. Like the room where she had encountered Moira O'Donnell the walls and floor were of bare stone, although a red rug, thread-bare in places, covered the centre of the floor. Around the edges of the room were various odd-looking contraptions. The only one which she recognised properly was a set of stocks – authentic-looking and open, just waiting for a victim to surrender to it. She continued to gaze around wide-eyed, noting racks hanging from all walls, each holding a selections of whips, chains and other torturous-looking items.

'I don't think this is really my cup of tea, Jordan,' she said, shaking her head doubtfully.

'You don't know anything yet, Angelique,' he replied. Circling the room he continued to light candles until the whole, inhospitable room was bathed in a soft yellow glow that relaxed Angelique, despite her trepidation. He pointed to a plain wooden chair. 'Take a seat and I'll get you something to drink.'

Angelique nodded and sat down. As she sat she crossed her legs tightly, only to feel them slide apart again. Trying to calm herself she concentrated on clenching her hands into fists, then relaxing them.

'Here.' Jordan handed her a silver goblet filled to the brim with a voluptuous claret. She sipped the wine appreciatively.

The warmth of the alcohol spread through her like wildfire, and she found herself staring up at Jordan, becoming mesmerised by his gaze.

Reaching down he relieved her of the goblet and set it on a side table next to his own. Then he took both her hands and helped her to her feet. 'This way, Angelique,' he murmured, 'it's time to begin.'

Feeling as helpless as a puppet, she allowed him to lead her across the room. He tethered her wrists high above her head, securing them to an iron ring fixed to a joist. The ring was just a little too high for comfort and she was forced to stand on tiptoe, despite her high heels.

'What now?' she asked, in a voice which she had intended to sound bold, but which echoed around the room in a nervous tremor.

Jordan raised an eyebrow and gave a devilish smile. 'Now?' he said. 'Now we are going to discover the real you.'

Angelique shivered, wondering what he meant. They had already made love and played with each other's bodies extensively. What other secrets could she possibly harbour? Unable to bear the way Jordan looked at her so knowingly, his curving lips almost mocking her, she closed her eyes.

His footsteps were a whisper of soft leather across the flagstones as he came closer and closer to her. Keeping her eyes tightly shut, she sensed his movement around her, the disturbance to the air, his masculine scent filling her nostrils, his body warmth enveloping her.

'Angelique. Angelique,' he called softly, his breath whispering across the sensitive membrane of her ears, caressing the exposed flesh of her neck and throat and disturbing the precariously balanced tendrils of hair piled up on top of her head. 'Tell me that you want to learn, Angelique,' he urged in a voice that was hardly more than an exhalation of breath. 'Tell me you trust me.'

For a long while she was silent. The harshness of her breath and the thumping of her heart against her ribs were the only sounds her body made. And then she spoke, agreeing to Jordan's request, telling him that she trusted him implicitly.

She was rewarded by the touch of his lips upon hers, his breath tasting sweet and fruity. He moved his mouth lower, his tongue trailing the tanned length of her throat as she strained her head back, avoiding her stretched arms as she offered more of herself to him. His lips caressed the sensitive flesh of her underarms and travelled across the hard ridge of her collar-bone. Touch my breasts, she willed, wanting so much to feel his tongue slide down her cleavage and delve beneath the thin fabric of her dress to discover the taut buds of her nipples.

As she desired so his touch rewarded her, his fingers parting the top of her dress until her breasts were fully exposed. Sharp darts of arousal stabbed her womb, sending a rush of moisture from her vagina as she sensed him looking at her. A moment later she felt the warm caress of his breath and then the soft wetness of his tongue as it lathed her nipples, his lips teasing them, sucking and pulling until she moaned aloud.

Her moans turned to whimpers as she felt his fingers caress her legs. Starting at her ankles he stroked her, lingering on the soft flesh at the backs of her knees, his fingertips describing small circles as they moved inexorably higher until they brushed the crease at the base of her buttocks. She wore no knickers and Jordan rewarded her wantonness with a squeeze and an appreciative murmur.

'You are already ahead of the game,' he said gruffly, his fingers probing between her buttocks and spreading them apart.

Angelique groaned, partly with pleasure and partly with shame as a cool draught of air caressed her exposed anus and dried the wetness between her parted legs. Not there, Jordan, she wanted to say but she couldn't speak. She felt helpless. Bound and helpless in his hands, like a sex toy. Just a body. A vessel for pleasure.

'Fuck me!' she begged, squirming in his hands. All she wanted right then was for him to touch her sex, to stroke her swollen labia and spread them apart. She wanted him to finger her and rub her clitoris and then to take her roughly, straight away. 'Please, Jordan. Fuck me,' she said again.

To her dismay she felt his hands leave her buttocks and sensed his body withdrawing from hers. Her eyes were still closed but now she opened them a little, noticing through the ragged shadow of her eyelashes that he had crossed the room and appeared to be deliberating over a selection of whips.

'No. Not that.' Her voice wavered and travelled shakily around the room again. Why couldn't she sound forceful for once?

'Yes, Angelique,' he said, flexing a small leather crop in his hands as he walked back over to her.

He held it up to her face and made her study it. Then he told her to kiss it.

'No. I won't. Do you think I'm mad?' She turned her face away from him but he stunned her by reaching roughly between her legs and plunging a couple of fingers deep inside her. He moved them slowly, waiting for her to respond. Squirming on his fingers she heard the wet sounds of her arousal and felt the heat build, driving her towards desperation. 'Don't do this to me, Jordan,' she begged, feeling helpless again and hopelessly aroused.

'You don't mean it,' he said, his thumb moving to her clitoris, stroking it expertly until she felt as though she would go mad with desire. Then to her frustration he took his hands away, smiling as she groaned with disappointment.

'What do you want from me?' she gasped, her throat feeling tight and hoarse, her chest aching. Trying unsuccessfully to flex her arms she let her head drop forward in defeat.

Ignoring her question, he reached up and unfastened her tethered wrists, rubbing them between his hands until Angelique raised her head again and smiled tremulously at him.

'Come here,' he ordered gently. Taking her by the arm he led her back to the chair and bent her forward from the waist so that her palms were resting flat on the hard wooden seat.

She shivered as he raised the back of her dress and a cold draught of air swept over her naked buttocks. The cold feeling didn't last for long. Straight away his hands began to warm her, stroking and caressing the light brown flesh until she felt the familiar warmth return to her lower body. Arching her back, she offered herself to him, hoping that he would touch her sex again, or penetrate her with his lovely, hard cock.

Jordan stepped back a little and looked at Angelique. From that angle he couldn't see her face, only the long sweep of her back and the curve of her hips and buttocks which jutted out invitingly. Smooth and round, her bottom seemed to beckon to him and just below, the pink purse of her sex contrasted nicely with the toasted skin of her thighs. He dropped to his haunches behind her and prised her open a little with gentle fingertips, just to see the proof her arousal for himself – the creamy nectar that filled her vagina and spilled over the puffy folds of her labia. Just for a moment he was tempted to taste her, but he forced himself to resist. First the punishment. Then the pleasure.

Chapter Seven

*A*ngelique whimpered as Jordan administered a couple of soft smacks to each buttock. She was surprised to discover how pleasant it was to feel the gentle tingle and spreading warmth that the palm of his hand left upon her softly quivering flesh. If that was all there was to it, then she could handle this sort of thing with no problem. Wriggling her hips, she urged Jordan to smack her again.

'Ouch!' she yelled, as she felt the first bite of the crop instead. 'What was that for, you bastard!' Behind her she heard Jordan chuckle softly, followed by a whistling sound as the crop cut through the air. 'Don't you dare do that again,' she warned, glancing at him over her shoulder and clenching her buttocks instinctively.

'Did you think I was just going to tap you on the bottom a couple of times and leave it at that?' he asked, slicing the air with the crop and smiling broadly as she winced.

Reaching behind her, she rubbed her buttock where it stung. 'I thought this was all about pleasure,' she said. 'That really hurt.'

'That was nothing.'

'Nothing? Well, it bloody well felt like something.' Angelique started to straighten up but Jordan stopped her.

'Please don't, Angelique,' he said. 'We haven't finished yet.'

For a moment she regarded him levelly, wondering whether she should ignore his plea and simply return to her room. She had enough pain – of the emotional kind – she didn't need any more. In a voice that was hardly more than a whisper she expressed her thoughts.

'Oh, Angelique, my darling,' Jordan exclaimed, moving around to the side of the chair and stroking her cheek with the back of his hand. 'I just want to make you happy. If I didn't think you had the capacity to enjoy this, I wouldn't have suggested it in the first place.'

Pursing her lips ruefully, she allowed him to stroke her cheek. Then she turned her head slightly and nuzzled his hand. 'Okay. But just take it gently to begin with. Remember, I am a novice at all this.'

When Jordan smiled she noticed how his eyes seemed more grey than blue in the flickering half-light.

'Yes. You are, aren't you?' he said. 'My little virgin, Angelique.'

His voice was tender, not mocking, and she allowed herself to smile back at him, her whole body relaxing at the same time. Bending her head, she arched her back again and asked him to continue.

This time the crop fell lightly. It stung, but not painfully so, and gradually the intensity increased in time with her groans of encouragement. The whole area of her bottom felt warm and alive, as though all the blood in her body had rushed there. Her sex craved the touch of Jordan's fingers, her vagina spasming around a non-existent cock as it created more and more moisture. The creamy fluid trickled over her swollen labia and down the insides of her thighs. Her legs trembled, the weight of her lust too much to bear.

'Please, Jordan,' she gasped at long last. 'I must have you inside me. I must come.'

Smiling knowingly, Jordan put down the crop and stroked his hands lovingly over her buttocks. The heat permeated his palms and his fingertips traced the slightly raised weals on her tender flesh before delving lower.

With a loud groan, Angelique thrust herself towards him in desperation. His touch was too light and too teasing. Her clitoris felt unbelievably swollen, straining beyond the protective layers of her flesh to receive some kind of gratification. Instinctively, she put her own fingers there, sliding them over the slippery folds of her labia and teasing the throbbing nub of flesh herself. Mmm! That was better, she thought. Her arousal mounted quickly as she stroked herself, efficiently bringing her gratification closer and closer until she was almost on the point of release.

Then Jordan stopped her.

Taking her wrist firmly, he moved her hand and placed it palm down on the seat of the chair again. 'Patience, Angelique,' he said softly. 'You must learn patience.'

Her response was another groan. Petulant she knew, but also anguished. It seemed as though she had never craved an orgasm as much as she did at that moment. When Jordan helped her to stand up and sit in the chair, she moved willingly, wanting desperately to arrive at the point where he would grant her that release.

Tucking Angelique's dress around her waist, Jordan carefully raised each of her legs and draped them over the arms of the chair.

Despite her overwhelming desire, Angelique still couldn't help blushing with shame. She was so spread open. So wantonly displayed that she couldn't possibly hide any part of herself from his piercing gaze. Closing her eyes against the sight of him looking at her, she sensed him drop to his haunches so that her wide-open sex was closer to his face.

'Beautiful. Quite, quite beautiful, Angelique,' he murmured, his fingertips stroking her so gently that she began to whimper with renewed desire.

Wicked, wicked Jordan knew exactly what he was doing. His fingers played her body deftly, as though she was a finely-tuned instrument and he the maestro. A shudder went through her as he rubbed the sensitive flesh around the straining bud of her clitoris, then flicked his tongue across it.

'Jordan, for God's sake, please!' she cried out, hating him for torturing her so mercilessly and at the same time adoring him for the pleasure she knew he would grant her eventually.

From time to time he would stop caressing her sex and turn his attention to other parts of her body: her toes, her inner thighs, her breasts and even the backs of her knees. He stroked and kissed her in all those places, keeping her arousal alive while allowing the urgency in her clitoris to abate a little. It was torment of the sweetest kind – drawn out and apparently never-ending. Finally, he turned his attention back to the core of her desire, his lips closing over the hard nub of flesh as his fingers sank deep inside her.

With a surge of excitement, Angelique felt the heat build up quickly inside her again, transporting her to another realm where her mind blanked out almost everything save the sensation of pleasure and the darkest of fantasies. Almost delirious with unresolved desire, Angelique wriggled further forward on the hard wooden seat so that Jordan could touch her more easily.

With her eyes closed, her mind filled only with the exquisite build up to orgasm, Angelique listened only to the hastening tempo of her own desire and failed to hear the quiet *swish* of the door followed by the soft tread of another person entering the room.

When he heard the door open and close, Jordan glanced up and mouthed a greeting to a stunned Deborah. It took the other woman a few minutes to take in the scene and then her natural instincts came to the fore. In moments she had crossed the room and knelt next to Jordan, her eyes conveying a silent message as she replaced his hands with her own.

Lost in the realm of ecstasy, Angelique felt nothing different apart from even more delicious gratification. Deborah's touch was light and skilful, her fingers gently probing inside the young woman stroking her throbbing clitoris at the same time.

Allowing her head to drop to one side, Angelique moaned softly. 'Oh, yes. Oh, God, yes, that's it!'

A smile flickered across Deborah's face as she brought Angelique to orgasm. It was so easy to pleasure another woman, so rewarding. And this one was truly beautiful, a real joy to touch and to explore. Leaning forward Deborah flicked out her tongue and lapped at Angelique's spasming vagina. Using her tongue like a tiny cock, she stabbed it inside the other woman's body while her fingers coaxed a second climax from her pulsating clitoris.

Jordan could hardly contain himself. If there was one thing that particularly excited him it was the sight of one woman pleasuring another, and Deborah was definitely mistress of her own domain. His fingers fumbled with his zip as Deborah reluctantly stood up, her fingertips still gently stroking Angelique.

At that moment Angelique opened her eyes, the surprise registering on her face as she saw Deborah snatch her hand away and she realised what had just taken place.

'Oh . . . Oh . . .' For once she was speechless.

'Okay, Angelique. Shush, darling. I want to make love to you now. Don't worry about Deborah.' As he spoke, Jordan knelt in front of her and stroked his swollen glans around the rim of her vagina, watching as it became streaked with her creamy juices.

Still feeling stunned, Angelique glanced at Deborah and then down at herself, all pink and glistening, ready to take Jordan's hardness inside her. It was what she craved. Damn the other woman!

'Jordan, Angelique, I'm really sorry. I'll go,' Deborah said, backing away from the two of them. Having seen the expression of anger and disbelief on Angelique's face, she realised she had grossly over-stepped the mark.

It was some consolation to her that Jordan glanced around and gave her an apologetic smile. 'It would probably be better if you did. I think Angelique and I would prefer to be alone.'

Angelique found herself nodding wordlessly as Jordan flashed her a look of pure intimacy. She had pulled down her dress a little at the front and Jordan's body shielded the rest of her from Deborah's gaze.

Later she would have to confront her feelings about what had happened. It was far too early to analyse why she didn't feel as horrified as she thought she should. And why, even now, as the red-head's long fingers curled around the door handle in the way a falcon uses its talons to grip a trainer's arm, she found her body missing the other woman's touch. In a minute only the lingering spiciness of Deborah's perfume would be testimony to the fact that for a few delicious moments Jordan had not been her only lover that evening.

The door closed and it was just the two of them again. Closing her eyes, Angelique sought Jordan out by touch alone, her fingers sinking into the heavy weight of his collar-length hair and massaging his scalp until she heard the final dull sounds of Deborah's footsteps fading away. In the next moment she felt the front of her dress being raised again and Jordan's lips against her own as further down his hardness sank into her with satisfying ease.

Their kiss muted a simultaneous exhalation of breath, the blissful moment of union carried on through a gentle thrusting and yielding that appeared flawlessly choreographed. It seemed incredible that in such a short space of time their love-making should have become so harmonised, as though they were two pieces of a jigsaw cut and shaped to a perfect fit.

Angelique felt her body tighten around Jordan as he knelt before her. One of her hands left his hair and she pressed the palm between his shoulder-blades to urge him closer to her. At the same time she deliberately tightened her vaginal muscles and attempted to pull him deeper inside her. She wanted more of him – all of him – with a desperate, almost savage intensity.

'Oh, God! Angelique. Oh, yes!'

Jordan's lips broke away from hers just in time for him to gasp the words and for Angelique to witness the way his face twisted into a rictus of ecstasy at the final moment. It made her feel so wonderful, so powerful, that it almost eclipsed the rapture of her own orgasm and she tightened her inner muscles still further. As soon as she was ready to let him go she would, but not before. If there was to be an element of control in their relationship there would also be give-and-take. And right now she was the one taking control.

While Jordan and Angelique played with and pleasured each other, two floors above them quite a different scenario was being enacted. At six o'clock that evening, twenty-seven-year-old Detective Sergeant Clive Porter had arrived at Thornbury Court with strict instructions to check in and then go straight to his room and wait. Now it was well past nine, he was on his third Scotch and soda and still none the wiser.

A joke was a joke and this time it looked as though it was on him. Still, he should have known better than to trust his colleagues. From the moment he had told them that he and his girlfriend, Cassie, were intending to tie the knot they had ribbed him something rotten. And even though it was almost six months later and the wedding was just around the corner, it seemed there was still some mileage to be had from his 'madness'.

The all expenses-paid night at this country hotel, in a plush room that made him feel as though he was immersed in a bowl of strawberries and cream, was part of his wedding present he had been informed. Of course, his first inclination had been to thank his workmates effusively and get on the phone to Cassie. She would love a bit of prenuptial bliss, he'd thought, his cock already stirring at the possibilities. Then he had found out his lovely young bride-to-be was not intended as part of the package.

'This is supposed to be your last week of freedom, mate,' D.I. Lavender had said to him. 'It's no time to be thinking about your fiancée. Plenty of time for that after you're married.'

A million buts and whys had leaped to Clive's lips only to be shouted down. It seemed all the plain-clothes lads at Roundwood wanted him to enjoy a night of luxury at a remote country hotel – alone. Clive wasn't stupid, there had to be something else. All of them were in on it. Whatever it was. And frustrating though all the secrecy might be, he had no choice but to go along with their instructions: enjoy a few drinks, a nice meal courtesy of room service, and the video channel offerings – and wait until *it* happened.

Having used the loo for about the tenth time that evening, Clive checked his watch. Then he leaned over the dressing-table to peer closely at his dark, clear complexion in the mirror. Pulling a rueful face at his reflection, he rubbed his hand over the black stubble on his chin. What was he, a sensible adult and member of Her Majesty's police force, doing holed up in a remote hotel at nearly ten o'clock at night with only himself for company? He had told his mum and Cassie that he was going on a stake-out – a convenient alibi for a night or two away that his colleagues used from time to time. Except this time he felt as though he was the quarry, the unsuspecting one.

The light rap of knuckles on the door brought him out of his reverie with a jolt. 'Turn down your bed, sir?' a feminine voice asked through the wood.

Straightening up quickly, Clive rushed to the door and opened it. On the threshold stood a small, curvy girl with white-blonde hair, china-blue eyes and fire-engine red lips. She was wearing a chamber-maid's uniform and a questioning expression. A true professional to the end, his assessment of her was quick and thorough and he felt tempted to jot down his impressions in the notebook he kept with him at all times.

Instead, he took a couple of steps back. 'Yeah. Er, yeah – 'course. Come in.'

He felt nervous and didn't know exactly why. Maybe it was something in the way she looked at him – without a hint of shyness or modesty – or the proportions in length of dress to thigh. The former being far too short for regulation wear, surely? And the latter way too long and shapely for him to keep his eyes from straying to them as she crossed the room.

'Lovely evening, isn't it?' she said, pausing to stare out of the tall mullioned window for just a moment before pulling a gold, tasselled cord to draw the red velvet curtains closed.

Her hips rolled under the short black dress as she moved to the bed, her actions calm and efficient as she folded back the red satin coverlet to expose a cream duvet.

Clive stared wordlessly at her, then shook his head. 'Lovely,' he breathed.

His eyes widened as she leaned right across the bed. Her dress seemed to flow with her, the lace-trimmed hem moving right up the backs of her thighs to expose the twin, cheeky mounds of her lower buttocks. Christ! Wasn't she wearing any knickers? Then she bent one leg and hooked the knee up, resting it on the top of the bed so that she could reach further across it and he saw that she was wearing a g-string. A small pouch of white cotton showed between her legs and he noticed the way the white thong disappeared between her buttocks.

He felt transfixed by the sight. It wasn't clear to him what she was doing. Why she found it necessary to stretch so far across the bed, or why she was taking so long about whatever it was. At the end of the day he couldn't care less. He could go on staring at those cheeks and that little white pouch all night.

When it came again, her voice startled him. 'You're from the West Indies, aren't you?' she asked without looking round.

He cleared his throat. 'No, Acton. But my grand-parents came from Jamaica originally.' It surprised him that he could talk so calmly.

Her buttocks quivered as a peal of infectious laughter rippled through her body. 'Sorry. That was stupid of me.' Easing herself back across the bed, she stood upright again. 'I like black men,' she said, turning around to stare straight at him.

This time her eyes held him. They seemed so pale. *She* seemed so pale – like the little china doll his sister Michelle had once been given for Christmas.

His grandmother had remarked on it, saying it was far too extravagant a gift for a six-year-old, and why didn't she ever see black dolls dressed that way? And his grandfather had shrugged and reminded her that in Jamaica very few of the dolls had blonde hair and blue eyes, to which the whole family, apart from his grand-mother, had burst out laughing. Now, instead of taking pride of place on his sister's dressing-table, this full-sized version was standing in the middle of the room, talking, smiling and making his cock go unbearably hard.

She was asking him if he still lived in Acton and he shook his head dumbly, managing to squeak out that he had moved up the M1 a bit after he had finished his training at Hendon.

'Ooh, so you're a policeman,' she murmured, slowly moving closer to him. 'It's a shame you don't seem to have your handcuffs with you.' Circling him slowly, she pretended to conduct a body search, patting his pockets and running her hands down his sides and over his buttocks and thighs.

His cock twitched and her gaze shifted instantly. 'I . . . er . . .' he stammered ineffectually, feeling a hot flush start somewhere in his boxer shorts and end up on his face. For once he thanked the good Lord for making him black, at least blushes were a bit less obvious.

A knowing smile lit up her face. 'Shush. Don't worry about that. Trust Polly.'

The young woman circled him again and then sank to her knees in front of him. With deft fingers she unfas-tened his belt, pulled it through the loops and slid down his zipper. Immediately, his cock sprang free – as eager and as hungry as ever – inciting a murmur of appreci-ation from its female audience of one.

As though in a trance, he watched as a pink tongue darted out of her mouth and snaked around her lips, wetting them thoroughly. Oh, God! She was going to . . .

His eyes closed as her mouth engulfed him and he rocked on his heels – all six-feet-two of him, feeling distinctly unsteady. To his chagrin, it took the young chamber-maid precisely two minutes and sixteen sec-onds to coax him to orgasm. Coax him? Christ, that was a laugh! He had barely been able to hold out for that long.

He wanted to say something. To apologise. But she was already rising to her feet and taking one of his broad, dark hands in her tiny, pink ones. Glancing down, he noticed that her bare arms were covered with a light dusting of golden freckles and hairs so white that they were hardly visible. His thumb moved over the back of her hand and stroked the hairs just above her wrist.

Polly glanced at him quizzically but said nothing. Instead she led him to the bed, turned him around and pushed against him gently so that he sat down with a sudden bump. Working his knees apart with her legs, she stood between them and ran her hands over his hair, her fingers skimming the short curls as though testing their springiness. With a slight giggle she ran her finger-tips around his ears, tracing the whorls as she gradually leaned closer and kissed him.

For a small woman she seemed to have a lot of power behind her actions. Every one of them was direct and confident and for once Clive felt weak and unable to resist. He realised that this situation was no accident and that not all the hotel's chamber-maids were likely to be as lovely, or as forward, as Polly. Obviously his mates had arranged all this and instead of feeling angry – as he might – or worried about Cassie finding out, he felt a blanket of calm descend over him. If this was his wedding gift from the boys at Roundwood he was going to enjoy it – every minute!

The fondant confection of Polly's kiss was something to be savoured. Soft and sweet her mouth moulded to his and guided him to a new level of enjoyment. Kissing was not something he and Cassie indulged in all that much any more. Since she had got out of the nurses' home and found her own place they had been able to dispense with the endless, frustrating hours of kissing and fondling on the sofa, in the car, or in the darkened secrecy of the cinema. With free time together limited by shift-work and anti-social hours, they tended to just get down to fucking without all the preliminaries. Having all night and being able to take his time was almost as much of a treat as the luscious Polly herself.

It was a delight to discover that under the short black dress her curves were all real and owed very little to padding, underwiring or skilful corsetry. All that covered the plump globes of her breasts was a brief, white cotton bra. It was hardly more than two triangles really – to match the single triangle that covered the thatch of pale curls at the apex of her thighs. And he adored the inviting way she giggled when he touched her, the backs of his broad fingers skimming the surface of her stomach and moving lower to stroke the slight swell of her belly.

'So soft,' he murmured almost to himself, feeling the tiny, almost invisible hairs on her torso tickle the back of his hand.

Polly stopped kissing the man in room forty-eight completely and arched her back, leaning away from him slightly so that she could see the expression of wonder on his face. He continued to stroke her torso, his other hand spanning her buttocks, keeping her close to him, making her feel possessed. It was odd that although she had been the one calling all the shots, his subtle mastery of her body almost put her in a position of weakness. She sighed with pleasure, feeling tempted to urge him on in some way but also recognising that he was not a man to be hurried. And yet there was a lot more pleasure to come – and she *had* only been assigned extra duties until three a.m. at the latest.

Reaching behind her back, she unhooked her bra and shrugged it off, throwing it on to the dressing-table nearby. With an inward smile she noticed how his huge, liquid brown eyes once again seemed mesmerised by her. Now his gaze was fixed to the sight of her plump

120

breasts jiggling in front of him as she shimmied a little for his entertainment. It came in handy sometimes being an ex-stripper. She might look the picture of innocence but she knew the all moves – the apparently innocuous gyrations and undulations that kept a man transfixed.

If there was one thing Polly took pride in, it was her body. Fit and firm, it pleased her, delighted her partners and served her very well. If it hadn't been for her looks and her personality she would never have got the job at Thornbury Court – and that went double for her former 'dance partner', Liz. Although it might seem odd to some to work part of the time as a genuine waitress and at other times as a pleasure provider – she hated the word 'prostitute' – it was a job she loved. And it beat night after night of strutting her stuff in sleazy Soho joints. Yeah, she was happy with her lot and now she was going to pass some of that happiness on to the lovely man in front of her.

With one resolute fingertip she pushed against his chest until he fell back and sprawled on the bed. In a flash she had straddled him, the soft curls of her pubis brushing his cock which had started to stir again and now hardened in earnest. Taking her weight on her hands, she leaned forward and began to stroke her tongue back and forth across his collar-bone. With skilful swirls, she traced a path through the mat of curls covering his chest and sought out his nipples. As she nipped at them and sucked them eagerly, she reached down with one hand and felt for his cock, delighting at its substantial size as she wrapped her fingers around the stem.

The beautiful man beneath her groaned and arched his back with pleasure, dislodging her mouth for a moment. Polly smiled. Men who were as responsive and appreciative as this one made her work all the more worthwhile. And enjoyable. She always made sure she enjoyed the experience, too. In fact, this was as good a time as any to 'up' the pleasure for both of them. Grasping his cock even more firmly, she positioned herself over him and slowly fed every centimetre of his gorgeous organ into her hungry body.

The familiar heat of lust swept quickly through her as she enclosed him completely and then began to move – alternately rotating her hips and sliding up and down. A moment later she felt a further surge of arousal as his hands slid deliberately up her thighs and sought out the pouting folds of her sex. Spreading her labia wide, he used one finger to describe enticing circles around the stem of her burgeoning clitoris, while his other fingers stroked and probed her dewy flesh.

Even as she rode him harder and harder, her desperately inflamed passion driving her on, his caresses did not waver. And although she tried desperately to maintain control, she felt her command of the situation slip from her grasp as easily as he slipped from her body.

To Polly's relief, her disappointment was short lived. Rolling her over on to her back and hooking her legs over his shoulders, he plunged into her again and again, his hands moulding her breasts as the weight of his body forced her knees back towards her chest. Now she was as wide open as she possibly could be, her sex straining against him on each inward thrust. His wiry pubic hair tantalised her exposed clitoris, sending urgent messages of desire zinging through her body.

She had wanted to make sure he reached his climax first, but she couldn't stop herself. The surge of pleasure was too strong. Dark, forbidden lust already had her in its clutches and there was no denying it now. Bucking and squirming, she felt desperate to reach the wave of release that she knew was just within her body's grasp. She couldn't wait for him, now it was too late. Her mouth opened wide to issue a long, drawn-out groan. Too late! Too, late! Oh, yes! Oh, God, yes! Her mind whirled in delirium as her body danced along to his tune. There was no faking it – she loved this job!

Feeling frustrated following her chance encounter with Jordan and Angelique, Deborah had decided to seek solace elsewhere.

'Christina. Christina, are you still awake?' she called out softly but insistently as she carefully pushed open the door to Christina's studio flat.

'Deborah? What a surprise.' Whipping off a pair of spectacles that she only wore for reading, Christina allowed a smile to spread across her face at the sight of her colleague.

Seeing that she was welcome, the other woman stepped into the room and closed the door behind her. 'I didn't mean to disturb you, but I was feeling at a bit of a loose end,' she said.

'Are you sure that's all?' Christina was nothing if not perceptive. Jumping to her feet she walked into the flat's small kitchen and opened the fridge. 'Want a glass of wine? I'm going to have some.'

Deborah nodded and sat down on the sofa. 'Yeah, thanks.' She picked up the book Christina had just been reading, glanced at the cover and raised an eyebrow. '*Gone With The Wind*?'

'So, what's wrong with that?' Christina said, sounding defensive. Handing a goblet of white wine to Deborah, she sat down on the sofa next to her.

Laughter accompanied the red-head's nod of thanks. 'Nothing is wrong with it. I was just a bit surprised that's all. I didn't have you pegged as a romantic.'

'You mean you think there's no room in my life for anything that isn't erotically charged? Well, I'll have you know this book is very erotic in its own way.' Christina took the book away from Deborah and flicked through the pages absently. 'You still haven't told me why you're really here.'

Having taken a huge gulp of wine, Deborah sighed and then told Christina all about her encounter in the cellar.

'I felt really embarrassed,' she concluded. 'And you know that's not like me.'

'I'll say!' The other woman couldn't help laughing aloud. 'Oh, come on Deb. It's not that terrible. I expect Angelique will forget all about it by the morning.'

Christina couldn't have been more wrong. After Jordan had taken Angelique back to her room, made love to her one more time and then left, she had lain awake, her mind going over and over the events of the evening – all of them.

The worst part was when she allowed her thoughts to return to the knowledge that another woman had looked at her and touched her intimately. Had brought her to orgasm. She didn't like to admit it, but even as the memory resurfaced, her body responded with as much eagerness as it had at the time. Hell, she had enjoyed it! Having another woman caress her had been bliss – the soft fingertips, the knowing, clever caresses and the flickering pleasure of Deborah's tongue had driven her quickly over the brink.

Jordan had not referred to the episode afterwards and for that she was grateful. But she knew he would eventually. He was probably dying to know what she thought, and suspected that he was already wondering how soon the three of them could repeat the experience. She couldn't help imagining what the other woman's naked body might look like. Deborah was tall and athletic, no doubt her stomach was ironing-board flat, the muscles in her shoulders, back and limbs taut, her breasts firm and her buttocks high and rounded.

Angelique shivered with renewed lust at the very thought. It was difficult to imagine any more of her but she wanted to try. Obviously a natural red-head, Deborah's pubic hair would be the same fiery colour, glossy curls shielding the soft pouch of her sex. In her mind's eye, Angelique saw Deborah lying on her back, knees bent up, legs spread wide. As though looking through the zoom lens of a video camera, she imagined moving closer between those open thighs, homing in on the inviting folds of her exposed sex. Silently the camera whirred and moved in closer still, lingering on the glistening lips as unseen fingers opened them out like petals. Each overlapping soft pink fold of flesh swelled and blossomed, the clitoris hardening, peeking coyly at the camera lens while just below the honeyed channel of Deborah's vagina pouted invitingly. Urging the camera closer still, Angelique imagined herself delving into that secret tunnel, watching as it widened and moistened in front of her very eyes – or at least the impassive eye of the lens.

Lost in a haze of lust, Angelique's fingers drifted to the corresponding parts of her own body. She writhed under her accomplished caresses, exploring Deborah in her mind while her fingers discovered herself. Now awakened, her desire to experience the other woman thoroughly was powerful and all-consuming. It would not be to thrill Jordan, or even to gratify Deborah. She would investigate this newly discovered facet of her sexuality for no other reason than to please herself.

Chapter Eight

*F*or the next couple of weeks Angelique found that her life wasn't quite following the route she had intended. For one thing, she had been disappointed to hear that Deborah was going away on a two-week management course. For another, the path to discovering her true origins was not running as smoothly as she had hoped. And lastly, it seemed Betty Simmons, the cook, was determined to throw up as many objections as possible to Angelique's attempts to reorganise the catering side of the hotel.

Angelique saw great potential for improvement, to introduce new dishes and create specialist menus that would make the hotel restaurant a draw in itself. Betty Simmons saw only interference and kept muttering darkly about 'little girls playing at work' and the 'folly of trying to fix things that were not broken'. No amount of persuasion or tactful cajoling on Angelique's part seemed to have any effect on the woman, and in the end, Jordan was reluctantly called upon to mediate to secure Betty's grudging agreement to cooperate with the hotel's new Catering Manager.

With a proper job to consume her energies, Angelique

found herself putting the mystery of her origins on the back-burner. Hotel life was so hectic. There always seemed to be something to do – often too much – and she quickly found that it was almost impossible to refuse a task that was not strictly part of her own job description. Manning reception, giving a helping hand in the kitchen when one of the staff went down with flu, polishing some of the hundred-or-so pieces of antique furniture and even weeding the odd flower border, or watering hanging baskets, all became part of her remit. Used to a relatively pampered existence, Angelique found her new life hard-going at first, and she often found herself having to dredge up the last of her energy reserves to enjoy an evening with Jordan. But it was worth it!

Having overcome her initial reticence about subjugating herself to him, she found herself responding with increasing enthusiasm. Every night, it seemed, Jordan had a new scenario planned for them. Sometimes there were just a few minor differences – such as handcuffs instead of leather restraints, or not being in bondage at all but simply expected to obey Jordan's instructions. Whatever the circumstances, the outcome was always the same, incredible, mind-blowing orgasms that left her feeling totally sated.

With Deborah away, Jordan was even busier than ever during the day. Angelique rarely saw him, except to take him a jug of coffee, or enjoy a quick sandwich lunch together. Being a naturally friendly person she sought out other people to chat with. Sandy could usually be relied upon to provide amusing conversation. Several times she found herself seeking him out on some pretext or another, and would then spend the next hour or so working side-by-side with him in the grounds as he regaled her with terribly wicked stories about the goings-on at Thornbury Court. And the two waitresses, Liz and Polly, were equally entertaining – their lewd insights

127

over a glass or two of wine in the hotel bar a pleasure not to be missed.

It seemed incredible to her that none of the hotel's employees seemed in the least bit fazed by the double life that went on under the creaking rafters. A-list guests were treated with equal deference in all public areas, even though their reason for visiting was often either the giving or receiving of total humiliation – that was strictly a behind closed doors activity. And there seemed to be an unwritten code among staff members that nobody would discuss the guests while they were in residence. Only afterwards were the more bizarre incidents shared with anyone who was interested in hearing the salacious details. Even then, none of the guests was ridiculed for their particular preferences, 'each to his own and good luck to them', seemed to be the Thornbury Court philosophy.

Christina put it most succinctly. 'Well,' she said, leaning her elbows on the reception desk and unconsciously wiggling her bottom, 'we only have this life. Better to get on and enjoy it than worry about other people's perceptions of right and wrong. As long as the only people getting hurt are the ones who want to be.'

Angelique laughed. 'I know what you mean. My father always used to hammer it in to me that life is not a rehearsal, it's the real thing.'

'Yeah. He was a very sensible man.' Christina's smile became a little wistful. 'I really miss him, Angelique, as I'm sure you do.'

It surprised Angelique that after all this time a lump could still form so quickly in her throat every time someone mentioned Harvey. With difficulty she swallowed and nodded.

A delicate hand reached across the polished wood and grasped her arm lightly. No words were spoken but when Angelique glanced down at the hand and then up to Christina's face she felt something indefinable tug sharply at her insides. If Christina had been a man, Angelique would have found herself thinking how desirable he was, how she might like to progress things between them. In short, she would recognise her response as sexual attraction. But Christina was a woman. So what was the emotion that suddenly gripped her?

With a start, she realised that Christina was asking a question.

'I'm sorry. I didn't catch that,' Angelique said, apologetically.

Christina squeezed Angelique's arm lightly and then took her hand away, leaving her feeling slightly bereft.

'I was wondering if you would like to come to my flat tonight. I could cook some pasta or something. Nothing fancy. Especially with you being a professional cook. And we could raid the wine cellar, Jordan wouldn't mind.'

Angelique smiled. 'A girls' night in?'

'Yeah. Exactly. I just thought it might be nice if we got to know each other a bit better. And I will admit I've been feeling a bit lonely with Deborah away.'

'Are you and Deborah good friends?' Angelique asked, already knowing the answer. The two women were always talking to each other and sharing secretive smiles.

'The best,' Christina grinned broadly. 'But there is plenty of room in my life for another friend and I think you and I are definitely on the same wavelength.'

Angelique smiled and in the next instant was interrupted by a harassed waitress who couldn't find the day's menus. 'They are on my desk!' Angelique called out to her. Then she turned to Christina. 'Thanks. I'd love to have supper with you tonight.' She grinned ruefully. 'Will seven-thirty be okay?'

'Seven-thirty will be perfect,' Christina said. 'See you then.'

* * *

A late finish meant that Angelique barely had time for a quick shower before going to see Christina. Anxious to get away from the straight-jacket feeling of the smart red suit she habitually wore during the day, she opted to relax in black leggings and a silk blouse in a bright fuchsia pink.

'Wow! That colour really suits you,' Christina said, her face wreathed in smiles as she opened the door to her flat.

Angelique found herself blushing a similar colour to her shirt. 'Thanks. It's an old faithful.' Her gaze quickly appraised Christina who was casually dressed in a tight red T-shirt which she wore tucked into black jeans. 'You look nice, too. Isn't it a relief to get out of work clothes at the end of the day and just chill out?'

'Absolutely,' Christina agreed. Treating her guest to a broad grin, she led the way into the spacious room that comprised the main part of her accommodation. Her bed was a double futon covered in plain black cotton, which she used as a sofa during the day. The only other main items of furniture were a second sofa – a battered black leather chesterfield – a few low tables and some built-in cupboards.

'I believe in the minimalist approach,' she explained needlessly as Angelique glanced around with interest.

'So I see.' Angelique smiled, and then accepted a glass of Chianti. 'I'm afraid I tend to go for clutter,' she admitted. 'Although it's more by accident than design. Whatever I do I just can't seem to keep my surroundings tidy.'

'Well, if you don't have much to start with then you can hardly make a mess,' Christina said, without managing to sound pompous. With a relaxed sigh she sank gracefully on to the futon, one leg tucked underneath her. She gestured expansively. 'Sit down. Make yourself at home, even if that does mean turning the place into a tip.' With a deliberate wink to show that she was only teasing she laughed aloud, throwing back her head to expose a slender throat.

Impulsively, Angelique responded by sticking out her tongue, and the two women collapsed into fits of laughter.

'Oh, God! I haven't laughed that hard in ages,' Angelique groaned, wiping a tear from the corner of her eye.

'Nor me,' Christina said. Then she muttered, 'Music, music,' and jumped to her feet. Walking over to one of the cupboards, she flung the door open to reveal a CD deck and stack of discs. 'Madonna okay?'

She glanced over her shoulder towards her guest. Angelique was feeling stunned by the strong feelings that had overwhelmed her as she watched Christina move about. There was no doubt in her mind now that her emotions had a strong sexual content. She instantly felt afraid that either Christina would make an overture which she would have to deal with, or worse still, that she wouldn't. Unable to speak for the moment, Angelique nodded dumbly.

Was it her imagination, or did Christina just give her a knowing smile?

The raunchy sound of 'Vogue' filled the room and Christina carried on into the kitchenette. 'I wasn't sure if you were a vegetarian so I bought ravioli filled with ricotta cheese and spinach. Is that okay?' she called out.

With Christina partially out of sight, Angelique was able to concentrate instead on the reassuring 'kitchen sonata' – the chink-chink of china, the clash of steel and the rhythmic beat of cupboard doors being opened and closed. The familiar sounds allowed her to recover her composure and eventually shout back that no, she wasn't a vegetarian but Christina's choice sounded absolutely delicious anyway. She also added that she was starving.

With greedy eyes she watched as about ten minutes later, Christina placed two plates heaped with pasta and a rich tomato sauce on the white breakfast bar that separated the kitchen from the living area.

As Angelique climbed on to one of the high stools that sat under the lip of the breakfast bar, Christina walked quickly around the room lighting candles and turning off the lights. Returning to take her own seat she sat down and glanced around with satisfaction.

'That's better,' she said, rubbing her hands together and then picking up her fork. 'I love candlelight, don't you?' She stabbed casually at the food on her plate and glanced up at Angelique.

The breakfast bar was so narrow their heads almost touched and Angelique couldn't help inhaling Christina's light floral scent, or noticing the generous dusting of freckles over the upper swell of her small breasts. Feeling slightly uncomfortable, she glanced down at her plate and found her eyes straying to Christina's hands, noticing how the long, slim fingers seemed to play around the handle of the fork rather than grip it, and how the fingers of the other hand drummed lightly on the counter top.

'Sorry. I'm always doing that,' Christina said. 'I play the piano you see and often find myself accompanying other people's music.' She laughed her customary tinkling laugh, which Angelique thought was reminiscent of wind chimes, and picked up her glass. For a moment she sipped delicately.

'Piano.' Angelique repeated, almost to herself. 'Piano, that's it!' Suddenly she jumped down from her chair and rushed toward the door. Just as she reached it she realised what she was doing and stopped in her tracks. Retracing her steps she climbed back on the seat and picked up her fork again. For a few minutes she forced herself to eat and tried to quell the surging excitement inside her. Then she steeled herself to answer Christina's questioning look.

'In my father's last letter he mentioned that there was

a key to solving every mystery,' she explained. 'You know about me being adopted and everything don't you?' she added. 'I just assumed . . .'

Christina nodded and reached out to touch Angelique's arm just as she had done that afternoon. 'Yeah. I know. Go on.' By the inflection in her voice it was obvious that she was intrigued.

Angelique felt shy and a bit foolish. 'For some reason, when you mentioned that you played the piano, I suddenly thought of piano keys and wondered if that was what he meant.' Shaking her head in disbelief at her own logic and her desperation to clutch at straws, she glanced back at Christina. It made her feel grateful that she looked as though she understood completely. There was no derision in her expression, none at all.

'As you know, Thornbury Court has the Piano Bar,' Christina said, 'and there is also an upright in the communal sitting-room.'

Angelique remembered seeing it and nodded. 'Would you mind if . . .?' she began but Christina was already on her feet.

'Of course not. As long as you let me come with you. I love mysteries.' Her pale blue eyes sparkled and for a split second Angelique was tempted to take her delicate face between her hands and kiss her softly smiling lips.

Fighting down the urge, she contented herself with a smile instead. 'Thanks for this, Christina. I'm sorry to spoil our meal.' She glanced at the barely touched food but her friend – which was how she thought of the other woman – already simply laughed off her apology.

'It doesn't matter. I can always pop it in the microwave when we come back. Or I've got some cheese and crackers. We won't starve. Come on, let's get on with our bit of detective work.'

Disappointingly, a thorough search of both pianos revealed absolutely nothing. Feeling near to tears, Angelique lifted the lid of the baby grand in the Piano Bar for the fourth time and peered inside.

'I think if there had been anything hidden inside either of them it would have been discovered by now,' Christina said. 'Did you check underneath the upright?'

Angelique gave a dejected nod. 'I've gone over them both with a fine toothcomb. Oh, bloody hell, Christina! I was certain I'd find something. I don't know what exactly, but definitely something. Some kind of clue.' She slammed the lid of the piano. 'Damn Harvey, the bastard! Why couldn't he just have told me the truth while he was still alive?' The frustration and disappointment was all too much for her and she burst into tears – much to the amazement of the handful of customers in the bar.

Putting a consoling arm around Angelique's shoulders, Christina led her gently away. 'Come on. Let's go back to my place and get plastered,' she suggested.

With a wan smile Angelique allowed Christina to lead her back to her flat. Once inside, Christina sat her down on the sofa again and handed her a glass of wine.

'Now drink that,' Christina ordered. 'Or would you prefer something stronger – a brandy, perhaps?'

'No. This is fine, thanks,' Angelique said, shaking her head and draining the glass in a few gulps. 'I will have another wine though.'

Quickly, all thoughts of food and even Angelique's earlier disappointment became blurred around the edges as the two women finished the first bottle of wine and moved on to a second. Christina sat next to Angelique and tried to cheer her up by relating one amusing anecdote after another. Gradually, Angelique started to succumb to the numbing warmth of the alcohol. She felt suffused by gratitude to the woman beside her.

'Oh, boy, I feel so much better now. Thanks to you,

Christina,' Angelique said, turning her head so that she could smile properly at her companion.

In that instant their eyes locked and unspoken messages passed between them – questioning and mutual assent. Leaning toward each other at the same moment their lips touched, hands fluttered and rested lightly on shoulders and eyelids closed.

It was a wonderful kiss, Angelique thought, gentle, sweet and undeniably feminine. And the fingers drifting over her upper back were light, the touch non-threatening and exploratory. Inside her head Angelique groaned and her response was transmitted by a slight increase in pressure against Christina's lips.

Christina reacted eagerly, one hand delving into the thick, silky mass of Angelique's hair as the other roamed her back and shoulders. This young woman wasn't Deborah by any means. Everything about her was different and yet there was something indefinable about Angelique that made Christina's heart leap about with excitement. Small serpents of desire wriggled inside her belly and she felt an almost overwhelming urge to throw herself across Angelique's lap and beg her to spank her.

'Christina, what is it?' Angelique felt the slight hesitation of her friend's indecision and pulled away, her eyes roaming the other girl's face and wondering how it was they came to be in each other's arms in the first place.

Long-lashed eyelids flickered for a second as Christina stared back at her. 'Nothing. A silly thought came into my mind, that's all.'

'What sort of silly thought?' Angelique reached up and ran a gentle hand over Christina's hair and down the side of her face. The other woman was so delicate, her bone-structure so fine that she made Angelique feel positively ungainly in comparison. That was crazy, because there wasn't an ounce of spare flesh on her.

Christina nuzzled Angelique's palm for a moment then pursed her lips. 'I don't know if you are aware of

135

the fact, but Deborah is more than my lover. She is my mistress. I just had a desperate longing to be spanked, that's all.'

Angelique stared back at the other woman and tried to imagine what it might be like to be dominated by Deborah. Oh, God, it must be wonderful! she thought. She cleared her throat.

'I do sort of know how you feel,' she said hesitantly, 'Jordan and I . . .'

Christina's face seemed to light up as she interrupted. 'Oh, yes, Jordan. He's marvellous isn't he, really knows how to crack the whip.' As she broke off to giggle at her intentional pun, she noticed Angelique wasn't laughing. Or even smiling for that matter. 'What's up – have I said something wrong?'

Angelique shook her head dumbly and pulled right away from Christina. Shuffling back on the sofa with her arms crossed protectively over her torso, she tried to sink into the corner.

At once Christina was full of concern. 'Angelique, I'm sorry. I didn't realise you and he were serious.'

'Well, I am. Obviously he isn't. Although to be fair he did warn me.' Angelique felt a hot flush rise in her cheeks. 'What the hell is going on in this place? Is everyone at it – all these kinky activities?'

Despite her annoyance with herself and her remorse at having upset Angelique, Christina couldn't help the smile that touched her lips. 'Just about,' she said, matter-of-factly. 'But I thought you knew that.'

Angelique sighed and glanced down at her hands. 'Yes. I did. I'm just being an idiot. For some inexplicable reason I thought Jordan sort of oversaw everything but didn't actually participate. Except with me.'

'Christ, really?' Christina blurted out. 'I thought you must know all about Jordan. He takes a very active part in the hotel's activities.' She reached forward to pick up the wine bottle from the low table in front of them and

refilled their glasses. Settling back again she eyed Angelique carefully. 'It would be very unrealistic of you to
expect a conventional relationship with Jordan. He is not
a conventional man by any stretch of the imagination.'

Angelique gave a rueful laugh. 'I know. And it's
idiotic really because that's one of the main reasons I like
him, why I'm attracted to him. Not to mention the fact
that just now I felt . . . I felt . . .' She hesitated.

'Yes?'

Glancing up, Angelique noticed that Christina was
looking at her expectantly. 'I felt very attracted to you.'
She took a deep breath and let it out slowly.

Moving as though in slow-motion, Christina put down
her glass, took Angelique's away from her and put that
down, then reached forward and began to unfasten the
buttons on Angelique's blouse.

As she glanced down Angelique felt mesmerised by
the sight of Christina's fingers deftly working the buttons
through their holes. Loving the sensation of pure silk
against bare skin, she wore no bra underneath the blouse
and was aware that her breasts were rising and falling
rapidly. She had to concentrate on curbing the rate of her
breathing and keeping it slow and even, conscious all
the time that her nipples were as hard as bullets and
aching to be touched.

The silk slid over her skin as she arched her back,
exposing her naked breasts to the other woman. Shrugging her shoulders slightly, Angelique felt the blouse
ripple down her arms to form a pool like melted rasp-
berry ice-cream on the black leather sofa. She exhaled
loudly, her skin prickling and forming goosebumps as
fresh air stroked across it, followed by Christina's light
touch.

'You do really want this, don't you, Angelique?'
Christina asked, her warm breath another welcome
caress.

Feeling as though her breasts swelled and throbbed in

response, Angelique nodded wordlessly. There was so much she wanted to say – to do – and yet her inexperience galvanised her into inaction. At that moment she felt as though she and Christina were joined by the invisible thread of Deborah's caresses. Each had experienced the same things. Each had felt the same woman's fingers upon the most intimate parts of their bodies.

'Deborah?' Angelique started to speak but Christina hushed her and placed a finger against her lips.

'Deborah won't mind if we enjoy each other tonight,' she murmured, apparently misunderstanding what Angelique had been about to say.

For a moment Angelique debated whether to say anything else. She decided against it. Instead she opened her mouth and sucked Christina's finger.

Christina took that as a sign to continue. A smile crossed her face and she licked her lips before bending her head to take one of Angelique's nipples between them. Gently she sucked and nibbled the tender bud of flesh and lathed the whole area with her tongue, taking her time before giving the other breast the same delicious treatment. Throughout it all Angelique clutched at her shoulders and moaned, arching her back to offer yet more of herself to Christina's mouth.

Inwardly, Christina smiled. She loved to receive pleasure but giving it was just as enjoyable, especially to someone as beautiful and responsive as Angelique. For once she was cast in the leading role and it was one she assumed eagerly. Perhaps when Deborah returned the three of them could . . .? The very thought made her feel unbearably hot.

The first light of dawn was already filtering through a gap in the curtains by the time the two women fell asleep in each other's arms. When Angelique awoke it was with a smile on her face. Beside her, Christina lay on her stomach, still snoring softly.

Angelique knew the young woman was not rostered on duty until later that afternoon and therefore had no reason to wake her. For her own part, she had nothing to do that couldn't wait awhile. Instead she allowed herself the luxury of remembering the night before, recalling each blissful minute second by second.

She could not believe the level of ecstasy that Christina had taken her to, time and time again. Nor could Angelique relate to the way she herself had responded, other than with wonder. Normally enthusiastic anyway, Christina's skilful caresses seemed to turn her into a hot, wet, writhing, wailing banshee of a lover. And at some indefinable point the idea of touching the other woman had ceased to make her feel nervous and instead excited the hell out of her.

If she had one regret it was that she wished she had shown a little more finesse. Christina's touch was light and gently coaxing, whereas Angelique felt spurred into action by the other woman's passivity, quickly taking over the dominant role. As soon as she had recovered a little from her first orgasm of the evening – brought about by the delicate touch of Christina's fingertips alone – she practically dived on her partner and ripped the clothes from her body.

As though a touchpaper had been lit inside her, she scrabbled desperately at the buttons on Christina's jeans and pulled the awkward garment down her legs while her partner divested herself of the red T-shirt. Underneath she was completely naked, a fact which, just for a moment, took Angelique's breath away. She couldn't believe the loveliness of Christina's body – the perfect symmetry of each line and curve, each ridge and indentation.

Exhaling loudly, she allowed herself the luxury of feasting her eyes on flawless beauty while Christina reclined on the sofa, a slight smile playing about her lips. It was obvious that she was proud of her body, and rightly so. And it was obvious she was more than happy to be the object of another's admiration.

Angelique noticed that by bending her knees slightly, Christina deliberately allowed her a tantalising glimpse of her charms. Her sex was a perfect pink pouch of delicate, sensitive flesh. Now Angelique looked there, her hands moving to Christina's knees to spread them apart, easing them wider and wider until she was completely exposed.

A sharp intake of breath signified Christina's arousal and diverted Angelique's interested glance to her face. 'You are beautiful, Christina,' she said softly, her eyes returning to the glistening folds of pink flesh and then back to gaze at Christina's face. To her delight, Christina blushed.

Oh, yes, Angelique thought with a surge of pleasure. What power she possessed in her fingertips, her lips, her eyes. The power to give enjoyment to another woman. Tentatively, she reached forward with both hands and spread Christina's outer lips wider still and then the delicate inner lips. Her clitoris was swollen and so hard, already emerging from its little hood to tantalise her. Stroking it with a single fingertip, Angelique watched with pleasure as it swelled a little more.

Christina whimpered. Yes, this was right, Angelique realised. Remembering easily how she herself liked to be pleasured, she rubbed two fingers lightly up and down the stem of the other woman's clitoris, increasing the speed ever so gradually until her partner was crying out with unleashed desire. Then Christina began to grind her hips, making it difficult for Angelique to keep up her rhythm but she persevered and in seconds she was left in no doubt that Christina was in the throes of orgasm.

'Phew, thanks,' Christina said with a tremulous grin as Angelique slid her naked body alongside her and stroked her torso.

Angelique smiled, feeling pleased and clever and more

140

than a little aroused herself. 'That was my first time,' she admitted.

A wicked glint sparkled in the other woman's eyes. 'I would never have suspected.' Her tone was deliberately grave which made Angelique wonder if Christina was simply teasing her. She was a tease, there was no doubt about that and very, very good fun. With a struggle, Christina sat up. 'Shall I make up the bed – would you like to stay?' she asked, touching Angelique's shoulder tentatively and stroking a questioning finger down her upper arm.

For a few blissful moments Angelique allowed herself to revel in the new sensations that simple caress awakened within her. It was amazing, but everything about the events of the evening just seemed completely right.

Turning her face up to gaze at Christina she nodded gently. 'I'd love to.'

Chapter Nine

*I*t was turning out to be a very warm summer. By mid-July temperatures were soaring and according to forecasts it promised to be one of the hottest summers on record. Gloomier predictions warned of drought and water rationing, but until that actually happened Jordan was determined that the grounds of Thornbury Court should be kept in tip-top condition. That meant employing a student to go around the grounds first thing in the morning, turning on the lawn sprinklers, then in the evening to turn them off and, in between times, drench the countless well-stocked borders, ornamental beds and planters that surrounded the whole building.

Sandy, backed up by Fergus, had complained that the flowers were in danger of getting sunburn due to being watered during the day, but really there was no other choice. Not unless Jordan employed two more people, or even three, and the hotel's cash-flow just wasn't up to it.

He was inspecting a worrying-looking crack that had appeared in the wall of the fountain, next to the croquet lawn, when he was surprised to hear Deborah's voice in his ear.

'Hi, stranger.'

Jumping to his feet, Jordan flung his arms around the red-head and planted very wet kisses on both her cheeks. 'Hi, yourself. Where have you been hiding since you got back – was the course good?'

Deborah rubbed at her wet cheeks and gave a wry grin. 'You're just like a puppy I used to have, Jordan. All eager and slobbery.' The grin softened to a fond smile and she reached up to stroke his hair. 'Yes, the course was good. I'll give you all the gen later, and surprise, surprise I've been with Christina. That little minx needed a good seeing-to, I can tell you.'

Jordan joined in her laughter, imagining that Christina's taut little bottom must be red raw.

'Did she tell you she and Angelique got it together while I was away?' Deborah continued.

That was a shock, and Jordan stared at her in amazement. 'No, neither of them thought to mention it,' he said. 'Well, well. Christina and Angelique.' He sat down heavily on the wall that he had been inspecting and pondered the implications for a few moments.

'I wouldn't worry about it, Jordan,' Deborah said, sitting down next to him. 'I mean, I don't think they are serious or anything. Christina was certainly eager enough to see me again.'

Shielding his eyes with his hand, Jordan stared up at the clear blue sky. 'Oh, I don't doubt that,' he said. 'I'm just surprised at Angelique. I mean, the way she reacted when you – well, you know.' Deborah nodded sagely and Jordan glanced at her and shrugged. 'I can't help wondering why she kept it from me.'

'Who knows?' Deborah got up and wiped her hands over the back of her smart black skirt. 'I wouldn't lose any sleep over it, Jordan. In fact, I'd be pleased if I were you. After all, if she's loosened up that much already it can only mean more enjoyment in the long-run.'

Jordan noticed how she tried to give him a reassuring

smile and that her relief was obvious when he responded in kind.

'You're right of course, oh wise and wonderful Deborah,' he said, his eyes twinkling mischievously. Slipping his arm around her waist he urged her in the direction of the house. 'Come on. While you've been slacking off, the work has been piling up.'

Deborah turned around and hit him playfully on the chest. 'Oh, great. Now I remember why I love this place.'

If Deborah had any doubts about why she had returned to the hotel – reluctantly leaving behind the beautiful and inventive Dutch girl she had teamed up with on the management course – she only had to listen to Jordan's friendly banter now. Or recall how, on her first night back, Christina had lavished kisses on her boots and literally begged for an orgasm. Failing that she simply had to look around her at the living splendour of a bygone era, the golden walls of the old house basking in the sun and the acres of well-kept gardens surrounded by sprawling fields and woodland. There were no end of reasons why she regarded Thornbury Court as her home. It would take a lot to make her turn her back on all that she had.

While Deborah was counting her blessings, Angelique was cursing the thorns in her side – namely the local suppliers who either could not, or would not, meet the orders she gave them.

'How can I be expected to produce that courgette soufflé thing of yours if I get sent aubergines instead?' Betty complained, hands planted firmly on hips as she stood in front of Angelique's desk, 'or *Blanquette de Veau* when the butcher can't tell his calves from his pigs?'

Angelique sighed. In all honesty she didn't know how to answer the woman because she felt just as frustrated. That was the trouble with being out of the country for so long. She didn't know who anyone was, or where the best suppliers could be found. And it seemed that, between them, the handful of top restaurants had a monopoly on quality supplies countrywide. Even decent asparagus and strawberries were proving difficult to get hold of – and it was traditional cream-tea time of year when fresh strawberries were essential. Thank goodness Sandy had the forethought to start a strawberry patch. It provided a good yield, but nowhere near enough if trade were to suddenly pick up.

Sometimes she thought of François and wondered how he was doing. Before leaving France, she had promised to keep in touch with him. However, since falling under the spell of the older, more experienced Jordan, the likelihood of Angelique maintaining contact with François was receding daily.

However genuine her professional concerns might be, if she looked deeper into herself she would be forced to admit that lately they had masked the real problem of discovering true origins.

It seemed to her she had been getting nowhere fast until, just a few days before, after she had spent countless frustrating hours going through every single box of paper's in Harvey's archive and finding nothing, Jordan had appeared and had calmly asked about the details on her birth certificate.

Surrounded by a sea of paper, Angelique had looked up, stared at him open-mouthed and suddenly realised what an idiot she had been. Caught up in Thornbury Court's peculiar *mélange* – from the frantic to the frankly erotic – she had completely forgotten to take the most obvious step in her quest. As soon as Jordan reminded her, a phone call to her mother in Paris and a bit of haranguing was all it took to have her original birth certificate winging its way to her.

Now, three days later, it had arrived.

When it appeared on her desk that morning, along

with her other mail, she suddenly felt apprehensive. As she dealt with Betty she managed to ignore its presence, but as soon as the cook left she found herself glancing anxiously at the long blue envelope bearing a French stamp and her mother's precise handwriting.

As she hesitated, she was relieved to be interrupted by another knock at the door. This time it was Jordan.

'What a relief to see you,' she said, letting out a long breath. 'This arrived today. I've been trying to pluck up the courage to open it.' She picked up the envelope, waved it in the air, then dropped it hastily on the desk as though it burned her fingers.

Jordan glanced at the envelope, then Angelique's stricken expression. 'Just do it, Angelique,' he urged. 'Or would you rather I opened it?' He walked across the room and moved to pick up the envelope, but Angelique stopped him and picked it up herself.

'No, it's all right, I'll do it,' she said, adding nervously, 'Here goes.'

Carefully separating the sticky edges of the envelope, she opened it and drew out the slightly yellowing document that was inside. It was folded over twice so she couldn't read any of the details and for a moment she held the paper against her chest, as though her heart was capable of absorbing what her eyes were reluctant to see.

'I'm scared, Jordan,' she said, tears glistening in her eyes as she looked up at him.

'Don't be. It can't hurt you. You've already suffered the worst pain. This is a way to heal yourself.' Jordan's voice was soft and persuasive.

Angelique also realised the sense in what he had to say. 'Okay,' she said hoarsely.

A lump seemed lodged in her throat and her hands trembled as she opened out the long sheet of paper and spread it flat out in front of her on the desk. With unwilling eyes she glanced down. There it was, all laid out in red ink: Certified Copy of an Entry of Birth, along with the certificate number. And underneath typed in black ink the details she already knew: her date of birth, twenty-four years earlier, her given name and sex.

Then there were those details she didn't know.

Automatically, she glanced at the next box: Name, and surname of father. She was disappointed to see that it simply contained the words: 'father unknown'. But the following column – details about her mother, at least held a little information: 'Jeanette Baker, unmarried, of no fixed abode'. Angelique sighed, the latter part was disappointing, but now she had a name to go on. And the next column, occupation of father, was even less informative. It simply contained the single word 'unknown'. At signature, description and residence of informant, Angelique's heart leaped. Her mother's name was cited again, together with the name and address of a nursing home: 'The Cedars, Boscombe Rise, Longley Green'.

She glanced up at Jordan excitedly. 'Longley Green – that's near here, isn't it?'

To her relief he nodded. 'About five or six miles up the road. I know the place quite well, including Boscombe Rise, but I don't remember seeing a nursing home there.'

Immediately, Angelique jumped to her feet. 'We have to go and look. I have to go,' she amended quickly, realising how much she took for granted.

'No. You were right the first time,' Jordan said, as he walked around the desk and took her arm. 'We will go and look.' He smiled gently. 'Come on, Angelique. What are you waiting for? Let's go and solve this mystery once and for all.'

Their optimism was dashed as soon as they arrived in Longley Green and had driven the whole length of Boscombe Rise. A handful of large houses lined the road either side, but none of them bore a nameplate which read 'The Cedars', and not one of them looked remotely like a nursing home.

'These all seem to be private residences,' Jordan said gloomily, slowing the car so that he and Angelique could peer up the long driveways.

She felt the familiar stirrings of frustration. 'Well, we can't give up,' she said. Sitting back dejectedly, she thought for a minute and then suggested that they stop at the nearest pub for a bite to eat. 'You never know. One of the locals might remember the place. After all, we know it was there twenty-four years ago.'

Privately, Jordan thought that Angelique was clutching at straws but he didn't like to disappoint her, and it was lunchtime. 'Okay, let's go for it. I could do with a bite to eat.' He smiled encouragingly, put his foot down on the accelerator and in no time at all they were pulling into the tiny car park of 'The Walnut'.

While Jordan and Angelique looked forward to enjoying the cramped conviviality of the pub's saloon bar, back at the hotel Rod Bennet, Thornbury Court's bell-boy, was not feeling quite as enthusiastic about the hours that lay ahead.

'Just what the bloody hell do you think I look like in this get-up?' he grumbled, as he pulled at the sleeves of the white tuxedo. They were clearly an inch too short and unkindly exposed his bony wrists.

'Mrs Livsey asked for a waiter who looks like Humphrey Bogart in Casablanca,' Lesley explained patiently. 'And if that's what Mrs Livsey wants, that's what she gets.' She pulled at the offending sleeves and then attempted to adjust Rod's bow-tie.

'Get off me, you faggot!' Rod grumbled, slapping Lesley's hands away. 'I look nothing like Humphrey Bogart and you know it. Plus the fact I'm a bell-boy not a waiter.'

148

Lesley frowned at the uncalled for slight and was about to retaliate when Deborah poked her head around the door. 'Aren't you ready yet, Rod? The kitchen just rang through to say that the trolley's all set to be taken up to Mr and Mrs Livsey.'

Rod frowned. 'I'll never be ready. Look at the state of me.' He held his arms out at shoulder level as though he was about to be nailed to a cross.

Deborah stepped into the room and eyed him carefully. He was so tall and thin, the uniform clearly did nothing for him and yet in all probability he wouldn't be wearing it for very long. In a calm voice, she pointed that fact out to him.

'Yes, well. There is that to it I suppose,' he conceded grimly. His eyes followed Deborah as she walked around him slowly. The very act excited him even though there was no hidden intent behind it. With a further tingle of excitement he remembered being told that Mrs Livsey was also a very competent dominatrix.

'It is a shame that Dave is still away,' Deborah said, referring to the waiter who normally serviced the Livseys. Then she glanced at Lesley who blushed automatically.

In a deliberately teasing manner, Deborah reached into her pocket, pulled out a leather thong and began to toy with it. Both Rod and Lesley were instantly rivetted.

'Dave wrote to me last week,' Lesley said, stammering badly. 'He said his mum is much better and should be allowed out of hospital by the end of July at the latest.'

'Good.' Deborah continued to play with the thong, drawing it through her fingers and winding it tightly around her hand so that it left deep red marks across her pale skin.

'I'm sorry I called you a faggot,' Rod said abruptly, flashing a smile at Lesley.

The housekeeper smiled back, one eye still on the leather thong. 'That's okay. No offence taken.' She meant it. Deep down she and Rod held quite an affection for each other. Under other circumstances they might even have become more than friends and workmates.

'Well done, boys and girls,' Deborah said in her school-teacher voice. 'Now, you are clear about the scenario for this afternoon, aren't you Rod?'

He nodded. 'I think so.'

Pausing only to wind the thong into a little ball and replace it in her pocket, Deborah walked over to the window and perched on the sill, arms crossed. 'As you know, Mr and Mrs Livsey are very old A-list,' she said. 'They've been coming here since Thornbury Court reopened and might even have been guests at the old hotel,' she said. 'Anyway, the scenario is always the same. Mrs Livsey likes to dominate. Mr Livsey likes to watch. But you are not to touch either of them, Rod. Is that understood?' Her eyes narrowed and she waited until he nodded and repeated that yes, he understood. 'Any sexual contact is strictly between the two of them,' she added. 'Although you will probably be required to watch. In a minute you will take up the trolley and serve them lunch. You will stand attentively to one side while they eat and you will obey all instructions, is that understood?' Again she paused until Rod nodded. 'If you make any cock-ups, so much the better,' Deborah said. 'Acts of clumsiness will give Mrs Livsey a good excuse to chastise you. How, where and when she punishes you will be up to her. A dungeon is at the couple's disposal but there is every possibility that this afternoon's activities will be confined to their suite. I understand a trestle and various other small items were ordered and taken up there earlier.'

She stood up and walked slowly over to Rod. Reaching down she grasped his testicles and squeezed hard, a cruel smile crossing her face. 'Do a good job, Rod, and I'll make sure that you are doubly punished later,' she said darkly.

'Oh, God! Yes, Deborah,' Rod gasped. 'I promise I'll be the worst waiter Mrs Livsey has ever dealt with.'

Releasing her grip, Deborah smiled thinly. 'Good,' she said. 'Very good. Now get on with it!'

While Rod Bennet was receiving his instructions for the afternoon, Jordan and Angelique had fallen into the easy company of some interesting people. Two of them, Dan and Susan, studiously mousy people in their late-twenties, were teachers at a local public school. And the third member of the little group was a very lively and eccentric middle-aged man who had immediately produced a business card – plain white with a fancy blue script which read: 'Martin Wreathe, Antiques & Bric-à-Brac.'

Of the three of them, Angelique took to Martin at first sight. For a start he looked interesting. A man of imposing build, he had a strong, animated face, long, straggly dark hair streaked with grey and a thick neck, almost the same width as his head, around which he had wound a blue-and-white fringed scarf. It did nothing for him and clashed horribly with his red-and-yellow check plus-fours, white T-shirt and brown suede waistcoat. If the police were ever to ask her to describe him, she would have no trouble at all.

Added to his less than conventional appearance was the fact that he seemed completely mad.

'Oh, yes I remember "The Cedars",' he chipped in, as soon as Angelique mentioned the reason she and Jordan were visiting Longley Green.

'Really?' She couldn't believe her luck and pulled her stool closer to the group's table, and Martin in particular.

'Yes. Nice pub, did a good ploughman's,' he said. Pausing to sip his beer, he sat back and wiped the froth away from his mouth with the back of his hand. 'Used to go there of a Friday night before my Jan skipped off with that steeplejack. Him and his big erections, I didn't stand a chance!'

Even though it was old ground for them, Dan and Susan flashed Martin a sympathetic glance while Angelique threw Jordan a look of anguish.

' "The Cedars" is the name of a private nursing home,' Jordan explained patiently. 'It was situated along Boscombe Rise. Must have closed down though because all the houses along there seem to be private residences now.'

Martin looked blank but Dan scratched his cheek for a minute, his face screwed up in concentration.

'Just a minute,' he blurted out. 'We did something last term on local history. I seem to recall we used old copies of the census. Do you remember what we did with them, Susan?'

Susan shook her head. 'I can't remember what we did – ' She broke off and her face suddenly brightened. 'Oh, yes I can,' she went on. 'We put them in the back of the stationery cupboard. Said we might use them for scrap paper.

'Look. I don't suppose we could have them, could we?' Jordan asked. 'I mean we'd be glad to make a donation to the school in return, or perhaps offer a free weekend at the hotel as a raffle prize or something. You name it.' He couldn't help noticing how Angelique's face brightened for the first time since their arrival at Longley Green.

Susan and Dan glanced at each other.

'That's really kind of you to offer, but you don't have to. They are only reams of paper after all,' Dan said.

Leaning forward, Angelique patted the back of his hand. 'They may only be bits of paper to you but they could help me find my real parents.'

Dan swallowed and looked embarrassed until Susan butted in. 'Well, I suggest we get another round in and then go back to the school and get them. If you decide to contribute something it's up to you.'

* * *

By four o'clock, Jordan and Angelique had finally worked their way far enough back through the census documents to find the information they were looking for. 'The Cedars', it turned out, had reverted to being plain old number 144 in the early nineteen-eighties. Throwing all the reams of paper into the back of the BMW, Angelique fastened her seat belt and Jordan spun the car around.

At the end of a long tarmac driveway, bounded on both sides by a wilderness of garden, sat a crumbling wreck of a house. Even though the sun was doing its best to brighten the place up it was obvious that major repair work needed to be done. The window frames were rotten and some panes of glass were cracked, while a number of tiles were missing from the roof and patches of damp showed on the brickwork.

'This place is a dump,' Angelique said under her breath as she walked gingerly up to the front door and raised the iron knocker. On the cracked and broken concrete step stood a couple of empty milk bottles. Unwashed, the yellowing streaks of milk inside the bottles gave off a foul odour. 'Phew. I feel sick and not just with nerves.' She attempted to joke but failed miserably. All she could think of was that this depressing, horrible place might be her only link with her real mother.

Her knock was answered by an old woman in a floral apron, carpet slippers and a badly-fitting blonde wig. She refused to invite either of them in, insisting that Jordan and Angelique must show their ID cards first.

'But we are not from the council, or British Telecom,' Jordan explained patiently for the third time. 'We understand this used to be a nursing home. "The Cedars". Is that right?'

The woman stared at them with a glassy expression for a moment or two. Angelique realised that she must be nearly blind, judging by the milky cataracts which obscured her pupils.

'We don't mean you any harm,' Angelique said softly. 'According to my birth certificate I was born here and then adopted. I just need to find out who my mother was and where she went to after she left here.'

The old lady toyed with her apron. 'There are boxes,' she said at last in a raspy voice. 'In the attic, loads of boxes of papers and such-like. I can't be doing with them but you can have them if you want to.'

Angelique glanced at Jordan. Then she turned to the woman again. 'Do the papers relate to "The Cedars"? Are they patients' records, that sort of thing?'

To her relief the woman nodded. 'Records, yes. Lots of them. You can have them, they're no use to me.'

Much as he wanted to help Angelique, Jordan didn't relish the prospect of digging about in a dusty old attic. 'If it's all right with you, I'll send a couple of my people to come and get the papers tomorrow,' he said, doing his best to ignore Angelique's crest-fallen expression. He handed the old woman a business card and carefully slid her fingertips over the embossed lettering. 'We run Thornbury Court Hotel,' he explained. 'It's just a few miles from here.'

'I know it,' the woman said, nodding. 'You send your people. Ten o'clock sharp mind, or I won't let them in.'

Solemnly, Jordan shook her hand. 'Ten o'clock,' he assured her, 'and I'll make sure they bring identical business cards with them as ID.'

The woman nodded again, obviously satisfied with the arrangement. 'I'll be glad to see the back of those boxes,' she said, already starting to close the door. 'All they do is make the place seem untidy.'

By eight o'clock that evening Angelique had got over her disappointment at having to wait until the following day to see the paperwork belonging to 'The Cedars'. It had been a blow not to come away with something there and then, but she could see Jordan's point. If the outside of the house was anything to go by, the attic and the boxes would be filthy and thick with dust and there probably wouldn't have been enough space in the car for all of them anyway.

'I'll get a couple of men to go over there with a van,' Jordan had promised her. 'You'll have the boxes by lunchtime tomorrow.'

Angelique smiled and accepted a glass of champagne. 'Why are we celebrating?' she asked, temporarily forgetting her mission in order to enjoy the aura of tension that had sprung up between the two of them.

Jordan grinned wolfishly. 'I think you know.'

The words made Angelique shiver. In a moment of heady madness, after she and Jordan had arrived back at the hotel and enjoyed afternoon tea together, she had agreed to watch Deborah chastise Christina that same evening. Jordan had hinted that he knew about Angelique's 'special' relationship with Christina and, after a moment's hesitation, Angelique admitted it and then told him everything.

'I almost felt tempted to spank Christina myself when she mentioned it,' Angelique said hesitantly. 'I'll be interested to see how Deborah goes about it.'

Jordan fought down his rising excitement. 'So, after only a few weeks you fancy yourself as a bit of a dominatrix, do you?' he said lightly. 'I thought you enjoyed being submissive.'

Angelique nodded. 'Oh, with you I do.' Her tone and expression were earnest and she leaned forward as she spoke, clasping the stem of her champagne flute between both hands. 'But there's something that appeals to me about actually being on the other end of the whip. I can't explain it, but you must know what I mean?' She gazed warmly up at Jordan who had relinquished his chair to cross the room and stand in front of her.

'Of course I know,' he murmured darkly. 'But I have only ever wanted to wield the whip. I never enjoyed taking punishment.'

'So you have tried it?' Amazement sounded in Angelique's voice.

Jordan nodded and took the wine glass away from her. 'Naturally, I tried it. I had to know how it felt to be on the receiving end.' Reaching down, he clasped her hands and pulled her to her feet. 'Before we go down to the cellar I have to make sure that you have been properly dealt with,' he said in a voice that made Angelique's whole body turn weak. 'Now take off your dress and bend over that table.'

He indicated a gleaming rosewood side table that stood just to the left of the tall window. The curtains were open and bright light still streamed into the room.

'Someone might see,' Angelique said hoarsely, unzipping the peach silk dress she wore.

Jordan nodded, walked over to her and took the dress. Draping it neatly over the back of a chair he paused to admire the way she looked. Tall in her high heels, slim and curvaceous she stood proudly in front of him, her breasts straining to break free from the confines of the peach satin corset she had chosen to wear underneath her dress. She wore no knickers, he noticed, with a flicker of arousal, only cream-coloured stockings and matching shoes.

'If anyone were to see you looking like that, they could count themselves as very lucky,' Jordan said.

The thought of being spied upon made her tremble nervously. 'May I draw the curtains?' she asked, moving to the window.

'No, you may not.' Jordan was firm.

'But, Jordan – '

'You may not. Now bend over as I told you.'

Knowing it was pointless to try arguing with him, Angelique bent over the gleaming table and rested on

156

her forearms so that her perspiring flesh left its mark. Turning her face to one side, she rested a cheek on the backs of her folded hands.

Despite his stern manner, Jordan's hand was very light that evening. Almost as light as the warm evening air which caressed the puffy folds of her naked sex and whispered around the honeyed entrance to her vagina.

'So wet,' Jordan murmured, his finger tantalising her outer lips, 'so very wet.'

Angelique felt herself melting, her breasts oozing over the cups of her corset to press into the wooden table-top, her juices drowning Jordan's hand as he stroked the whole of her warm sex. Easing her legs further apart, she pressed her face into the crook of her left arm and stifled an anguished groan. Her mind screamed out to him to stop, and yet not to stop, to cease tantalising her and yet to go on. How much could she bear? She would never know. But Jordan would take her as far as he wanted her to go before he would grant her release. Each time it was almost too far – but not quite.

'Arch your back for me, my darling,' Jordan said. 'I want to see all those wicked little places of yours.'

Her face and throat flamed as she obeyed him. God, it was such sweet torture, displaying herself to him in this lewd and provocative way. Unbearable agony made all the more arousing for the fact that he described to her exactly what he saw. She didn't need a mirror to know her own body. Jordan's descriptions told her everything.

He spoke of her flesh, every fold, every quivering and swelling part of her. 'You should see yourself, Angelique,' he said. 'You should see how wide open your vagina is. And look at how much creamy moisture you have made! It is incredible. You should see how it coats your red, swollen flesh. How it glistens on the soft petals of your labia. And your clitoris, Angelique. Oh, your clitoris. It is so, so swollen and cheeky too – the way it peeps out at me between those lovely lips of yours. It wants me to touch it, Angelique. It begs me to touch it. Do you want me to? Do you want me to stroke that naughty little part of you?'

Angelique stifled another groan. He was saying those things again. And she was so hot. God, she was hot. She shifted her weight from one foot to the other, and back again.

'Your buttocks jiggle when you do that,' Jordan said. 'Do it again.'

Feeling hotter still, Angelique complied. She was desperate for him to touch her again. To touch her clitoris. But stubbornness made her refuse to beg.

He walked around to the front of her and raised her head. Staring into her eyes he smiled. 'Stand up, Angelique,' he said softly. 'I want to see your breasts.'

Feeling a little stiff, she straightened up and adopted a stance that was deliberately defiant – chin up, shoulders back, chest out. The cups of her corset no longer concealed her breasts properly and she held her breath as Jordan's deft fingers soon finished the job, tucking the cups under the firm globes and flicking her rosy nipples into life.

'Such lovely breasts,' he murmured, gazing at her. 'Such a lovely body.'

He walked around her slowly and she breathed in deeply, feeling more desperate than ever under his close scrutiny. Pausing in front of her, he reached out and stroked the silky thatch of hair that covered her mound.

'This is lovely – but too thick,' he said. 'I would like you to shave it.'

'No.' Angelique shook her head immediately.

'Not all of it,' Jordan said, ignoring her dissent. 'Deborah could do it for you. She's an expert at such things. I'll ask her, shall I?'

'No,' Angelique repeated. 'I don't want her to touch me again.'

'Yes, you do.' Jordan breathed the words softly against

158

her face. 'Yes, you want her to touch you. You desperately want her to touch you. You want her to chastise you as well, don't you?'

'No!' Angelique mixed desperation with anguish to make her voice sound hoarse.

With an enigmatic smile, Jordan shook his head slowly from side to side.

Angelique felt as though all her will-power was sliding away from her, slithering down her body and out through the soles of her feet. Seeping away into invisible cracks in the carpet-covered floor.

'Well, we'll see,' Jordan said to her. He unzipped his trousers and motioned to her to sit up on the table. 'First of all we'll enjoy a good fuck, and then we'll see, won't we?'

Breathless with desire, she eased herself on to the table and spread her legs wide. It was no good, she only had enough strength left in her to do one thing properly, and disagreeing with Jordan came a very poor second.

Chapter Ten

To Angelique's consternation, Jordan seemed to be taking a particularly uncompromising stance that evening. Pleasurable though everything was, they were definitely doing things his way. No arguments. No half measures. Although it went completely against her assertive and stubborn nature, she found a certain relief in allowing him to be the master in every way. It meant she could enjoy each and every moment for what it was. She didn't have to think. There was no room for guilt to sneak in. And she was not expected to perform but just to accept the delights Jordan chose to heap upon her.

And what bliss they were. Each time she and Jordan fucked, Angelique thought it was the best ever – and this time was no exception. Reclining upon the table top, with her legs spread wide, she accepted every thrust of Jordan's beautiful cock with a passion which did not abate easily. Even when her legs tired and she felt weak from countless orgasms, she still craved more.

Eventually they came – together and explosively – and Jordan leaned over her, tenderly stroking a damp tendril of hair away from her face. 'That was fantastic,' he said. 'You are fantastic, Angelique. I often suspected when you were younger that you would grow up to be a formidable woman.'

Angelique laughed. 'Formidable? That makes me sound like a battleship of a woman.' She paused, for a moment recalling her first impressions of Moira O'Donnell, before adding, 'Certainly not one who feels as though she might dissolve like sugar in hot water every time a certain man just looks at her.'

'Would that certain man be me?' Jordan asked. His voice was tender but he looked slightly troubled.

Seeing the change in his expression, Angelique asked him if anything was the matter. He nodded. 'I worry that you are becoming too dependent – on me and on Thornbury Court.' His concerns about the financial situation of the hotel never left him entirely.

Despite the fact that Jordan was still resting limply inside her, Angelique struggled to sit up. 'I am never dependent on anyone,' she said, her bold statement causing her to reflect briefly on her feelings about her father. Her thoughts were easily transmitted to Jordan simply by the look in her eye. 'I shall never rely on anyone else apart from myself ever again,' she added defiantly.

'Don't be bitter, Angelique,' Jordan warned, easing himself away from the silky comfort of her body, 'and don't lose that air of innocence whatever you do.'

This time when she laughed it was tinged with disbelief. 'Innocent – me?'

Jordan didn't meet her eye as he zipped up his trousers and smoothed out the creases, but he nodded. 'You think you know it all, don't you?' He put out his hand. 'Come.'

Jumping down lightly from the table, she felt the weakness in her legs as her knees buckled. 'Come where?' she asked.

Reaching out to her, Jordan stroked his hands across her breasts and adjusted the cups of her corset again so that they were tucked in, leaving her upper body completely exposed.

'We have a date with Deborah and Christina,' he said. 'Or had you forgotten? I think perhaps after tonight you will have lost a little more of that innocence – but in a positive way.'

Lost in the rapture of their love-making, Angelique had forgotten. But now that Jordan reminded her what was still to come, her stomach churned and she felt a familiar tingle between her legs.

'My dress,' she murmured, glancing around, but Jordan shook his head and took her arm.

'You will go down to the cellar just as you are,' he said.

'What?' Angelique was shocked, she couldn't parade around the hotel half naked.

Typically, Jordan shrugged off her concerns. 'By using the secret passages we are very unlikely to come across anyone else – and if we do, they will not be "vanilla" guests,' he said, meaning guests who were not on the A-list.

His tone and demeanour brooked no argument it seemed. With a slight shrug of consent, Angelique allowed herself to be guided along the maze of hidden corridors and down several winding staircases until they reached the converted cellar. Just as she was becoming accustomed to walking around in her corset, stockings and shoes, a figure appeared at the other end of a long passage.

'Jordan!' she hissed, clutching his arm.

They and the figure drew nearer to each other and it soon became clear by the broad build and swaggering gait that the other person was Fergus. Angelique was horrified. She clutched at Jordan again and tried to use his body to shield her.

'Don't be ridiculous, Angelique,' he said calmly. 'Fergus has seen plenty of women's bodies before.'

'Not mine!' Angelique hissed. 'He hasn't seen my body and I don't want him to. Look at me.' She glanced down at her naked breasts, the nipples hard as bullets in the cool air that permeated the cellar, and further down to the triangle of glossy chestnut curls at the apex of her thighs.

Taking her instruction literally, Jordan looked, his eyes making a slow appraisal that sent rivulets of moisture trickling from her vagina.

Unfortunately, Fergus also paused to admire the unexpected view. He had drawn close enough to hear Angelique's anguished appeal to Jordan and to appreciate the fact that here was a young woman who, for whatever reason, had chosen to expose most of her body. To a connoisseur such as Fergus, it was a heaven-sent opportunity to feast his eyes.

As Fergus drew almost level with them, Angelique felt her blushes start at the tips of her toes and shoot up to the roots of her hair. She couldn't let him see her like this, yet she had nowhere to hide.

Her hands fluttered nervously over the front of her body, trying to shield her breasts and pubis simultaneously, but Jordan grasped the tops of her arms lightly and held them behind her back.

'Naughty, naughty, Angelique,' he said mockingly. 'Let Fergus have a proper look at you.'

'Jordan ... You ... I ...' she stammered in dismay but as usual he was uncompromising, holding her gently but firmly.

Wave after wave of shame swept over her and hot on its heels came another sensation which was almost as unbearable. While Fergus stood right in front of her, his insolent gaze carefully scanning every quivering part of her body, she felt an undeniable surge of desire. Her breasts rose and fell rapidly on her heaving ribcage and to her mortification trickles of her own juices ran down her inner thighs.

Fergus noticed immediately and a wicked smile touched his lips, increasing Angelique's discomfort and the amount of moisture her tingling vagina produced. He and Jordan exchanged knowing glances. Then Jordan nudged her buttocks gently with his thigh causing her trembling legs to falter. As they parted, she was uncomfortably aware that Fergus' gaze shifted and she felt his eyes stroking her sex as surely as if he had put his hand between her legs. Her stomach fluttered and her heart raced.

'Please, Jordan,' she gasped.

Releasing her at long last, Jordan put his arm around her shoulders instead and pulled her against him. Grateful for the warmth and comfort of his body, Angelique listened as Fergus explained that he was on his way to another of the converted rooms in the cellar to assist a couple of guests in making their own 'blue movie' – an anniversary present to themselves. He and Jordan discussed it for a few minutes, cracking a couple of jokes about 'super studs'.

Shoving his hands deep into his pockets, Fergus gave Angelique a cheeky nod goodbye and sauntered away.

For a moment she was speechless. Then she found her tongue. 'How could you, Jordan? I was mortified. Absolutely mortified.'

Jordan stared back at her with an amused glint in his eyes. 'You loved it.'

'I did not.'

'Yes, you did. You loved it. Look at this.' Reaching down he stroked a hand between her legs then held it up to her face. Creamy, viscous fluid coated his fingertips. 'You are soaking, darling,' he said, matter-of-factly. 'Don't tell me you didn't enjoy it.'

Swallowing deeply, Angelique stared back at him. She could still see his fingers out of the corner of her eye and could smell the musky sweetness of her own arousal.

'Shouldn't we be getting a move on?' she said

hoarsely, unwilling to give him the satisfaction of agreeing with him. 'Deborah and Christina will be waiting.'

As it turned out, Deborah had not bothered to wait for an audience before she got on with the business of chastising Christina. It had taken her some time to get the young woman properly bound and chained to a free-standing metal frame. But by the time Jordan and Angelique arrived she had already managed to mark Christina's her buttocks with a light network of thin red lines. When the heavy oak door creaked open she glanced around without breaking her rhythm. Christina was already facing in that direction so both women set eyes on Angelique as soon as she stepped nervously over the threshold.

The first thought that ran through Angelique's mind was what on earth had Deborah done – was still doing – to Christina? It was horrible to see her friend being so cruelly abused. And yet in the next instant, when the young woman groaned loudly with delight, Angelique felt suffused with erotic longing. It was a yearning to treat Christina in the same way and also a craving to be chained up next to her and receive the same treatment.

As though he could read her thoughts, Jordan's voice was soft in her ear. 'What do you think, my lovely Angelique?' he said. 'Do you wish to dominate or be dominated? Is Deborah the mistress or are you?'

It was one of the few times in her life that Angelique felt torn by indecision. And yet, if she stopped to think about it, what a ridiculous decision it was to make. It almost made her laugh aloud and so she stopped herself from thinking about it.

Instead she whispered, 'I don't know.'

While Angelique grappled with her desires, Deborah took the initiative. 'Come over here, Angelique,' she ordered in an imperious voice.

Angelique's head snapped up as Deborah spoke. Her

heart began to thump. Would she obey? Could she? Slowly she turned and placed one foot in front of the other.

'Head up, shoulders back!' the red-head snapped, and Angelique responded immediately.

When she was within a foot or so of Deborah she stopped in her tracks. Suddenly she realised what she was doing and felt overcome by the humiliation of her situation. Deborah was simply another woman, she reasoned, an employee of the hotel, one of her members of staff. She had no right to issue orders.

'Do you call that good posture?' The confident tone cut through Angelique's thoughts. A sudden pain shot through her breasts and she glanced down to see that Deborah was pinching her nipples.

'How dare you. . .' Angelique began in outrage, but Deborah silenced her with a glare.

'Do not speak,' she said. Her fingers and thumbs tightened on her nipples, forcing Angelique to whimper.

Angelique's cheeks flamed as she stared back at Deborah as defiantly as she could. Further down, her body was also betraying her. Shame showed in her face, the rosy flush spreading down her throat and across her chest. And lower still her aching nipples sent tiny messages of desire darting down to her sex which throbbed and moistened in response. Please don't, she groaned inwardly, please don't let me enjoy this.

To her relief, Deborah let go of her nipples and took a step back. 'Show me your clitoris,' she ordered.

Angelique was stunned. What? Her mind was screaming. *What?*

'Do as she says,' Jordan said.

With a slight start of surprise Angelique remembered that he was standing just behind her. She shook her head slowly and defiantly. 'I'm not – ' she began.

Jordan spoke up again. 'Do it, Angelique. Do it to please me.'

'No!' Angelique pleaded with him. Turning her head she saw his expression was as implacable as the look Deborah bore.

There was something terribly futile about her unwillingness to cooperate, she realised. For one thing she wanted to gratify Jordan. For another she wanted, surprisingly, to please Deborah and also to thrill Christina who was still watching avidly. And most of all she was aching to find out just how far she, Angelique Hemsley, was willing to go in all this. Did she truly have the guts to take her pleasure when, where and with whoever she desired?

With trembling hands she reached down, her fingertips parting the silky thatch of curls as she felt for her outer labia. Slowly, ever so slowly, she parted the puffy lips, spreading them wide apart so that the swollen nub of flesh concealed beneath was now exposed to Deborah's view. Holding herself open like that seemed to Angelique to be the most degrading thing she had ever done. And yet, as she stared at the ceiling and bit her bottom lip to quell her trembling, she couldn't deny the tell-tale signs of her own arousal.

To Angelique's utter shame the red-head sank to her haunches in front of her and scrutinised her exposed clitoris. A sound of approval broke from the other woman's lips. A low, guttural sound that sent ribbons of desire spiralling upwards and outwards from Angelique's pulsating flesh.

Out of the corner of her eye, Angelique noticed Jordan walking across the small, stone-flagged room. He stopped behind Christina's bound and naked form and began to stroke a hand across her buttocks. Harsh, aching envy immediately consumed Angelique. The envy that Christina should be receiving Jordan's caresses was tinged with another envy – why should he be the one who touched Christina that way when she desired the other young woman so much herself? Oh, God, I must be going mad, she thought. To be standing in the middle of a converted cellar exposing my most private parts to one woman while I go through agonies watching my male and female lovers together. I must be insane!

More wetness trickled down the inside of her thighs and this time she welcomed the additional rush of heat to her cheeks as Deborah's eyes widened. Obviously she had seen it. And that meant only one thing – that she knew Angelique was enjoying every bit of her humiliation.

They had been in the cellar for well over an hour. Angelique knew that because she had heard a distant grandfather clock strike the hour twice. Deborah had finally left her alone and given her permission to sit on a hard, straight-backed chair while she finished chastising Christina. And Angelique had been forced to watch as the young blonde girl squirmed and moaned her way through an unbelievable range of punishments. The paddle, the tawse, the cane and the crop were each used upon her soft, willing flesh until she was begging for release.

'You will give Christina the gratification she craves,' Jordan said to Angelique. 'You will go over there now and caress her to orgasm, is that understood?'

Dumbly, Angelique nodded. She wanted to touch Christina. From her vantage point she had seen how wet and swollen the other woman's sex flesh had become during the treatment Deborah had meted out. Now she longed to be the one to grant Christina her release.

On shaking legs she crossed the shadowy room, the disturbance to the air causing the countless fat, ivory-coloured candles to flicker in their wrought-iron holders. As she came closer to Christina, she noticed that the young woman was dressed in bondage clothes: strips of black leather bisecting areas of her pale gold flesh. Thick leather cuffs enclosed her wrists and ankles and thin silver chains attached to them held her spread-eagled to the rudimentary pine frame.

'Hello, Christina,' she whispered softly as she drew close. Her breath disturbed the fine white blonde hairs that feathered around the young woman's neck and ears, and Christina shivered.

Angelique didn't need Christina's reply. Nor did she need the young woman to tell her what she wanted, or what she liked best. Stroking her right hand over Christina's belly and down between her legs, Angelique's fingers sought the hard bud of her clitoris. Within seconds the young woman was shaking and whimpering uncontrollably as wave after wave of orgasm swept through her. Two fingers of Angelique's left hand buried deep in the velvety tunnel of Christina's vagina felt the rhythmic spasms of her crisis and Angelique found herself sighing with elation at having created such an effect.

A slight draught touching her buttocks told Angelique that someone had moved behind her. She was not surprised when a hand snaked between her own legs. Shuffling back a couple of paces, she managed to spread her legs wider and arch her back so that the questing fingers could do more. Out of the corner of her eye she saw Deborah moving about which meant that the fingers which now stroked and probed her remorselessly belonged to Jordan. With a groan of delight, tinged with relief, she arched her back further and ground her burning sex against his hands.

Deborah came to stand next to her just as she started the rise to orgasm. Jordan's fingers were deep inside her, tantalising her most sensitive flesh, while his other hand kneaded her buttocks rhythmically. Dark thoughts invaded Angelique's mind as she forced herself not to look at Deborah, but to concentrate on pleasuring Christina while receiving her own gratification.

'Leave Christina now, Angelique,' the red-head said softly, moving her hands as she spoke.

'No, I want to – ' Angelique gasped even though she knew it was useless to argue.

Already the force of her orgasm was upon her, driving her into a shadowy tunnel where bright lights suddenly exploded and she was rocked by shockwaves of extreme pleasure. She felt Deborah's hands cup her breasts and her mouth enclose one of her nipples. The soft, wet lips sucked. The pearly teeth nibbled. And all the time Angelique was powerless to resist.

When she awoke, late the following morning, the first thing Angelique did was replay the whole experience over in her mind. Instinctively, she slid a hand between her legs and stroked her tender sex flesh as the memory of pure bliss encapsulated her mind.

Jordan had backed her against the unforgiving stone wall and had slid his hard cock inside her, while Deborah and Christina looked on – the other two women pleasuring each other while she and Jordan fucked like demons. It had been an incredibly erotic episode and she felt liberated by it. But not totally. Deep down inside she was grateful that Jordan had not actually had sex with either Deborah or Christina. Somehow, she still didn't think she could handle that scenario just yet, although she was sure the time would come eventually.

An hour later, Angelique bumped into Jordan downstairs in the hotel's reception area, just in time to witness him giving instructions to two men carrying dusty old cardboard boxes that seemed to be falling apart. Pieces of paper fluttered down from the open boxes and as Angelique stooped to pick them up she realised that these were the records from 'The Cedars' nursing home.

Excitement leaped within her as she glanced up and Jordan nodded in reply to her silent question.

'I have told the men to put the boxes in your office,' he said. 'I hope you don't mind. There are quite a few of them.'

'Mind?' Angelique laughed as she stood up and brushed the dust from her hands. 'I can't wait to start delving into them. Thanks.' She stood back as two more men entered, their arms also laden with boxes. 'I had a great time last night,' she whispered, almost as an aside.

Glancing down at her, Jordan smiled a twinkling, blue-eyed smile. 'I'm glad. So did I,' he said. 'Let's hope it was just the first of many more similarly pleasurable evenings.'

Silently, Angelique nodded. Like Jordan she looked forward to expanding their sexual horizons together but still felt slightly apprehensive about how far he would expect her to go.

The contents of the boxes from 'The Cedars' turned out to be almost as disappointing as the ones which had contained her father's papers. However, as Angelique worked her way methodically through them, several interesting items eventually came to light.

Firstly, she came across her mother's file. Most of the papers inside the yellowing folder related to the changes in the woman's actual physical condition during her pregnancy and two-week stay at the nursing home. By reading through the medical notes, which included pre-natal care, Angelique was able to form a picture of the person who had given her life.

Jeanette Baker, her mother, had been five-feet-seven-inches tall and weighed only one-hundred-and-twenty pounds at the start of the pregnancy, which meant she had been very slim. Her blood pressure had been normal and she had suffered all the usual childhood ailments and had been vaccinated for rubella. Then there was the additional information that she didn't smoke but liked to drink a couple of glasses of good wine every day.

171

Angelique grinned to herself at the implied inflection when it came to the word 'good'. Perhaps she had inherited her gourmet inclinations from her biological mother.

To Angelique's surprise, there were also quite a few details relating to herself in the file including the length of labour: eighteen hours, time of delivery: 1.15 a.m. – and most surprising of all, a couple of photographs of herself as a foetus, taken during routine scans. In the doctor's notes there were several mentions of the 'father' being present and of 'extras', such as a personal midwife, being paid for by him. The mere mention of that particular mystery man set her heart thumping and quite a few times she was forced to stop reading so that she could catch her breath properly.

Eventually, having perused it for quite some time, Angelique gave the file a fond pat and put it to one side. Rummaging through the box that had contained the file, she quickly came to the conclusion that the rest of its contents were similar records belonging to other patients. Putting the box aside, she turned her attention to the others and was just beginning to become really disgruntled and sick of being covered with dust and grime, when she came across a couple of boxes which seemed to contain copies of the medical care bills.

It seemed to take ages, and she missed lunch entirely, but eventually Angelique found the first of several bills relating to her mother's care. Each of them had PAID stamped across them, and the date in big red letters that had faded to pink. More importantly, each of them bore the signature of the man who had settled the accounts – Anthony D Fordyce.

Once again her heart began to race, obviously her father had paid the bills. If Anthony D Fordyce wasn't her actual father, then he would have been closely connected with him – possibly an accountant or personal assistant. Angelique sat back on her heels and stared at the small pile of papers which she still clutched in her right hand. Whoever he was didn't matter, she had another name to go on and that was enough for her for now.

By the time Jordan came to her office to see how she was getting on and to find out why she had failed to keep their lunch date, Angelique was hovering on cloud nine.

A cursory search of the other boxes had revealed nothing of apparent interest. But in the last box – which she thought was absolutely typical of her luck – she found an old brown envelope containing a single key. There was no indication what the key was for, or to whom it belonged other than some hastily scribbled initials on the reverse side of the envelope. They were a bit faded but looked as though they read ADF. It was a long shot, but could the key and the initials belong to her father? Without knowing what the key related to it was unlikely that she would ever know the answer for sure.

Almost beside herself with excitement, Angelique showed Jordan everything in the order that she had found it, including the key which, of course, she saved until last.

Jordan made no comment as he glanced through the medical file and flicked through the bills, but when he saw the key he threw Angelique a shrewd look.

'You know what that is for, don't you?' he said.

'No.' Angelique shook her head. 'I haven't a clue, but I think it might have belonged to my father.' She showed him the initialled envelope which she had thrown in the wastepaper bin.

Holding the key up to the light, he studied it carefully. 'If I'm not mistaken, this is a key to a safety deposit box,' he stated matter-of-factly, unaware that Angelique's stomach was clenching and unclenching with barely contained excitement.

'Where, what box?' she asked quickly and was disappointed to see Jordan's casual shrug.

'Who knows?' he said. 'Are you sure there was nothing else in the envelope – not a convenient slip of paper giving the name and branch of a bank and the box number?'

Feeling thoroughly dejected, she shook her head dumbly.

'Then you have a fair amount of detective work ahead of you,' Jordan said. 'But the situation is not completely hopeless. It just means that you will have to trawl around all the banks to see if they recognise this particular style of key.'

Angelique thought about this and then her face brightened. 'The chances are it will be a fairly local bank,' she stated, thinking aloud.

Irrational though it was, she felt annoyed at the way Jordan immediately shot her theory to pieces. 'Not necessarily. Even if it did belong to your father, the likelihood is he worked and banked in London. You might have to cast your net a bit further afield in the banking world than the "big four" in the high street.'

What he said made perfect sense, of course, and that infuriated her even more. Before Jordan had put his head around the door to her office she'd thought the mystery of her true parentage was as good as solved.

Apparently anxious to console her, Jordan walked across the room and took Angelique in his arms. Resisting for only a moment, she gave herself up to the incomparable bliss of his kisses and caresses and once again felt thankful that he had very special ways of making her forget her frustrations for a little while.

By the time she walked into the Piano Bar that evening, Angelique felt suffused with renewed hope. Whichever way she looked at it she had much more to go on now: another name – possibly that of her natural father, or at least a close associate of his – and the key, no doubt the very same key to which Harvey had alluded so cryptically in his last letter to her.

Humming softly to herself, she chose a seat at the bar and when she glanced to her right was surprised to see the unmistakable figure of Martin Wreathe, poised to take the seat next to her.

'Oh, fancy seeing you here,' she said somewhat unoriginally.

Thankfully, Martin didn't appear to notice. 'It's no accident,' his gravelly voice rasped. 'I remembered something about that woman you were looking for and so I thought I'd better let you know, sharpish.'

'What? About my mother – Jeanette Baker? Is that the woman you mean?' Angelique knew she was gabbling but could hardly contain her immediate excitement. At that moment the barman handed her a glass of vodka with tonic and she drank half of it down before she realised what she was doing.

To her relief, Martin nodded in answer to her questions. 'Yes, Baker, that's the one. I don't know why I didn't remember her at the time because you look a lot like she did, the same hair and everything. And that mouth is the same. I'll remember that mouth until my dying day.'

Angelique blushed. Men often made comments about the fullness of her lips and how attractive it was the way they formed a natural pout. Feeling extraordinarily grateful to the woman she had never met for bequeathing her such remarkable features, she ordered drinks for both of them and prompted Martin to continue.

She was thankful that he was not a man to beat around the bush when it came to relating the facts. Launching straight into his recollections, he told her how, twenty years ago, a Miss Baker had come into his shop to enquire if he undertook house clearances. She explained that she lived locally but was due to emigrate to Australia.

'The house was only a small terrace,' he said, running his fingers through his wispy hair, 'but there were some nice pieces of antique furniture. She told me a friend of the family had given her the items to help her furnish the house. A very kind man, she said. I thought maybe he was a boyfriend or something, a sugar-daddy type.'

Angelique was both excited and intrigued. 'What makes you say that?'

Martin shrugged. 'I don't know really. It was just the way she spoke about him I suppose. Like he was someone she looked up to but who showed her all these little kindnesses.'

'You must have talked quite a lot,' Angelique said.

Surprisingly, Martin's face became flushed and he gulped his beer hastily. 'Well, when I – that is to say, we – undertook the house clearance, I went along to sort of, you know, oversee things and we got talking a bit.' He glanced down at his hands and Angelique noticed how the network of thread veins covering his cheeks turned a deeper red. 'She was a very pretty young woman. Looked just like you do now and about your age too I should think. And I haven't always been this old and ugly.' He paused to laugh ruefully and winked at Angelique when she opened her mouth to refute his words. 'It's okay, I'm no bowl of fruit, I know. In my younger days I was quite a handsome young buck. Anyway, I don't know if things have changed all that much but in those days, given the opportunity, a single young man and a single young woman would quite often get talking.'

Angelique laughed at this. 'Stop teasing. You know full well nothing has changed,' she admonished. 'Did she happen to mention the name of this sugar-daddy, or which part of Australia she was headed for?'

'Yes to the first and no to the second,' Martin said, as

Angelique's heart leaped with excitement and then plummeted again. He scratched his head for a moment. 'It was an unusual name, something to do with that actor – now what was his name?' Patience didn't come naturally to Angelique, but she tried her hardest not to prompt Martin. Another round of drinks later her fortitude was rewarded. 'James Stewart!'

Angelique was stunned. 'James Stewart was my mother's boyfriend?'

Martin stared at her uncomprehendingly for a moment then laughed a great, rumbling laugh. 'Oh, bloody hell! No, not James Stewart. That rabbit of his, the invisible one, he was the one?'

'My mother was having a relationship with an invisible rabbit?' Angelique thought she had every right to feel confused at that moment.

'No. The rabbit's name was Harvey. That was his name. Harvey.'

'Harvey!' The name shot from Angelique's mouth so vehemently that Martin flinched. 'Sorry, Martin.' She gave him a wobbly smile as she tried to compose herself.

Feeling as though she owed him some kind of explanation, she told him about Harvey Hemsley being her adoptive father and about the mystery surrounding her biological parents, which she felt no closer to solving now than she had weeks ago when she first found out. Right at that moment she felt an overwhelming urge to tell Jordan what Martin had just revealed. And when Lesley came into the bar Angelique asked her if she knew where Jordan was that evening.

'No, sorry, Angelique. Nobody tells me anything,' Lesley said, her bright scarlet lips making a slight pout. Suddenly she noticed Martin looking at her and simpered as coyly as any woman. 'Aren't you going to introduce me?'

Stifling a grin, Angelique went through the formality of a proper introduction. For a few moments the three of them chatted about the weather and how lovely the grounds of Thornbury Court were looking. And Martin mentioned that he had just taken delivery of a small group of some nineteenth-century garden statuary which might look nice dotted around the place.

'I'll mention it to Jordan tomorrow,' Angelique promised. 'I know money is tight at the moment but perhaps I can persuade him to come down to your shop tomorrow and have a look.' She was anxious to be able to repay the antiques dealer in some way for all his help.

A moment later Lesley was called away to cover for the evening receptionist while she took a short break. Martin watched the retreating figure – tall and straight-backed in her habitual plain black dress. Then he turned to Angelique and winked broadly.

'Damn fine-looking woman, that Lesley,' he said. 'I think I might make this one of my regular haunts from now on.'

Chapter Eleven

'**S**o the plot thickens,' Jordan said to Angelique the
next day when she told him about her conversation
with Martin Wreathe. They were sitting side-by-side in
a pagoda-style gazebo in Thornbury Court's own Japan-
ese water-garden. The pagoda was reached by crossing
an ornate wooden bridge, painted red and decorated
with gilded dragons. And surrounding the small, equally
ornate pagoda were several lily ponds containing shoals
of enormous koi carp.

As she watched the slippery golden fish darting about
in the sparkling water, Angelique gave a deep sigh. 'I
honestly don't know what to think now,' she said,
turning her head to give Jordan the benefit of her soft
hazel-eyed gaze. 'Do you think it's possible that Harvey
was having an affair with my real mother?'

Jordan stared levelly at her. 'Honestly?'

Angelique nodded. 'Honestly.'

Stretching his long legs out in front of him, Jordan
glanced down and idly flicked away a speck of lint from
the cream-coloured silk trousers he wore. Angelique
suspected he was stalling, trying to work out what to
say to her that would cause the least hurt.

'Just give it to me straight, Jordan,' she said, hoping she sounded braver than she felt.

'There is no doubt that your father – Harvey, that is – loved women,' he replied carefully. 'He used to say, and I feel inclined to agree with him, that all women are beautiful but only a few wear their beauty on the outside. Nevertheless, at that time he was deeply involved with another woman. I think it is possible but highly unlikely, that he was actually having some kind of "relationship" . . .' He paused and, crooking two fingers, made inverted comma signs in the air before continuing. '. . . with your natural mother at the same time. Or any other woman for that matter. Harvey may have been highly sexed but he was monogamous by nature.'

For some odd reason Angelique felt herself give an inner sigh of relief at this disclosure. She had begun to think that her beloved father had been nothing more than a libidinous satyr of a man, ready and willing to fuck anything that moved. She laughed, and with the laughter came another overwhelming sense of relief.

'I think I just let a lot of tension go,' she admitted to Jordan, glancing up at him. Her heart quickened as she noticed a familiar expression on his face.

'Care to off-load a little more?' he asked, his narrow-eyed look full of meaning.

Angelique glanced around. 'What – do you mean here?'

'Of course, here.' Jordan began to stroke a finger slowly up and down her arm.

Immediately, Angelique felt her body respond to him and she breathed in deeply. 'You know I want you all the time,' she said.

'I know.' His words did not sound arrogant. They were spoken softly and Jordan followed them up with a deep, searching kiss that set Angelique's heart racing.

Gently, he put his arms around her and pulled her on

to his lap. As he kissed her, Jordan let his hands roam carelessly, stroking her upper arms, her shoulders, her breasts through the thin white cotton of the sun-dress she wore.

Tingles of pleasure coursed through Angelique's body as she squirmed on Jordan's lap and delighted in the pure bliss of his caresses. He didn't know it yet, but underneath her dress she was completely naked. She hugged the knowledge to herself, knowing how captivated he would be when he discovered her little secret.

It didn't take him long to find out. Questing fingers creeping under her dress soon met with bare flesh.

'Angelique, you are a little minx,' Jordan growled in her ear as he slowly unfastened the buttons down the front of her dress, from neckline to hem. Peeling back the two sides of her dress, he exposed her naked body to his gaze.

A cooling breath of fresh air wafted over her and she felt her nipples harden in response. With tender hands he cupped her breasts and rolled the hard pink buds of her nipples between his fingers. His touch was so exquisite Angelique could hardly bear it. Beside her she could hear the occasional splash of water but, when she looked, the sun glinted sharply off the surface of the pond forcing her to close her eyes to block out the glare.

'Keep your eyes shut,' Jordan murmured. 'Concentrate on using your other senses instead.' Raising her arms above her head, he allowed his fingertips to skim the sensitive flesh of her underarms. 'How does that feel?'

'Wonderful,' Angelique breathed. 'Ticklish but wonderful. I can feel it all the way down to my toes.' She smiled as Jordan's tongue followed the trail his fingers created.

Again her patience was severely put to the test. Sitting there, almost in the open air – her body exposed to the elements and anyone who might happen along – she felt vulnerable and yet curiously wanton. A large part of her couldn't care less if the entire population of Buckinghamshire stopped to gawp. She was there with the man she wanted most in the whole world. It was a marvellous day and she felt gloriously abandoned. Why worry – why not just go with her desires? The words in Harvey's letter which had instructed her to do just that floated into her mind and she latched on to them as permission to enjoy herself fully.

The day – her whole future – felt heavy with promise and a delicious feeling of abandon overtook her. Lost in a sense of hedonism she stretched her half-naked body, wanting to feel the muscles extend and pull and the fresh warm air caress her exposed flesh. As she arched her back, her fingertips and toes grasping for thin air, the silky ends of her hair swept the wooden seat and she felt a thrill of arousal as she realised what a tempting offering she displayed to Jordan. The smooth sweep of her throat and torso, the enticing globes of her full breasts and the glossy thatch of hair at the apex of her thighs were all intended for his delectation. And it came as no particular surprise to her when, a moment later, Jordan whispered how beautiful she was and how much he wanted her. On the outside she blushed prettily at his compliment, while inside an intense heat flared up, melting her completely.

'Take me, Jordan,' she urged hoarsely. 'I want to feel you inside me right now. I can't wait.'

He made a tut-tut sound, but there was laughter in his voice when he spoke. 'Angelique, you are such an impatient young woman,' he said lightly. 'I thought I had you trained a little better than this.'

'Trained!' Angelique narrowed her eyes and practically spat out the word but her outrage was followed by a soft chuckle and then a serious tone of voice. 'I don't want you to train me, Jordan. I just want you to fuck me.'

Even a determined man like Jordan knew when he

was beaten. As he unzipped his trousers and slid his hardness inside her he murmured soft words into her hair – phrases that would have sounded loving but for their content. 'I would love nothing better than to keep you as my sex slave, Angelique. To be able to mould you to my erotic ideal and to have you obey my every whim would be ecstasy,' he said. Sighing softly he thrust a little harder. 'Ah, what a fantasy. But that is all it can be. I think you are too strong a woman to cede totally to me, or to anyone else for that matter. Perhaps it is time you explored other exciting facets of your sexuality.'

Deliberately blocking her ears to his words, Angelique concentrated solely on her own efforts as she rose and fell rhythmically, her body impaled on his erection. She loved to enclose him and grip him tightly with her vagina, her thighs which gripped his and her arms which she wound around his neck. Mindlessly clutching at handfuls of his hair and whimpering incoherently, she rode him, feeling supremely powerful and yet helplessly weak at the same time.

Jordan trapped Angelique's gaze with his own. Her eyes were hazy and yet alert to what he was about to say. 'I want to see how dominant you can be, my darling,' he crooned, stroking her breasts and torso until she groaned with desperation and pressed herself closely to him. 'Within the next day or so I will arrange things so that you can flex your muscles in that respect.'

His words surprised her but before she even thought of replying, he grasped her around the waist – arresting her own movements – and thrust deeply inside her. Giving up control to him, she found herself quickly transported to another blissful plane where nothing else mattered besides the strength of her desire and the pursuit of total gratification.

Sensation heaped upon sensation as his cock slid inside her honeyed channel up to the hilt, and then withdrew slightly before plunging in even deeper than before. Angelique gasped, her thigh and stomach muscles quivering as she struggled to keep pace with him.

Around them the scented air from the profusion of plants and shrubs that surrounded the water-garden became overlaid with the distinct aroma of sex. Lavender vied with musk for supremacy in an intimate, oriental corner of a very English estate, while its owners strove to teach mother nature a thing or two.

Unlike Angelique, Deborah didn't bother hiding her surprise when Jordan spoke to her later that day and told her that he wanted Angelique to test her skills as a dominatrix.

'I would suggest Christina as her "victim",' Jordan said, 'but I don't think it would do Angelique any good to try and dominate someone for whom she feels compassion. I want her to feel completely unconstrained by personal feelings.'

With a slight laugh, Deborah leaned across her desk and patted Jordan's hand. 'After the other night I don't think Christina's backside could take much more. She's still got a few marks to show for that session.'

Both of them fell silent for a moment, remembering. Then Jordan broke the silence. 'Are we expecting any guests who might be suitable?'

'Mr Rackham is making his quarterly visit the day after tomorrow,' Deborah said. 'He has asked for the school-room – says he fancies being a naughty boy again. Do you think Angelique would make good headmistress material?'

Jordan pondered her question. 'You make an excellent headmistress – the grand-mistress of headmistresses, in fact,' he joked. 'I find it difficult to imagine anyone else taking your place!'

For a moment, Deborah's smile faltered. 'Perhaps you

should start imagining it, Jordan,' she said. 'I can't promise to be around for ever.'

She didn't continue but he sensed there was a lot more she wanted to say. To be honest, it scared him to ask. The thought of Thornbury Court without Deborah was too dreadful to contemplate. While he was conscious that it put unfair pressure on her, he still voiced his thoughts.

'I'm not planning to leave, Jordan,' she said, much to his relief. 'But you know as well as I do that things can change at the drop of a hat.' She paused and wistfully remembered the Dutch girl. 'I can't help feeling there is a lot of life out there in the big bad world that I'm missing out on by being holed up here.'

'Thornbury Court isn't a prison, Deborah,' Jordan snapped. 'You are free to come and go as you please. And you usually do.' The barb was unnecessary and the red-head looked understandably hurt by it.

'Don't start using your master tactics on me, Jordan,' she warned icily. 'They won't work.' Glancing up she noticed his contrite expression and her face immediately softened into a smile again. 'Let's not fight,' she said. 'I know you've got problems. Have you spoken to the bank recently?'

Jordan shook his head. 'No. At the moment I'm letting sleeping lions lie.'

Deborah's lips twitched. 'Don't you mean dogs?'

'No,' Jordan said emphatically, standing up and walking over to the window to gaze out over the neatly trimmed lawns. 'I mean lions. Those bastards would rip me to shreds in seconds if I let them.'

Reclining in her chair, Deborah regarded him thoughtfully. She wasn't sure if it was her imagination playing tricks on her but in the clear light of day she thought he was starting to look closer to his real age. With a pang she realised that if their financial problems couldn't be resolved the youthful, ever-optimistic, dynamic Jordan

185

could eventually become embittered and a mere shadow of his former self.

'Did you mention the hotel's difficulties to Angelique?' she asked.

To her disappointment Jordan shook his head. 'Not yet, but I will,' he said apologetically. 'Up until now the timing hasn't been right, but I plan to speak to her about it by the end of this week at the latest.' He turned away from the window, shoved his hands deep in his pockets and flashed Deborah a broad grin that looked completely genuine.

'Now remind me about Mr Rackham,' he said, reclining against the window-sill. 'From what you've said so far I think he could be ideal for Angelique's debut.'

Frustration was gnawing at Angelique's good temper. As Jordan had predicted, each of the big four high-street banks provided no help whatsoever in her search for the safety deposit box that matched the key she had found.

Each time she had stepped through the portals of one of the banks and crossed the ubiquitous industrial carpeting to the desk that bore the sign 'Customer Care', she came away with the overwhelming urge to change the words to 'Customer Couldn't Care Less'. Although strictly speaking she wasn't actually a customer of theirs, it was still no reason for the haughty clerks, to treat her enquiries with such blatant disinterest.

If she didn't have a host of better things to do she would have felt tempted to complain to the managers. As it was, on each occasion, she turned on her heel as imperiously as she could and marched out of the bank, head held high. It was only when she reached the pavement outside that she ground her teeth in frustration and fought against the overwhelming urge to dissolve into floods of tears. Fuck them, the bastards – fuck them all! she thought.

Feeling unaccountably homesick all of a sudden, she

returned to the car park where Jordan's BMW awaited her. By the time she reached it she had managed to cheer herself up with the prospect of returning to the peaceful haven of Thornbury Court, opening a bottle of really good Bordeaux and unburdening herself to Jordan. Stopping by the side of the dark blue car, she opened her handbag, felt around in it and only came across a few old till receipts. Now where were the damn car keys?

'Excuse me, lovely lady.' The heavily accented voice accompanied a darkly-tanned hand which swooped over her shoulder and dangled a familiar keyring in front of her face. 'I believe these belong to you.'

Whirling around, Angelique found herself nose-to-nose with one of the best-looking men she had seen in a long time. Overtly Latin in appearance and classically handsome, the unexpected sight and sound of him made her feel homesick all over again. François hadn't been the only Frenchman with whom she had fallen heavily in lust during her time in Paris – their silky smooth accents, their classic shrugs and pouts, all endeared them to her in a unique way.

'I'm sorry, what . . .?' she began, noticing the way a thick hank of jet black hair hung over his face. It took every ounce of will-power to stop herself from brushing it back over his high, slightly leathery brow.

'I said, I believe these are yours. You dropped them in the bank,' he repeated, jangling the keys again before pressing them into her hand. Almost to her disappointment he swept his hair back from his face and smiled endearingly.

She gulped. 'That was very kind of you,' she said faintly. 'I wouldn't have known where to start looking for them.'

Thrusting his hands deep into the pockets of his tan suede trousers, the stranger continued to smile. 'I expect you want to repay me?' he said, his dark eyes glinting in the strong sunlight like chips of black marble. 'Come and have a drink.'

'I should be inviting you,' Angelique murmured.

The stranger's smile grew broader. 'Thank you. I accept.'

For a moment she wavered, feeling sorely tempted. It had not been a good day and a pleasant drink with a handsome man who knew nothing about her, or the difficult time she was currently going through, could be a welcome relief.

Finally, making herself sound regretful, she shook her head. 'No, I'm sorry I can't,' she said, and deliberately glanced at her watch to make it look as though she had an appointment to keep. 'In fact, I'm late already.'

It was flattering that he didn't give up easily. 'Tonight then?' he suggested. 'Or tomorrow – next week?' His voice petered out as she stared resolutely back at him.

She shook her head and uttered a single word answer. 'No.'

His look of amazement made her want to laugh aloud. 'No?' he said incredulously. 'No?'

For a moment she hesitated, wondering if she should try to placate him in some way. But why should she? She didn't owe him any explanations. All at once she felt a renewed optimism. Angelique Hemsley was her own person. There was no longer any reason for her to feel as though she should be satisfying other people's wants all the time. Pleasing herself was what counted and having the courage of her convictions.

Shrugging off the persuasive hand on her arm, she smiled sweetly but with a determined glint in her eye. 'That's right,' she said firmly. 'My answer is "no".'

Returning to the hotel, Angelique soon discovered that the best laid plans have a habit of not working out when they depend on the cooperation of other people.

'I'm sorry, Angelique,' Deborah said, when Angelique

asked if Jordan was around. 'He had to go out this evening. He has a meeting with the conference manager of a big company which could mean a lot of business for us.'

Angelique smiled. 'It's okay, I won't go to pieces without him,' she said, trying not to sound as irritated as she felt.

Deborah laughed and offered Angelique a drink, which she accepted gratefully before dropping casually into a leather visitor's chair. While Deborah poured the drinks, Angelique explained about her frustrating afternoon.

'Oh, God. Tell me about it,' the red-head said, handing her a cut-glass tumbler of neat Scotch. 'I hate banks. Especially at the moment.'

Angelique frowned. 'The hotel is in trouble, isn't it?'

'Yup.' Deborah nodded and tried to sound optimistic. 'Don't worry, something will turn up. It always does.'

'I could probably invest a bit more,' Angelique said, sipping her drink. 'Harvey left me a small fortune really. Although most of it is tied up, I could get an accountant to go through it all and tell me how I can release some capital.'

'I don't know if Jordan would like that,' Deborah began, but Angelique silenced her with an unladylike snort.

'Bugger Jordan! I can do what the hell I like with my own money.' Just the thought of not being allowed to contribute made her mind up for her. 'No, I've decided,' she said, reclining in her chair and crossing her legs. 'I'm going to hire an accountant tomorrow and present Jordan with a *fait accompli*.'

A low whistle issued from between Deborah's lips. She had to admit, Angelique had balls. 'Okay, you know what you're doing,' she said. Then she added almost too casually, 'Has Jordan mentioned the other thing to you by any chance?'

'Other thing?' Angelique threw Deborah a surprised glance across the desk.

Deborah seemed to hesitate before replying. 'Jordan has told me you have a desire to dominate someone,' she said.

'*Jordan* has a desire for me to dominate someone,' Angelique cut in. 'I don't really know how I feel one way or the other.'

For a fleeting moment Deborah remembered how submissive Angelique had been the other night in the dungeon. 'He is usually a good judge of character,' she said, trying to convince herself as much as anyone.

Angelique shrugged. 'So, what of it?'

There was an ominous pause before Deborah answered. 'Tomorrow a Mr Rackham will be checking-in to the hotel. He is a regular A-list client who harbours a whole catalogue of fantasies, all of them involving his submission to a female dominant.' She glanced at Angelique.

'Go on.' Trying to appear nonchalant, Angelique recrossed her legs and sipped her drink.

'Okay,' Deborah continued. 'The plan is this. Mr Rackham wants to be a naughty schoolboy. Jordan thinks you are cut out to be the stern headmistress. I think you could probably cope with it, but what do you think?'

Angelique swallowed deeply as hysteria welled up inside her. She, a stern headmistress to a complete stranger in short trousers? It hardly bore thinking about!

'If you and Jordan both think I could do it, I'd like to give it a go,' she said calmly, surprising herself. 'Just tell me what I have to do.'

Finding an accountant was easy. Mr Kemp, the solicitor, had given her a few names and Jordan confirmed two of them as very good choices. In the end only one of the two could give her an appointment straight away.

Sandy-haired Gordon Shipley was everything she

expected from an accountant. Thirty-something, bespectacled and wearing a grey pin-striped suit, he perched on the edge of the chair she offered him and only looked relaxed when he was number crunching on his portable computer.

'Some of these investments are a bit dodgy,' he said, his eyes scanning the documents which Mr Kemp had given her. 'I'd get out of this one pretty damn fast if I were you. And this one. And this.' He jabbed at names on the list with a broad-tipped finger. The nail was clean but well-bitten, she noticed. Mr Shipley obviously lived on his nerves.

'What I need to know is, can I release some of the money fairly quickly?' she asked. 'I want to invest it in this place.' She glanced fondly around her office, the room already as familiar to her as the small, book-lined study in her mother's apartment in Paris.

To her relief he nodded and gave a fleeting smile which she supposed was the best she could hope for. 'If you decide to engage my firm, I'll handle your affairs personally,' he said. 'It goes without saying I'll do my very best for you.'

At his use of the word 'affairs', Angelique smiled inwardly. If only he knew the extent of her affairs. Would his hair turn as grey as his suit if he learned that in less than eight hours time she would be assuming the role of headmistress and would get to cane a complete stranger? Someone not that dissimilar to him, if Deborah's description of Mr Rackham was anything to go by.

While Gordon Shipley continued to peruse the documents in more detail, Angelique ordered a fresh pot of coffee and poured them both a cup. He gave a distracted nod of thanks but a few moments later glanced up.

'Do you know the contents of the safety deposit box?' he asked.

Angelique's heart gave a little jump. 'How do you

know about that?' she countered, trying her best to sound calm.

The accountant tapped one of the sheets of paper in his hand. 'The details of the late Harvey Hemsley's bank account and safety deposit box are given here. His account has been closed and the funds transferred to you but the box still remains.'

For a moment Angelique had to fight to control her breathing. Was this the same box for which she had the key? Surely not. She had found that key among the things from 'The Cedars'. Reaching into her handbag, she took out the key and showed it to Mr Shipley. 'Would this be the key for it by any chance?'

To her dismay he shrugged. 'I wouldn't know just by looking at it. You would have to take it to the bank,' he said.

She held her breath, waited for the thumping of her heart to subside a little and then asked the sixty-four-thousand-dollar question. 'Which bank?'

It was so obvious. Angelique wondered why she hadn't considered it before. Harvey had held an account at the same small merchant bank which handled all the hotel's banking requirements. Going there had entailed a trip into central London, but Angelique hadn't been prepared to wait. She was desperate to find out if the key in her possession was the one which fitted Harvey's safety deposit box. And if so, she was dying to know what secrets it held.

When she explained the situation, Deborah had been happy to lend Angelique her own car – a nippy, red Peugeot which took her right to the doorstep of her destination in just over forty minutes. Luckily, she found a parking meter right outside the bank, and within minutes she was being attended to.

A young woman in a well-fitting kingfisher-blue suit brought the box to her. It was nothing out of the ordinary. Plain grey metal with a lift-up lid. Trembling with nerves, Angelique tried the key. It turned easily and with a racing heart she opened the box and peered inside.

If she had been expecting cash, or precious jewels she would have been horribly disappointed. All the box contained was an oblong manilla envelope which bulged intriguingly. Taking the envelope and putting it into her tan leather handbag, Angelique locked the box again and thanked the banker.

'As you are probably aware, my late father's account has been closed,' Angelique said, zipping her bag shut. 'Is it possible to open an account in my name instead? There will be the box to pay for, of course, and I could do with a good merchant bank to handle my financial affairs.'

The young banker knew exactly who she was dealing with and that the woman seated opposite her was currently a paper millionairess. 'Of course, Miss Hemsley,' she said with a bright smile. 'I'll just get the necessary forms.'

Within the hour Angelique was back at her desk at Thornbury Court, the envelope held between her trembling hands. With a jolt of relief, she glanced up as the door to her office opened and Jordan entered.

'Oh, thank God it's you!' she said, trying but failing to smile properly.

'I hear you've been doing some detective work,' Jordan said, taking a seat opposite her and glancing at the envelope. 'What is that, evidence?'

Angelique shook her head. 'I don't know what's in here. Here I am with yet another envelope that I'm too scared to open.' She tried to make light of it and briefly filled him in on the details of her meeting with the accountant, his disclosure about the safety deposit box and her subsequent trip into town.

Reaching across the desk, Jordan squeezed one of her hands. 'Do you want me to open it?' he offered.

'No, that's okay. I'll do it.' Angelique glanced resolutely at him and then at the envelope. 'Here goes nothing,' she murmured, her fingers working the tacky edges of the envelope apart.

Inside were more pieces of paper. Most of them were old and yellowing and many of them referred to Harvey's original investment in Thornbury Court. Then there were several other documents, equally old and yellowing but this time with an entirely different subject matter – Angelique. Or to be more precise, the circumstances of her adoption and the certificate of adoption itself.

Quickly her eyes scanned the pages. Much of it was legal jargon, too confusing to be of any interest but there were certain details that stood out. With a finger she pointed out the evidence of her bloodline to Jordan.

'That Anthony D Fordyce was my father,' she said, showing him a letter from the man in question giving his permission for Angelique to be adopted by Harvey.

'And your mother worked at Thornbury Court, look,' Jordan said, showing her a paragraph further down the page.

Angelique read it, then sat back in her chair and sighed deeply. 'She and Harvey could have been having an affair then,' she said dejectedly.

To her surprise Jordan laughed. 'No, don't be ridiculous, how could they? Harvey had nothing to do with Thornbury Court then. He didn't invest until much later, when you were already well and truly his daughter, remember?'

'Oh, God, I'm so stupid! Of course.' Angelique stared back at him with wide eyes. 'I keep forgetting that this place was a hotel well before you inherited it and my father, I mean Harvey, became involved.'

She glanced back at the sheet of paper which lay between them on the desk. 'Do you think my blood father was a guest here? Did the hotel have an A-list then like it does now? And was my mother involved in all that sort of thing? Was she an earlier version of Deborah, do you suppose?'

'It is possible,' Jordan said. 'As far as I know the converted cellar and the A-list were already well and truly established as a popular feature of Thornbury Court before I inherited it. In fact, when I took over there was an old chap, like an old retainer, who put me wise to everything that used to go on here. It was his suggestion that I endeavour to keep up the Thornbury Court "tradition."' He laughed. 'Some tradition.'

'I'll say.' Angelique joined in his laughter. She felt relieved now. Relieved that she knew who her real father was and had solved the mystery of the key. The next step was to track down Mr Anthony D Fordyce and confront him. Either he would reject her, or welcome her as his long-lost daughter. Whichever way it went at least she could stop wishing and wondering. At least she would know where she stood at long last.

Chapter Twelve

*I*t was almost seven o'clock when Deborah tracked down Angelique in the Piano Bar.

'Dutch courage,' Angelique said as she pointed to a tall glass of Scotch and soda. 'I can't face Mr Rackham without some kind of booster.'

Deborah gave a dry laugh. 'It's not his face you should be thinking about,' she said, grinning broadly as Angelique groaned then picked up her glass and took a large gulp.

'I don't know if I can go through with this,' she murmured, feeling the anxiety that gripped her abate a little as the alcohol did its job.

Deborah was brusque. 'Of course you can,' she said firmly. Taking Angelique by the elbow she hauled her off the bar stool. 'Now come with me. It's time to get ready. Oh, and you can bring that if you want to.' She couldn't help noticing the way Angelique reached out for her drink as she began to drag her away from its comforting presence.

Down in the cellar a 'school-room' had already been prepared. With a couple of old-fashioned flip-top desks and a blackboard affixed to the wall, as well as a teacher's large wooden desk positioned right at the front of the room, it looked very authentic. On the walls were various maps and cross-section diagrams of parts of the body: the lungs, the heart, as well as a couple of parts that Angelique did not recognise. And on the blackboard someone had chalked a number of Latin verbs.

'*Amo, amas, amat . . .*' Angelique murmured to herself, then jumped when Deborah tapped her on the shoulder.

'This is for you to wear,' she said.

Angelique's eyes widened when she saw the red rubber dress that Deborah held up in front of her. In her other hand were a pair of red leather thigh boots.

'No teacher I ever met went to school in that sort of get-up,' Angelique said.

'This is not like any school you've ever been to,' Deborah pointed out. 'This is more like a school of correction.'

'Or the school of hard whacks,' Angelique chipped in, to which her companion laughed.

'Something like that,' Deborah concurred. She handed the dress and boots to Angelique who took them without a murmur. 'Now I'm just off to get changed myself. I decided it would probably be helpful if I stuck around, just in case you need a little support – amoral or otherwise.' She smiled then gave a huge sigh. 'God, I love this job!'

Angelique was stunned by the passion behind Deborah's parting shot. In the short time she had known her, it hadn't escaped her attention that Deborah was a natural dominatrix, but her sheer enthusiasm for her role was amazing to someone as relatively unsophisticated as Angelique.

By the time Deborah returned, Angelique had managed to squeeze herself into the dress. This was thanks in no small way to her own determination to succeed at anything she did, coupled with a plentiful amount of talcum powder. Eyeing her reflection in the large mirror that dominated one side of the school-room, she had to congratulate herself on her appearance – formidable and yet sensuous, her height accentuated by the six-inch stiletto heels on the boots. What pleased her the most was that her naturally sinuous form was made all the more curvaceous by the flattering properties of the rubber, which moulded and flattened her body in all the right places.

Dressed from neck to toe in a black PVC cat-suit and matching spike-heeled boots, Deborah looked equally stunning.

'Wow!' The exclamation came from both women at the same time and after a brief pause they laughed in unison.

'You look good, Angelique,' Deborah said, nodding approvingly as she walked around her companion and made a visual assessment.

'If I look good, you look amazing,' Angelique cut in generously. 'If I didn't know you better I'd be trembling in my boots.'

Deborah grinned like a cat. 'That is the general idea. We want Mr Rackham to be quaking and stuttering like any other gauche little schoolboy who has been hauled up before his superiors. When he has to answer to us I expect to see tears in his eyes.'

She sounded so assertive that Angelique gulped. 'We can't keep calling him Mr Rackham,' she said. 'Somehow I find it difficult to reconcile the name with the image I have conjured up for him.'

The red-head nodded, her outfit creaking as she moved about the room, opening cupboards and drawers and extracting a few useful items. 'When he arrives we won't,' she assured Angelique. 'We'll call him Bobby instead. As soon as he walks through that door he loses his everyday identity. Role-playing is what makes this work.'

Angelique followed her gaze and then glanced at her watch. Half an hour and counting.

When the duly appointed hour arrived and a timid knock sounded at the door, Deborah glanced at Angelique as though to say, 'This is it.' Up until that point, Angelique had managed to remain quite calm but now a hundred butterflies seemed to emerge from their chrysalises at once and flutter madly about in her stomach. A little higher, her heart began to pound against her ribs. Like an actor with stage fright her throat went dry and she felt horribly sick, but as soon as Deborah opened the door and commanded the hapless 'Bobby' to enter, a veil of serenity descended over her and she allowed her eyes to narrow.

'You, boy, over here!' she rapped out sternly, surprising herself.

Immediately the 'boy' shuffled forward, his movements ungainly and unwilling, his expression sheepish. Angelique looked at him and found herself surprised all over again that he wasn't at all what she had been expecting. For some reason she had pictured Mr Rackham as a tall, thin man, not unlike Rod Bennet, the hotel's bell-boy. The reality was the complete opposite.

Of medium height and almost as round as he was tall, he sported a traditional schoolboy's uniform of grey knee-length shorts, white shirt, grey socks and grey and yellow striped tie. His blazer, also grey, was obviously a little on the small side as the buttons looked strained to bursting point over a well-developed paunch.

Angelique's strict tone cut through the tension that surrounded the three of them. 'I said over here, boy!' she rapped out sternly. 'Stop dawdling or it will be the worse for you.' She gave a humourless laugh and picked up the cane that lay on the top of her desk. Unlike the straight garden canes she had seen being used at Thornbury Court before, this was a typical old school cane,

199

much thicker than the other kind and with a curved handle. She slapped it against her open palm and watched with a frisson of pleasure as Bobby jumped visibly at the sound it made.

'Feeling a little worried, are we, boy?' she said.

Bobby's heavy jowls wobbled as he nodded fervently.

'Then you will have to make sure you conduct yourself well,' Angelique added. For good measure she sliced the air with the cane and felt another bolt of delight zing through her as the 'boy' in front of her cowered.

Now she had him in her clutches, so to speak, Angelique faltered a little. She wasn't quite sure what her next move should be, but thankfully Deborah came to the rescue. Grasping the quivering Bobby by the scruff of his neck she applied enough pressure to force him to kneel down in front of Angelique.

'My, my, Bobby,' Deborah mocked. 'You are the worst-behaved boy we have seen in some time. Isn't that so, headmistress?' She glanced at Angelique who gave a growl of agreement and glowered when Bobby looked up. 'You really have become so bad – so very, very bad – that you can't even remember your manners when you are here,' Deborah added scathingly. 'Now that's not right is it, Bobby? Surely you know what you must do next?'

To Angelique's surprise Bobby nodded fervently, bent forward and began to lick the toes of her boots. Playing along with the scenario, she raised first one foot and then the other so that he could also lick the heels.

'Good boy, Bobby,' Angelique said in a slightly softer tone to Deborah's. 'Perhaps there is hope for you after all.' She picked up the cane and tapped it on his shoulders, rather like the Queen conferring a knighthood. 'I think it is about time you learned your lesson properly. Disobedience in class is a punishable offence. Bullying the other boys is a punishable offence. Talking after lights out is also a punishable offence. Do you have

an excuse for your consistently appalling behaviour?'
She glared down at Bobby, who was now practically
prostrate in front of her, and assumed a disdainful glare
as he raised his head and shook it slowly from side to
side.

'No, ma'am,' he whispered hoarsely. 'No excuses. I'm
just a bad boy.'

Angelique pursed her lips and drew herself up to her
full height. 'Just as I thought. Very well, stand up and
bend over that desk.' She pointed to one of the pupils'
desks and then stalked across the room to stand beside
it. Tapping the cane impatiently against the side of her
leg, she waited until Bobby struggled to his feet, shuffled
over to where she stood and slowly bent forward from
the waist, his fingers gripping the opposite side of the
desk.

This was it now, she thought. So far so good – but
there was no going back. Glancing at Deborah just for a
fleeting moment, she was gratified to receive her nod of
encouragement. Then, just as she raised her arm to
deliver the first blow across Bobby's grey serge-covered
behind, Deborah stepped forward.

'Might I suggest a little less leniency in this instance,
headmistress?' she said. Reaching forward, she deftly
unfastened Bobby's shorts and tugged them down to his
ankles. These were swiftly followed by the large pair of
white cotton boxer shorts that he wore.

Shocked at Deborah's action, Angelique averted her
gaze for a moment. When she glanced back it was to be
confronted with what looked like two huge mounds of
white blancmange. For a moment she felt revolted and
then she remembered her role. A swift glance at Bobby's
red face told her how humiliated he felt and she was
surprised to feel a wave of empathy. Her own experiences as a submissive told her he was probably already
well on his way to being in seventh heaven. There was
no way she was going to disappoint him.

Absently, she flicked the buttock nearest to her with her fingertips and watched as it wobbled for a moment before settling down to a slight quiver. 'This is going to hurt you far more than it's going to hurt me,' she mocked as she bastardised the usual cliché. To her delight, Bobby groaned and waggled his hips slightly in a pleading manner which she also recognised. She sliced the air with the cane a couple of times then brought it to rest across his buttocks. 'Right, prepare for your punishment!'

Despite feeling more in control than she had ever felt before, her first few strokes were tentative to say the least. Thankfully, Deborah was on hand to mouth words of encouragement, and in no time Angelique had administered six of the best. For a moment she paused to simply stroke her fingertips along the slightly raised red lines that bisected the white flesh. With a glow of achievement she couldn't help marvelling at the fact that it was she alone who had created them.

'Are you feeling sorry for your misbehaviour, boy?' she barked suddenly, tightening the thread of erotic tension that joined the three of them.

Bobby jumped and glanced around at her with a fearful expression on his still red face. 'No, ma'am. Not really,' he gasped.

'Then six more it is,' she said, flexing the cane in front of his face. 'But first you may kiss the cane and beg for your punishment.'

She nodded silently as Bobby duly planted a rubbery-lipped kiss on the bamboo and begged hoarsely for the next stage of his punishment.

Deborah stepped in. 'I wouldn't let him off too lightly if I were you, headmistress,' she murmured. 'There is no doubt this boy is a scoundrel and his punishment should be as memorable as possible so that he doesn't break any school rules again.'

Noticing the hopeful look which had flashed into

Bobby's eyes when Deborah spoke, Angelique nodded slowly. 'An excellent idea, but what do you suggest?'

A cat-like smile curved Deborah's lips. 'Oh, the dunce's corner I think, ma'am,' she said confidently. 'How much more humiliating can you get than that?'

Bobby started to groan and plead but the two women ignored him. Each taking him by the arm they led him – stumbling and tripping over his pants and trousers which were still around his ankles – over to the corner of the school-room where a large pointed hat, marked with the traditional 'D' for dunce awaited them.

'Strip and then put this on,' Deborah said, taking over.

The level of tension in the room increased yet again and Deborah's glance flickered over to the mirror on the wall. 'I think we have an audience,' she said quietly.

Glancing firstly at Deborah and then in the direction of the mirror, Angelique felt a sudden rush of excitement. It had to be Jordan watching them she reasoned and if that was the case she wanted to put on her best performance for him.

As soon as Bobby had removed all his clothes and donned the dunce's hat Angelique ordered him to stand in the corner, shoulders back and chest out. Her assessing glance swept over him and quickly noted that for a large man he had quite a small penis.

'What do you call this?' she said scathingly, tapping the end of his erection with the cane. Immediately, it jerked and became a fraction larger.

'I'm sorry, ma'am,' Bobby said. Although he looked thoroughly miserable the small droplet of viscous fluid that oozed from the little slit at the tip of his glans told a different story.

Angelique tapped it again and then swiped the cane across the fronts of his thighs. 'Not good enough,' she said. 'Try harder next time.' She swiped him again and again and gradually Bobby's cock grew larger and the purple glans began to glisten under a thin film of his juices.

Once again, Angelique felt a certain empathy with her hapless victim. It surprised her that she felt so aroused by the whole thing. Bobby was revolting to look at and yet that only seemed to add to the appeal of punishing him. She didn't want to hurt him badly but she felt no qualms about mistreating him. Even though he was the client, the one who was paying for his appalling treatment, it was almost as though he had been provided for *her* amusement.

She wondered again about the voyeur, or voyeurs, behind the two-way mirror and the knowledge that someone else was watching only added to her arousal. Even the tight rubber could not disguise the hardness of her nipples. And the scarlet hue of her dress almost matched the flush of desire that spread across her chest and up her throat to touch her cheeks. Her eyes sparkled. Her natural pout became more pronounced as she pursed her lips in mock annoyance with her 'victim'. And all the time her sex swelled and blossomed and oozed moisture, reminding her that there had been no room for underwear beneath the unforgiving rubber.

A familiar creaking sound alerted her to the fact that Deborah was becoming impatient. In a carefully disguised tone she suggested that perhaps the headmistress was feeling a little fatigued, having been faced with such a disobedient boy, and might appreciate a little rest while she, Deborah, took over for a while.

Angelique nodded gratefully and sat in the large oak and leather chair behind the headmistress' desk. Now it was time to watch the mistress of mistresses at work.

By the end of the session Angelique felt too aroused to do anything more than nod with gratitude when Deborah suggested that she escort the naughty boy back to his dormitory. She had watched him being beaten with the cane, spanked with the flat of Deborah's hand and subjected to all manner of degrading acts. Crawling around on all fours like a dog had been bad enough, his large rump quivering and swaying from side to side as he moved. But when Deborah ordered him to masturbate in front of them Angelique had been forced to damp down her own urge to do the same.

Glancing at the mirror often, she had willed Jordan to come into the room. She couldn't have cared less if the two of them had an audience. All she wanted right at that moment was to feel his cock inside her and his hands caressing her body.

Deborah allowed Bobby to put on his boxer shorts and then led him from the room. Angelique smiled weakly at them as they left. Bobby had thanked her profusely and she had assumed an imperious expression as she accepted his gratitude. Now they were gone she slumped in the chair, her legs splayed and stroked her hands idly over her body.

She liked the feel of the rubber. It was so smooth and soft, like butter. And she loved the way it accentuated the sinuousness of her body and moulded itself around the hard little buds of her nipples. At times, she even fancied that she could make out the shape of her pubic mound underneath the skirt of the dress. Walking over to the mirror, she paused to admire her reflection, forgetting for a moment that there might still be someone on the other side.

With careless hands she stroked her body, her fingers moulding the rubber around her swollen breasts and tweaking her nipples until they jutted out even further than before. Sliding down her stomach, across her belly and over her hips and buttocks, Angelique's hands served to excite herself. She was beautiful. She felt beautiful, and *felt* beautiful encased in the soft rubber.

Rolling up the hem of her dress, she stopped when it reached the tops of her thighs and just the very tip of her pubis was visible – no more than a little 'v' of chestnut curls. Moving her feet apart slightly, she felt a little more steady on her high-heels and considered her reflection as her fingers toyed with the silky curls that hid the pouting lips of her sex.

Now she remembered the possibility of a voyeur and hoped that Jordan was there. Are you watching me, my lover? she wondered as she played with herself. Can you see how aroused and ready for you I am? Feeling bolder she rolled up the hem of the dress a little more until the whole triangle of curls was exposed. Then she began to caress herself in earnest. Without false modesty, she acknowledged that the sight of her own semi-naked body was arousing. She turned herself on and if that was the case, what was she doing for Jordan right at that moment?

Reaching down she pressed her fingertips into the moist slit between her swollen outer labia and pulled the fleshy lips slowly apart. Tilting her hips slightly, she displayed herself to the mirror. Her clitoris was so swollen it looked to be close to erupting into spontaneous orgasm and the rest of her sex was red and juicy, like the flesh of a passion fruit. Succulent but without all the pips, she mused as she held her labia apart with the fingers of one hand and stroked her index finger of the other hand over the glistening folds of flesh.

Desperate to touch her clitoris, she forced herself to ignore the demanding bud and instead slid the tip of her index finger around and around the rim of her vagina. Tremors of lust gripped her as she forced herself to touch slowly and lightly. She felt anxious to finger herself properly, to sink several of her own long digits into the spongy depths of her vagina and stimulate herself. Instead, she forced herself to simply stroke her exposed sex with her fingertips, lightly arousing her burgeoning flesh until she was panting with the desire for release.

She wondered why Jordan hadn't put in an appearance

yet. Surely even he couldn't hold out much longer? He could see how desperate she was – *if* he was on the other side of the mirror. What if he wasn't? What if her only choice of lover was herself? At that moment it seemed like the cruelest of possibilities.

Giving in to the urge that gripped her, Angelique touched her clitoris with a tentative fingertip. She jumped and the aftershock rippled through her, almost as intense as an orgasm but not quite. 'I want to come,' she moaned quietly as she rubbed herself a little harder, two fingers sliding up and down either side of her clitoris.

A rush of her juices soaked her sex and she slicked some of the creamy nectar over the straining bud that now threatened to explode. Her buttocks clenched. She drove two fingers deep inside herself and felt her vagina spasm as her orgasm almost ripped her apart. Oh, God, yes! she thought. She rocked unsteadily on her heels as wave after wave of unabating pleasure swept through her.

Still she stroked herself and spread her body open wider. Through heavy-lidded eyes she watched as more juice trickled from her and coated her fingers. Then, gradually, the tremors began to die down and she slowly removed her hands and sank gratefully on to the nearest chair.

'Well, well, you are a voluptuous young lady, aren't you?' The clipped, very English tone cut through the haze that surrounded Angelique and she forced herself to turn her head towards the sound. It took a few moments longer for her to find the strength to open her eyes and when she did she found herself confronted by the sight of Fergus, the gardener, and a tall, well-dressed man whom she had never seen before.

In a rush of embarrassment at being caught in such a lewd position she hurriedly rolled down the hem of her dress until she was satisfied that she was decent. Then she sat up straighter and eyed Fergus and the stranger warily. She realised she could smell herself on her fingers and quickly sat on her hands in case the two men should happen to notice the tell-tale aroma.

The stranger laughed softly. 'Don't bother to be embarrassed on our account,' he said. 'We enjoyed watching your little performance through the two-way mirror.'

Angelique was horrified. 'You don't mean . . .?' she began and flushed bright red as Fergus grinned.

'All of it,' he said. 'Your stint as headmistress and afterwards. When you, er – well, you know?'

Feeling as though she was caught in a dreadful nightmare, Angelique inclined her head. 'I know,' she said faintly. Her mind screamed with humiliation and an overwhelming desire to put as much distance between herself and the two men as possible. Unfortunately, Fergus was standing right in front of the door and the stranger was just in front of him blocking her escape route.

Although she knew she was staring blatantly, Angelique assessed the stranger's appearance. About the same height and build as Jordan, he was probably about five years younger. His hair was similar in shade to her own and as far as she could tell his skin was lightly tanned. His dark pin-stripe suit looked as though it was hand-tailored, and his black brogues looked similarly hand-made. She imagined he could find his way around Jermyn Street blind-folded.

'If I wasn't busy, I'd take time out to put you out of your misery,' Fergus said cockily, interrupting her thoughts.

Angelique stared wordlessly at him. Was it her imagination or did he just thrust his crotch at her? she wondered. She glanced down at it and couldn't help noticing the large, tell-tale bulge under the loose cream-coloured trousers. Despite the maelstrom of feelings that coursed through her, she felt ashamed at the way her vagina automatically tingled at the sight. Her body all too often displayed a will of its own!

'Well, I expect I'll live,' she murmured in an ironic tone. Turning her attention back to the stranger who had moved a little closer to her, she couldn't resist asking who he was.

'My friends call me Jock,' he said, extending a broad hand towards her which she took in her own small, trembling one and shook half-heartedly.

It was hardly surprising that she had little strength left and assumed he would understand. 'What does everyone else call you then, Jock?' she responded pertly.

It infuriated her that he simply gave an enigmatic smile and tapped the side of his nose. 'State secret,' he said. 'Everyone at Thornbury Court is a friend of mine, so everyone here calls me Jock. You too if you wish.'

Burying the sarcastic retort that instantly sprang to her lips, Angelique got up and wobbled unsteadily over to the far side of the room where a cupboard held the clothes she had been wearing originally.

'If you don't mind, I'm going to go up to my suite,' she said as calmly as she could. 'I hope you gentlemen will excuse me?' She also hoped Fergus would catch the sarcastic inflection she added to the word 'gentlemen'.

Jock nodded, a slight smile touching his lips as though he had been the one to notice her irony. Just for a moment Fergus looked as though he intended to block her exit. However, Angelique gave him such a withering look that he backed down and stepped briskly away from the door.

'Jock used to be one of our regular guests,' Fergus said, just as she reached for the door handle. 'With Jordan away and Deborah otherwise engaged it has been left to me to show him our new, improved facilities.'

Angelique listened to what Fergus didn't say and turned around again hurriedly. 'Oh, I do apologise,' she said to Jock. 'No one told us you were coming here tonight otherwise we would have made certain that you were well taken care of.'

'I am being well taken care of,' he replied with a much broader smile that creased his lightly tanned face and touched the corners of his sea-green eyes. 'I like to do things on the spur of the moment. It keeps people on their toes, don't you know?'

The way he spoke made Angelique laugh aloud. 'Oh, absolutely,' she said. Then she turned to Fergus. 'Have you seen all there is to see down here? Perhaps Jock would appreciate a night-cap.' She glanced at her watch and saw it was already past midnight. Where had the time gone?

To her relief Jock declined. 'No, thank you. That is very hospitable of you but I really can't stay. I still have a box to go through tonight.'

Fergus ignored Angelique's raised eyebrow and added cheekily, 'I think Jock picked a good night for his surprise visit.' As he stared insolently at her, Angelique could hardly fail to pick up on his meaning.

She cleared her throat and shifted uncomfortably from one red leather-shod foot to the other. 'Yes, well, if you'll excuse me. I'll just go and put on some more appropriate clothing,' she said. 'Fergus, please buzz my room if Jock should change his mind about that night-cap. I think, as management, I should be available if he wants to discuss anything to do with the hotel or its facilities.'

Looking as though he felt suitably chastened, Fergus nodded. 'Will do, ma'am,' he said, and tugged his forelock deliberately – to which Jock laughed aloud and Angelique had to force herself not to respond. With all the dignity she could muster she gave Jock a fleeting smile, then left the room.

Chapter Thirteen

The light rap on the door to Angelique's suite an hour later surprised her. She had just about given up on the possibility of being summoned downstairs to the bar for a drink with Jock and had been planning to go to bed. Now she jumped up and padded over to the door. Opening it, she peered out cautiously and when she saw no one was there, stepped right out into the hallway to look up and down it. To her surprise it seemed completely deserted. Then, just as she was looking one way, Jordan sneaked up on her from the opposite direction and surprised her.

'I'm glad you're still awake,' he said in her ear.

'Oh, my – Jordan!' she exclaimed breathlessly as she held a hand against her chest. Beneath her palm and the thin, blush-pink cashmere jumper she wore, she could feel her heart beating wildly.

Laughing at her obvious surprise, Jordan picked her up and carried her back over the threshold. Closing the door behind them, he pulled her into his arms for a long, searching kiss. Finally, still gasping for breath but for a different reason, Angelique pulled away from him slightly and eyed the small black box in his hand.

'Video-tape,' he said in answer to her questioning expression.

'Video-tape?'

Jordan pulled the tape from the box and walked over to a tall walnut cupboard opposite the intimate gathering of sofas. Opening the cupboard he revealed a TV and video player which Angelique had not yet bothered to use.

'Yes, a copy of your performance with Mr Rackham,' he said. 'Or should I say Bobby?' He made a tut-tut sound and added, 'What a bad boy he was, Angelique and what a great headmistress you were.'

She glowed inwardly at his praise. 'Really?'

'Really.' Jordan nodded. 'I've already skimmed through a bit of this,' he said, 'and I must admit I was tempted to carry on watching. Nevertheless, I couldn't resist coming up here to share the whole thing with you.'

He pressed the play button on the remote control pad and sat down on one of the sofas, pulling Angelique down beside him as he did so.

Snuggling against him, Angelique glanced up as the tape leaped into life and familiar parts of the hotel appeared on the TV screen. 'I presume the hotel has some kind of close-circuit surveillance system?' she said. 'I've seen all the little cameras dotted about the place but I didn't realise they recorded everything.'

'Oh, yes,' Jordan said, sliding his hand up under her jumper and encountering bare flesh. 'But most of what they record is everyday stuff. Just occasionally, especially in the cellar, the cameras pick up something really worth watching.'

Angelique blushed. She couldn't help wondering for how long the tape ran and whether it had picked up her little display of self-gratification at the end of her session in the school-room.

'Each tape records for four hours,' Jordan told her

212

when she asked him. 'A new one would have been loaded at eight o'clock and replaced at midnight.'

On hearing this, Angelique paled a little. Noticing her expression, Jordan asked her what was wrong. She glanced at the TV screen and noticed that the tape was showing the moment when Deborah handed Angelique her costume for the evening.

'Did you skip right though to the end, by any chance?' she asked and felt a flicker of relief when Jordan shook his head.

'No. As I said, I watched for a couple of minutes and then felt anxious to come up here and watch it with you.' As he said the word 'anxious', he glanced down to the crotch of his navy trousers which bulged appealingly.

'I see,' Angelique said gravely. She reached out and began to unfasten them. 'Perhaps I should relieve sir of his "anxiety" before we go any further. I am worried that by the time we reach the end of this tape you will have ruined a perfectly good pair of trousers.'

'Oh, modest as always, Angelique,' Jordan said with a grin and then groaned as her deft fingers released his erection and began to caress it gently.

The way she deliberately ran the tip of her tongue over her pouting lips almost proved to be his undoing. If there was one thing about Angelique that was guaranteed to get to him it was her mouth. Now she tantalised him by flicking the pointed tip of her tongue over his glans, her eyes twinkling wickedly as his cock twitched in her light grasp.

'Aha! Time to feast, I believe,' she said darkly and made a perfect 'o' with her lips which she lowered over the roseate plum of his glans until she had engulfed him completely.

With trembling fingers Jordan reached for the remote control and pressed the pause button, then he buried both his hands in Angelique's hair. Gasping with barely restrained arousal, he clutched at handfuls of her silky tresses as she raised and lowered her head, sucking and licking him the whole time as desire surged within him.

Angelique sighed with happiness as she felt the proof of his arousal for herself – her fingertips sensing his juices rising just beneath the taut skin that covered his shaft. She enjoyed pleasing him in this way and she loved the shape and texture of his circumcised cock. Just running her tongue around and around the glans gave her the utmost satisfaction, especially when he groaned and arched his back in response as he was doing now. And she loved to grip his rigid shaft and press her tongue along the underside of it as her other hand caressed the delicious weight of his testicles. Even to run a single fingernail along the sensitive path of his perineum, from scrotum to anus, thrilled her almost as much as it did Jordan.

Glancing up she saw that Jordan's head was thrown back in ecstasy so that she could only see the smooth sweep of his throat and the sandpapery tip and underside of his chin. Increasing her efforts, she allowed her eyes to flicker up to his face several more times until he finally filled her mouth with his juices and then glanced down to see her gazing up at him.

Angelique's expression bordered on adoration. Yet when she raised her head properly and licked the droplets of come away from the corners of her mouth, Jordan noticed how wicked her eyes were and how her lips now curved into a foxy smile.

'You little witch,' he murmured fondly, his hands still buried in her hair. Cupping the sides of her head he pulled her up until her face was level with his. She immediately yielded to his kiss, accepting his words as a compliment and the sensual pressure of his lips as a gesture of his appreciation.

'The tape, Jordan,' she said huskily as they broke apart. With one hand resting protectively over his cock

214

and the other holding the remote control, he and Angelique watched her debut as a dominatrix.

By the time the tape came to an end both Jordan and Angelique looked as though they had just re-enacted every single erotic moment, even though the passing of time had forced them to fast-forward through a great deal of it. When it came to the part where Angelique had walked over to the mirror and begun pleasuring herself, Jordan had thrown her a surprised glance but quickly reverted to watching the scene unfold. Fortunately it stopped short of Fergus' arrival with Jock, although Angelique immediately told Jordan what had transpired. To her chagrin he burst out laughing.

'Oh, dear, Angelique,' he said, wiping a stray tear away from the corner of his eye. 'You always try so hard not to be quite as decadent as the rest of us and yet you consistently succeed in acting the complete opposite.'

'But I thought it was you behind the mirror,' she explained for the third time, to which Jordan chuckled all the more.

'I'm flattered, of course,' he said. 'And I wish I had been there watching you. Unfortunately the angle of the camera is not quite as revealing as it could have been in this instance.'

'I could repeat my performance,' she offered, her voice thick and treacly as she detached his arms from around her and rose to her feet. 'I could imagine there is a two-way mirror between us now.'

Jordan swallowed deeply and found himself trapped in her gaze. With a surge of lust he noticed how her hazel eyes darkened almost to black as the pupils dilated.

Keeping his attention upon her, Angelique stroked her breasts sensuously over the soft cashmere. Underneath she wore no bra, her sensual nature loving the way the natural fabric caressed her bare skin. As soon as she touched her breasts, her nipples hardened and swelled, the taut buds clearly visible through the thin jumper.

This time the linen skirt she wore was much longer and not as easy to deal with as the rubber dress she had worn earlier. But, as her jumper was thigh length, she decided to dispense with the skirt completely. In moments she had whipped the cumbersome garment away from her body and thrown it carelessly across the room.

For a brief instant, Jordan followed its flight with his eyes and then turned back to see that Angelique now stood before him clad only in the jumper. He could still see the outline of her nipples clearly and could also make out the jutting mounds of her breasts. He already knew she was naked under the jumper and imagined her breasts jiggling about unfettered as she moved, the soft fibres of the cashmere arousing her nipples even more.

Sensuous caresses took her hands down and across her torso in unending trails. As she moved so the hem of the jumper lifted slightly, revealing a tantalising glimpse of glossy chestnut curls every now and then. As an experienced voyeur, Jordan was surprised to find himself in the position of not knowing where to look. Her eyes mesmerised him so that he could hardly look away and yet when he did her pouting mouth drew his gaze back to her face time and time again. Conversely, when she stroked her body, or plucked at her nipples over the thin cashmere, even when she squeezed the plump mounds of her breasts together, he could not bear to tear his gaze away from that particular part of her to the exclusion of all else.

Inching back into the depths of the sofa he allowed himself the luxury of a travelling gaze – a visual assessment of her that made his heart pound and his cock weep with tears of viscous fluid. Stroking himself absently, Jordan continued to watch Angelique. He felt strangely detached, as though he sat outside his own body, and was intrigued by the way she touched herself. Her fingers were so deft and so clever he couldn't help marvelling at their skill as they delved into the mass of curls and reappeared coated with the creamy proof of her arousal. And when she parted her labia for him and exposed her inner most flesh for his visual delectation, he felt a surge of renewed desire for the woman in front of him, as though she were a complete stranger opening herself up to him for the very first time.

He longed to touch her and yet forced himself to hold back. The floor was hers and it was up to Angelique to call the tune. When she wanted his caresses he was certain she would let him know.

If she had felt aroused before in the school-room, it was nothing compared to the way she was feeling now. To have Jordan sitting right there in front of her, his cock stiffening and rising proudly even before she had really begun was the best of all worlds. Better than a two-way mirror, his captive presence was erotic in the extreme.

She could hardly bear to exhibit such restraint as she caressed her own body slowly, her delicate, knowing fingers lingering over each tiny part of her. Still dressed in the jumper, she moved deliberately so that its hem raised above the apex of her thighs and exhibited the triangle of her pubic hair. Between her legs she could feel her sex lips already thick and moist with arousal and it took her all her will-power not to touch them until she was satisfied that she had caressed every inch of her torso.

Then, when she eased those puffy lips apart and felt Jordan's gaze upon that exposed part of her as keenly as a beam of light, she shuddered with desire. Every minute portion of her felt alive – burning to be touched and to be licked and sucked. Her breasts ached to be fondled and felt overblown and heavy beneath the delicate cashmere, her nipples straining to break through the thin fabric. And her vagina felt moist and open, ready to take fingers or a cock – or both. A groan escaped her lips and she delved into the moist slit between her legs and thrust two fingers up inside herself.

For a moment she rocked her pelvis and ground her fingers deeper and deeper into herself. Lost in her own personal erotic nirvana, Angelique did not hear the small whimpering sounds she made, nor feel the trickles of her own juices running down her inner thighs. Feeling thoroughly wanton she dropped to her haunches and opened her knees wide. Her hands began to work feverishly between her legs, stroking and caressing the swollen flesh of her vulva as she sank a third finger up to the knuckle inside her vagina.

'Oh, Christ, Angelique!' The anguished cry seemed to come from somewhere far away and she glanced up, the sight of the pale blue ceiling and ornate white plaster mouldings coming back to her through blurred eyes.

A shadow seemed to block out her vision and then strong, masculine hands covered her own and moved them away. A hard body pressed her backwards until she lay flat on the floor, her legs still bent, soles of her feet flat to the floor. Hot breath rasped in her ear as she felt a familiar hardness nudge at the desperately swollen folds of her labia and sink into the willing chasm of her vagina.

'Oh, yes. Oh, perfect bliss,' Angelique gasped, her eyes suddenly opening wide to encompass Jordan's face and enslave him in her gaze.

Underneath the familiar weight of his body her hips worked – rocking and grinding so that her movements stimulated every part of her hungry sex flesh. There was no more room for words in her head or on her lips. Primeval lust took over where seduction was snatched away. She couldn't tantalise without suffering the consequences. And what consequences! A rhythmic jousting of bodies, thrusting and parrying until both combatants were reduced to gasping, quivering wrecks, each the victor.

As desperate as he was for his own release Jordan held back and forced Angelique over the edge of her desire instead. Watching through heavy-lidded eyes, he saw the abandoned way in which she reacted as her orgasm ripped through her like a bolt of lightning and engulfed her in its peculiar heat and light. It delighted him beyond belief to see her in the grip of so much pleasure, her limbs thrashing, her expression one of pure, mindless ecstasy.

Transported on an apparently never-ending roller-coaster of pleasure, Angelique rocked and moaned, feeling as though the exquisite sensations were almost too unbearable to endure. But endure them she did and finally she felt the rhythmic contractions of her vagina milk Jordan of his juices. Forcing her eyes to focus properly, she watched as her body tipped him over the very same precipice from which she had just fallen.

Euphoria contorted his face as a harsh groan broke from his lips. Beads of perspiration glistened on his brow and across his well-defined cheekbones as he continued to thrust for a moment longer and then he slumped, visually and physically. She saw the evidence of how she had drained him and loved him for his acquiescence. Using her vaginal muscles, she gripped him as tightly as she could until she was forced to release his wilting penis and allow him to repossess it.

They slept for hours after that. Both of them nestled in the womb-like comfort of her large double bed, not entwined together but each of them occupying their own space. Having joined together and become one, they now ceded to their own separateness.

Nevertheless, it was not a lonely night for either of them by any means. Drowsy fingers sought each other across the narrow divide of linen and occasionally one would roll over and drift into the other. On those occasions one pair of lips fleetingly brushed the other's mouth and then the wayward body rolled back to its original position. So perfectly choreographed were their movements during sleep that they both woke at midday feeling as though they had spent the whole time making love.

The next day, after a leisurely lunch outside on the terrace, Jordan reluctantly left Angelique to her own devices while he attended yet another meeting with the bank. Knowing what she knew and being determined to invest more of her own money in Thornbury Court, Angelique had asked if she should be present at the meeting but he shook his head.

'It's not that I don't want you to be there,' Jordan said hurriedly when he noticed her frown, 'but I would rather they didn't know about your plans to invest. That's a last resort as far as I am concerned and I don't want the bank to know the hotel has another source of funds.'

'That makes sense,' Angelique conceded, 'although I can't understand why they are being so difficult.'

'Nor can I.' With a resigned shrug, Jordan stood up and put his hand briefly on Angelique's shoulder. Dropping a light kiss on the top of her head he promised he would let her know how things went as soon as he returned.

No sooner had Jordan left, than Deborah arrived to take his place. Idly dipping her finger in the froth on the cup of cappuccino she had brought with her she gave Angelique a broad wink.

'Last night,' she rapped out, licking the finger and pointing it at Angelique, 'not bad. Not bad at all.'

'Thanks.' Angelique smiled and picked up her own coffee cup. 'It was quite a novel experience but I think I'll soon get the hang of it. I'm already looking forward to next time.'

To her surprise Deborah blushed slightly before she spoke. 'I'm glad about that,' she said, looking more sheepish than ever, 'because your next time may be sooner than either of us expected. And with a much more demanding client than Mr Rackham.'

Nervous tremors coursed through Angelique but she forced herself to look calm. 'Really?'

Sunlight glinted off Deborah's hair as she nodded. 'Usually I handle this client but surprisingly he asked specifically for you,' she said.

'For me?' Angelique knew she was beginning to sound really moronic but she was stunned, she didn't know any of the clients.

When she said as much to Deborah, she waved away her incredulity. 'This client knows you. And he is one of our VIP clients. A real peach of a man.'

'Knows me?' Angelique murmured softly. 'Who is he?'

Deborah drained her coffee and stared straight at Angelique seated opposite her. 'We all call him Jock,' she said.

For a moment Angelique wobbled in her chair. 'Jock? But I only met him last night, with Fergus,' she said, sounding as surprised as she felt.

'I know. He told me all about your chance encounter,' Deborah said with an obvious smirk. 'But you must have made an impression. First thing this morning he was on the phone to me asking all about you.' She paused to take in Angelique's open-mouthed expression before continuing. 'The thing is he likes to indulge in a little bit of everything. I wasn't sure if you were ready to handle it.'

There was a long silence while Angelique digested what Deborah had to say. 'What do you mean by "everything"?' she queried at long last.

Deciding honesty was the best policy, Deborah leaned forward, clasped her hands on the table top and assumed

221

a business-like expression. 'Domination by him,' she replied candidly. 'A little domination by you perhaps. Certainly sex in all its forms. Just between the two of you though,' she added quickly. 'No orgies or anything like that, but Jock can be demanding. He would expect to spend the whole night with you.'

'When you say "whole night" ... ?' Angelique began in a faint voice that was hardly more than a whisper.

Deborah cut in brusquely. 'When I say, "whole night", I mean a leisurely dinner with a couple of bottles of champagne, followed by a little esoteric entertainment and then bed, or wherever.' Forming a pyramid with her fingers, she leaned closer to Angelique. 'Jock is a remarkable and cultured man,' she added. 'His tastes are sophisticated. He loves women and expects them to look and act like women when he is with them. Mark my words, Angelique, if Jock takes a fancy to you – and by the looks of things he already has – you could end up with a very charming and eligible regular client.'

Hesitant about pushing Angelique too far at this stage, she didn't bother to mention that the fees Jock paid Thornbury Court were almost as indecent as his passion for kinky sex.

Deep inside Angelique felt nervous at the very idea of spending a night of unbridled lust with a man who was a virtual stranger and who would be paying for the privilege. On the other hand, a devilish voice whispered to her that it might just be fun, that Jock was a nice man and obviously well-heeled.

'Thornbury Court could certainly do with the money,' Angelique said as though she could read Deborah's mind.

Deborah was obviously taken aback, Angelique thought with an inward smile. Obviously she had expected Angelique to decline straight away – no ifs or buts.

Silently, Deborah nodded. Then she said, 'But you've

got to feel right about this, Angelique. At the end of the day it is sex for money, not because you fancy the guy.'

Angelique smiled. 'To tell you the truth, Deborah,' she said, 'when I met him last night I did fancy him. Isn't that funny?' She started to laugh but soon fell sober again when her companion didn't join in. 'I'm not so naïve that I don't appreciate the seriousness of what I would be doing,' she added calmly. 'And I don't know what Jordan would make of it.'

There! Now Angelique had managed to put Deborah's other major concern into words.

'I honestly don't know either,' the red-head murmured. 'Normally he would just treat it as a job of work for an employee and tell her, or him, to use their instincts and just get on with it. With you it will probably be different.'

'Why?' Angelique asked, her dead-pan expression hiding the fact that her heart had started to thump and her stomach cramped painfully.

Deborah gazed steadily at Angelique. 'I think you know why, but I'll spell it out anyway,' she said. Pausing to take a deep breath and noticing that Angelique seemed to be holding hers. 'He seems to really care for you, Angelique,' she added softly. 'Oh, I know he cares about all of us at Thornbury Court, that we're his "family" – he often calls us that. And perhaps he has slightly deeper feelings for myself and Christina because we've shared a lot of experiences over the years and I don't just mean of the sexual variety, you know?' She waited until Angelique nodded before continuing. 'Having said all that, I have never known him to spend as much time with one woman as he has with you. Or to behave in such a protective manner towards her. Even with myself and Christina it has always been business first and pleasure later.'

Angelique gulped, not trusting herself to think about

the 'pleasure' part of Jordan's relationship with the two women.

'Since your arrival, Jordan has hardly spent any leisure time with anyone else,' Deborah continued. 'And I know that he has cancelled a couple of appointments with female clients just so that he could spend the time with you instead.'

'Am I supposed to feel guilty about that?' Angelique cut in sharply.

Deborah looked stunned. 'No. Of course not. I'm just telling you how it is, that's all. There is no reason for you to feel guilty about anything you have done here, or may do in the future.'

Angelique knew she meant with Jock. 'Okay,' she said slowly. 'So how do you think Jordan will react if I say I want to – er, "service" Jock as a client?'

To that, Deborah laughed aloud. 'Aha! That's the sixty-four-thousand-dollar question, and one to which I have no answer. Basically, your guess is as good as mine. He can be quite an enigma can our Jordan.'

'Don't I know it,' Angelique said, smiling back at Deborah. She reclined in her chair and stared up at the cloudless blue sky for a moment before looking back down and pinning the other woman with her gaze. 'I guess the only way to find out is to tell him when he gets back.'

'So you do want to go through with it?' Deborah asked. 'I have to let Jock know pretty quickly because he's talking about coming to stay at the hotel this weekend.'

'This weekend?' That took Angelique by surprise. For some reason she had expected a little longer to get used to the idea. When Deborah nodded Angelique added, 'I think I can handle it. I will definitely let you know by the morning, if that is okay?'

'Sure, that's okay,' Deborah said. 'But what if Jordan puts his foot down?'

'Huh!' Angelique made no secret of the way she felt about that idea. 'As much as I like Jordan and as much as I would hate to hurt him, I am my own person. If I decide to go through with this thing with Jock, then no one will change my mind.'

Being of a determined disposition, Angelique was stunned by Jordan's apparent ambivalence to the situation. He returned from the meeting at the bank feeling slightly more optimistic and was quick to seek Angelique out to tell her how it went. They wandered out to the terrace as they had that lunchtime and as soon as he stopped talking she told him her news.

'I am pretty certain I could handle it, Jordan,' she said brightly. 'After all, he is an extremely valued client by all accounts and I have met him and found him to be absolutely charming.'

To her surprise Jordan gave a rueful laugh. 'Oh, yes. Charm is something Jock has bags of, as well as good looks,' he said. 'The other thing he has is money and plenty of it. God, if he wasn't so damn nice I would hate the bastard!'

'What does he do?' Angelique asked.

'Not much. He doesn't have to,' Jordan replied, pausing to order a jug of Pimms for both of them. 'He inherited his wealth and is a *bona fide* Member of Parliament. Duly elected by his constituents whose ancestors used to toil as serfs on his country estate. Makes you sick to think about it really.' Shielding his eyes with his hand, Jordan surveyed the rolling lawns and further afield, the dark green fringe of woodland that bordered the grounds.

'I guess some of us have it and some of us don't,' Angelique said in a mock Bronx accent.

'Some of us have it handed to us on a plate, you mean,' Jordan said.

Angelique glanced sideways at him. It wasn't like

225

Jordan to sound envious of someone's good fortune. 'I thought things went well at the bank. Why are you on such a downer?'

Typically, he shrugged. 'I suppose I am a bit bothered about this thing with you and Jock,' he said at long last. 'The thing is he has it all – except you that is. But after the weekend he really will have it all.'

'He is only going to borrow me for one night, Jordan,' Angelique pointed out softly as she touched his arm. Waiting until he turned his head to meet her steady gaze she said, 'I'm not planning to elope with him. I just want to do my bit for Thornbury Court. Why should I have special privileges?'

Fighting back the desire to say, 'Because you are special,' Jordan said, 'Because you are not used to all this. Hell, barely a month ago you hadn't even felt the kiss of the whip, or the slap of a palm upon your delectable behind.'

'That was then and this is now, Jordan,' Angelique said. 'Let's face it, I've had to do a lot of growing up in the past few months. I just look on this as another stage.'

'You might regret it in the morning,' Jordan warned as he reached out to her.

Leaning sideways in her chair, Angelique allowed Jordan's arms to enfold her and she rested her head against his chest just for a moment before looking up. 'If I do I won't let it get to me,' she assured him. 'Take each day at a time is my motto these days. Even if one day doesn't go exactly to plan there's always the next.'

'God, I never realised you were such a wise little being,' Jordan said fondly. Glancing down at her, he stroked a stray tendril of hair away from her eyes. 'If you intend to go through with this, do you mind if I make a suggestion?' He paused while Angelique shook her head and he smiled broadly. 'Make sure all your erotic skills are finely honed. We have a couple of days and nights at our disposal, you can practice on me.'

'Oh, you!' Angelique exclaimed before she burst out laughing. Jordan had sounded so serious for a moment that her stomach had tightened into a fierce knot. Now it unravelled quickly and she relaxed again in his arms. 'Of course I'll practice with you,' she said softly. 'Who else would I choose to "hone me" than the maestro himself?'

Chapter Fourteen

*D*espite her bravado, by the time Saturday evening
actually arrived Angelique was a bag of nerves. A
courier had delivered an intriguing package from Jock
which now lay on her bed. And Jordan had called up to
her suite to wish her good luck and to remind her of
their date for the following afternoon – a picnic down by
the lake, just like the old days.

Thinking about the old days made her feel unbearably
nostalgic and she had to fight back the urge to dissolve
into tears. This was ridiculous, she told herself. The
decision to spend the night with Jock had been entirely
her own. Yet the prospect made her feel a little strange
and she suddenly felt a rush of empathy with the heroine
in the film *Indecent Proposal* who sold herself for one
night for a million dollars. From what Deborah had told
her, Angelique expected to receive quite a few indecent
proposals from Jock before the night was out.

Champagne seemed the only answer to her slump in
spirits, the sparkling alcohol providing a pleasant lift.
Downing her first glass with haste, she poured a second
and walked over to the bed. She put the glass down on
the table by the side of the bed and then stroked a

thoughtful hand over the package. Gift-wrapped in grey and cream striped foil and decorated with silver streamers, the oblong package had a lift-off lid which she raised to reveal oceans of soft grey tissue. Beneath the tissue was a dress so magnificent that it took her breath away.

With trembling fingers she reached into the box and pulled the dress out by its shoestring straps. In cream silk-jersey the sheath dress had a boned and pleated bodice – designed to mould and accentuate the breasts – and a long, fluid skirt that was split to the thigh on each side. Another layer of tissue paper concealed a second surprise – a filmy set of lingerie, scant cream lace so fine it looked and felt like gossamer, and a pair of pale cream hold-up stockings with deep lacy welts.

She marvelled at the clothes as she slipped each wonderful garment on to her excited body and was amazed by the fact that each item fitted to perfection. It horrified her to contemplate how much the whole outfit must have cost, and so she didn't. Instead she thought about the way she should wear her hair to do justice to the dress.

Having fiddled about with it for some time, drinking another glass and a half of champagne in the process, she decided to wear her hair pinned up in a loose top-knot from which escaped a few stray tendrils. The simple style added height and accentuated the swan-like grace of her neck and the smooth sweep of her shoulders. Glancing over her shoulder, Angelique noticed how the back of the dress dipped slightly to a point just below her shoulder blades. The colour showed off her tan to perfection and the champagne added a sparkle to her eyes.

'You are beautiful, Angelique,' she said to her reflection, repeating the words often spoken to her by Jordan. 'Beautiful, desirable and sensuous. A gift to any man.'

Her own words brought her up short. Giving herself to a virtual stranger for money was a scary thought.

Despite her attempts at false bravado, her insides tingled and squirmed, forming one tight knot behind her navel and another which squeezed her heart. The antique telephone jangled, disturbing her thought haze and as she picked up the receiver and held it to her ear she heard the news she had been expecting and at the same time dreading: Jock had checked in and was now waiting for her in reception.

She descended the main staircase on trembling legs which would hardly support her, one hand drifting down the satin sweep of the mahogany banister as she walked.

Jock stood at the foot of the staircase, hands clasped behind his back, feet planted firmly apart at shoulder width. He was wearing an elegantly tailored dress suit and underneath a white shirt with a wing collar and waistcoat in violet slub silk. His bow tie matched the waistcoat and when he brought his arms around to the front and reached his hands out to take hers she noticed his cuffs were fastened by a pair of gold and amethyst cuff-links.

His hair was slicked back away from his finely chiselled face and when he looked at her his green eyes sparkled with undisguised pleasure. 'Angelique, you look absolutely amazing,' he said, greeting her formally with a kiss that floated into the air just a fraction away from her left ear. 'I love the dress. It suits you as I knew it would.'

'You have excellent taste,' she replied with a faint smile.

Standing there in the reception of Thornbury Court, dressed in an outfit chosen for her by a virtual stranger and knowing her body had been paid for in much the same way made her feel distinctly odd. He treated her courteously, guiding her across the lobby and outside to a waiting chauffeur-driven Mercedes limousine with just the slightest pressure of his hand upon her elbow, and yet the inescapable fact was that this was no ordinary date.

The restaurant he had chosen was small, intimate and close to Westminster. At first she had been surprised that he didn't intend for them to dine at Thornbury Court and then she realised it was probably better this way. No distractions. No disconcertingly familiar scenarios. This was not about her and Jordan, this was business. She had a large stake in the hotel and Jock was its most valued client.

Business or no, it didn't mean she couldn't enjoy herself and she was more than happy to accept Jock's offer of a second glass of wine. They were drinking an excellent Le Montrachet. The Premier Cru white wine was a perfect accompaniment to the generous platter of rock oysters which he had ordered as a starter, and Angelique smiled appreciatively as she lifted one from its bed of crushed ice and tipped it down her throat. Another sip of wine followed the slippery trail of the shellfish and she sighed with pleasure.

'I love to see a woman enjoying herself,' Jock said, helping himself to another oyster, 'especially when it comes to food and sex. The two are inextricably linked, you know?'

Angelique nodded and went on to tell him about the cordon bleu course she had taken, and a little of her life in France.

'Funnily enough it was the simple dishes that I enjoyed eating the most,' she told him, pausing to polish off another oyster. 'You can keep your complicated recipes that cost a fortune and take hours to prepare. I'd rather have a bowl of soup à l'oignon gratinée, or pot au feu any day.'

Jock laughed. 'And now you are back in England to complete the other half of your education?' he said, giving her a knowing smile that stirred up the anxiety inside her which had lain dormant for the past hour.

'I actually came over here to find out the details of my inheritance and to try and discover who my real parents are,' she said, anxious to correct him. She could see her admission shook him slightly. The lustful sparkle in his eyes died just a little and he took several large gulps of wine before prompting her to continue.

Over a second course of pheasant mousse and then a main course of roast saddle of lamb she told him everything. At the end, when the waiter came to clear away their plates and she declined dessert, just opting for coffee and a liqueur instead, she noticed Jock looked as though he was lost in thought.

'Penny for them,' she said softly, patting his hand. Her inhibitions had relaxed considerably thanks to excellent food and wine and she felt grateful to him for the attentive way he treated her. Nothing was too much trouble and while she was speaking he hadn't looked the slightest bit bored.

Jock glanced at her and a brief smile touched his lips. 'I'm not certain but I think I know your father,' he said.

Stunned into silence by his disclosure, Angelique simply stared at him.

'The name is not a common one,' he added when he thought she'd had ample time to digest what he had said. 'Therefore, chances are the Anthony Fordyce I know of is the same one you are looking for.'

'Oh, bloody hell.' The words were expelled from Angelique's lips on a slow exhalation of breath. Her stomach knotted tightly and suddenly she felt a pressing need to urinate. 'Please excuse me,' she said hastily, rising to her feet. 'I must use the lavatory.'

Jock indicated a door at the back of the room and she nodded gratefully before walking quickly in that direction.

By the time she returned to their table she felt much better and told him so.

'I think it was the shock,' she said, sitting down again and picking up the snifter of Calvados which the waiter had brought in her absence. 'I felt as though my whole body had literally turned to water.' She laughed ruefully and sipped the brandy.

'While you were gone I gave the matter some thought,' Jock said, sipping his own brandy. 'I've got no qualms about approaching Sir Anthony on your behalf, but if he denies paternity I don't know how we will be able to judge if he's telling the truth.'

'*Sir* Anthony?' Angelique repeated.

Jock nodded. 'Yes, Sir Anthony Fordyce is a member of the House of Lords,' he said, matter-of-factly. 'Before his retirement from the House of Commons and subsequent knighthood, he served as the MP for a small constituency quite near to Thornbury which – thanks to changes in constituency boundaries – has since been divided up. That's another reason why I'm positive this must be the same man. Having the same name and an ex-constituency less than ten miles from the hotel is a bit more than coincidence, wouldn't you say?'

'Yes, I would,' Angelique breathed. 'Oh, God. What if it's true? What if it is him?' Suddenly she shook her head. 'No, it can't be. To find him just like that would be too easy. Life is just not that simple.'

'Sometimes it is,' Jock said, leaning forward and taking one of her hands in his. He stroked it gently until she stopped trembling. 'Fate has a way of stepping in and lending a helping hand. Putting you and I together like this was perhaps more for your benefit than mine.'

Angelique stared at him wordlessly. Then she glanced down at her hand which still lay in his broad palm. It was time for them to get back to the real business of the evening but thanks to his kindness her fears had almost evaporated.

'Would you mind very much if we went back to the hotel now?' she said.

The long, dark, chauffeur-driven limousine glided elegantly through the familiar London streets and on to the motorway. In the back, Jock pulled Angelique to him and began to kiss her, his hands exploring her gently as he did so.

Angelique's first instinct was to pull away. Then she had to remind herself that this was part of her job. Relaxing a little, she returned his kiss and sighed when a stray hand brushed her nipple through the delicate fabric of her dress. It hardened immediately and she heard Jock utter a low groan of desire.

As though a touch-paper had been lit inside both of them, their tentative caresses turned to passion.

His reaction was a full on, boiling lust for Angelique that drove him to push her down so that she lay flat on the seat with her legs bent and wide apart. The splits at the sides of her dress allowed her to sprawl wantonly, one high-heeled sandal-shod foot making its mark on the pristine leather seat, the other planted firmly on the floor.

'God, you look incredible!' Jock said hoarsely, his eyes unable to leave her body.

Kneeling on the floor between her parted legs, he slowly ran his hands up the insides of her thighs. Angelique moaned and squirmed a little but he didn't stop. When his fingertips reached the gauzy fabric that covered her crotch she shuddered and the gauze darkened where her juices soaked into it. For a moment he was content to simply stroke her mound over the outside of her knickers – his fingers disturbing the curly bush beneath. Then, as the wetness between her legs increased – the dark stain spreading outwards – he felt himself gripped by lust. In a moment his eager hands ripped the

234

insignificant garment away to reveal the full extent of her charms to his avid gaze.

For the briefest moment, Angelique felt stripped of far more than just her underwear. She managed to regain her composure only to feel it slipping quickly away again as Jock's fingers began to explore her blossoming sex. His touch was light yet determined, his fingers prising the soft petals of her sex flesh apart until she was completely spread open and exposed. She could feel her hardened clitoris standing proud, the sensitive bud pulsing with the dull ache of desire. Just below it her vagina itched for his touch and grasped Jock's fingers eagerly when they entered her.

The doubts she'd had about the whole evening receded as fast as water down a plug-hole to be replaced by sheer erotic instinct. Her body moistened and swelled in readiness for sex and moments later she welcomed Jock's hard cock inside her as if it were the most natural thing in the world for her to do.

Outside the hushed confines of the limousine, the unknowing world slid past: trees and houses shadowed by nightfall. Inside the car Angelique and Jock were invisible.

The dark tinted windows did an excellent job, hiding their frenzied coupling from prying eyes. Only the chauffeur caused Angelique the slightest concern. She wondered what he must be thinking, what he could see every time he glanced in the rear-view mirror. And yet, if she was being honest, she didn't really care all that much. She was enjoying Jock and he seemed to be enjoying her well enough. A satisfied client was all that mattered. That and her own fulfilment, of course.

It took very little time before Angelique felt the familiar gathering of erotic sensations that heralded orgasm. With one foot still on the floor, she wound her other leg around Jock's waist and urged him deeper inside her. Her clitoris seemed to scream with passion, the swollen bud rubbing remorselessly against Jock as he thrust and ground.

It was difficult to keep her eyes open. The lids felt too heavy with desire and she conceded to the will of her own body to close them. Without distractions her other senses were heightened. She could feel the soft hide seat beneath her naked buttocks and her clenching hand. Her other arm was thrown carelessly above her head and she grasped at thin air – air which filled her nostrils with a peculiar scent. 'Gentleman's Club' she would call it if she were able to bottle it. The distinct aromas of polished leather and wood predominated, with subtle undertones of male cologne and expensive cigars. As for sounds, these were varied and yet all subtle: a medley of groans and sighs and pleasurable whimpering, the occasional slap of Jock's body against hers, the smooth running of the car engine and the faint sticky sound of the tyres rolling over heat-softened tarmac.

Jock gripped her waist and began to thrust faster, bringing her back to reality and concentrating her mind on the pleasure building between her legs. Urging her pelvis up to meet his thrusts, she gasped and felt the first breath-taking wave of orgasm. In that split second her self-control abandoned her and she lost herself in that one erotic moment. Bright lights exploded, followed by a moment of oblivion. And then they were home, the soft scrunching of gravel beneath the tyres telling her they were back at Thornbury Court.

Hearing the happy sounds coming from the bar as they entered the hotel, a harmonious melody of chattering voices and the chink-chink of glasses, Angelique felt tempted to suggest a night-cap, but Jock clearly had other ideas. Taking her gently but firmly by the elbow he guided her up the staircase and along the hallway to his suite.

He opened the door and stood back while she entered

the elegantly-appointed sitting-room but instead of inviting her to sit he continued straight across the room to a door on the other side.

'Come with me, Angelique,' he said, holding out his hand.

She thought she detected a note of excitement in his voice and knew where they were headed. Suddenly, her legs turned to jelly. Back there in the limousine the sex had been wonderful. Wonderful and totally straight. Now he expected other things. She remembered Deborah's words.

Stage two of their evening was to be the esoteric part, and the prospect made her shudder. Submitting to Jordan was one thing but could she allow Jock to dominate her as readily? And Deborah had mentioned that her companion also enjoyed being dominated. Again, Angelique only had experience of chastising someone with Deborah's help and encouragement, never alone. Could she do it? Was she really up to the challenge?

Jock obviously sensed her hesitancy because he walked back to where she stood and clasped her shoulders lightly. When he touched her she shivered and an enigmatic smile flickered across his face.

'Surely you are not frightened of me, Angelique?' he said.

For a moment she gazed at him in silence and then shook her head. 'Not really,' she replied. 'Not frightened of you. If anyone scares me it is myself.' With an inward sigh of annoyance she realised she shouldn't be telling him this. He was a client, not a lover. She had to remember that.

'Don't forget I have already seen that other side of you, Angelique,' Jock murmured darkly, his fingers tightening around her shoulders. 'And I can't wait to stripe that delectable little arse of yours. I want to hear you beg for it, Angelique. I want to hear you beg.' His voice was low and as deeply shadowed as the unlit room and all she could do was listen in silence. Jock released his grip on her shoulders and took her hand instead. 'Come on now. Let me experience that other Angelique.'

Down in the cellar she was surprised to find that the room allocated to them was not a dungeon as she expected. Instead it had been made to look like a farmyard of some description, with hay bales stacked against one wall and straw littering the stone-flagged floor.

She glanced around, feeling slightly nervous still and unsure what to do next. There were the usual array of whips and other implements on the walls and she was surprised to see a dry-stone wall about five feet long had been built inside the room. It was to the wall that Jock now led her.

'Strip and bend over here,' he said calmly, patting the top of the stones.

Angelique hesitated and then began to unzip her dress. As it slithered down her body she grabbed it hastily to stop it falling to the floor and getting dirty. She glanced up as she folded the dress neatly and draped it over the back of a plain wooden chair. Jock was watching her, his hands once more clasped behind his back, feet planted squarely apart. It was unnerving being watched like that as she undressed. She felt as though she were in the presence of a stranger again, someone whom she didn't know if she could trust.

'All of it,' he said darkly, still staring.

With trembling fingers, she reached behind her and unhooked the bra. Shrugging it from her shoulders, she remained bending forward from the waist as she removed her stockings. Then she straightened up and steeled herself to look back at Jock. Good, his expression seemed to say. Just that. Good.

'What should I do now?' she asked, resisting the urge

to try and cover her nakedness with her hands. His expression had returned to being totally inscrutable and she felt nervous. Nervous and excited.

'I told you,' he said, stepping forward. 'Over the wall.'

On shaking legs she walked over to the wall and bent over it. The cold, harsh stone made her wince. Some of the edges were rough, others sharp. They prodded her flesh and made her feel uncomfortable. She sensed Jock step up behind her and felt his fingers tap her inner thighs. Without a word she moved her feet apart, wider and wider until Jock stopped tapping her.

Embedded somehow in the top of either end of the wall were metal restraints like thick handcuffs, and now Jock stretched her arms apart and snapped the restraints around her wrists. She wriggled helplessly, cursing the unforgiving stone in her mind. As a gesture of thoughtfulness, Jock placed a small, flat pillow beneath her head. Turning her head sideways she rested her face on it and gazed at the far wall where the door to freedom tantalised and tormented her.

He trapped her ankles in similar restraints and it was then she felt the slow build-up to desire. Here she was now, manacled and spread open, her body a willing vessel, nothing more than a plaything for this enigmatic man whom she hardly knew. She couldn't be held responsible though. Oh, no. Her will was not her own any more. It had been handed over to Jock along with her body. Whatever happened now would not be her responsibility, and in its own way that very thought was liberating.

She heard him moving about the room. His leather-soled shoes made a slight scuffling sound on the straw which littered the floor. In her mind's eye she saw him deliberating over the choice of whips and other implements on the far wall and felt her stomach clench with trepidation.

'Tell me you have been a naughty girl, Angelique,' he

said, his voice sounding strangely ominous in the hushed privacy of the cellar.

Her reply came out as little more than a nervous squeak as she told him and her buttocks clenched involuntarily when she heard him approach. Ouch! A slight sting to her left buttock told her he was ready to begin.

'How naughty have you been, Angelique?' he asked, flicking her right buttock with the crop in his hand. 'Very naughty – or extremely naughty?'

She knew what he wanted to hear. 'Extremely naughty, Jock,' she said. 'I've been so naughty I need to be punished badly. I need you to show me the error of my ways.' Closing her eyes tight she held her breath and waited.

There was a thin whistling sound as the crop sliced the air and landed across both buttocks. Angelique flinched but made no sound. It happened again, and then a third time and on this occasion a small whimper broke from her lips. Heedless of the turmoil in her mind, her body was starting to respond as it always did when Jordan chastised her. She could feel the tingling in her labia and the first tell-tale trickle of juices. The moisture tantalised her awakening sex, making the torment harder to bear. Three more times Jock striped her buttocks with the crop and then she felt his fingers stroke her, following the marks on her soft flesh.

His lips pressed against her bottom as a hand snaked between her legs and sought out her clitoris. Deft fingers played with the swollen bud until she began to groan and rock against his hand and mouth. A soft, wet tongue dived between her buttocks and laid a trail from her anus to her vagina, titillating and lapping at her excited flesh. Then he left her. High but certainly not dry, and just on the point of coming.

Her disappointment was audible.

She heard him chuckle. 'Not yet, my dear girl,' he said. 'You must earn it.'

Earn it – how? she wanted to scream, but in the next moment she felt the different, but no less arousing sensation, of a rubber paddle striking her buttocks – and then she knew.

It was only when she was sobbing for release that Jock finally relented and slid his tongue over the desperately swollen folds of her labia.

Nudging her clitoris with the tip of his tongue he felt the young woman shudder, and in the next instant she came in great, wracking waves that made her scream aloud. The piercing sound reverberated around the old stone walls. And as Angelique spasmed around his probing fingers and ground her clitoris against his mouth, Jock recalled certain sounds reminiscent of his childhood. In the old Scottish castle where his family spent their summers, the sound of leather against flesh and the anguished moans of desperation and release had almost been as familiar as the wail of bagpipes. Until he had become old enough to know better, he had believed his mother's claim that it was the wind which was responsible for those sounds.

Rising to his feet, he regarded Angelique as she lay limp and dishevelled, spread-eagled on the wall. Dry-stone walls like this one bounded all the fields on his country estate and it had long been a fantasy of his to put one of them to use like this. Thank the lord for the Thornbury Court Hotel. Without such a facility so many of his fantasies would never have been turned into reality.

Angelique opened her eyes and smiled wanly at Jock. He had unfastened the shackles around her ankles and now he was attending to the ones on her wrists. Her limbs felt stiff and sore and her breasts and stomach stung where the unforgiving stone had chafed the skin. Despite her discomfort, she couldn't deny that the

241

orgasm, or rather series of orgasms, that Jock had finally given her had been totally mind-blowing, and in a moment or two she was sure she would be ready to turn the tables on him.

Groaning a little, she stood up straight and rubbed her body with her hands.

'I say, I'm awfully sorry about that,' Jock said when he saw all the marks on her torso and limbs.

His sudden reversal in demeanour came as a surprise and – just as Angelique was about to assure him that it was okay and she would live – she suddenly had a better idea. Narrowing her eyes, she raised her head to look at him.

'Oh, mark my words, Jock,' she said in a deliberately cold voice. 'You will be sorry. Really sorry.'

It made her smile inside to see how taken aback he was by her own *volte-face*. Gone was the innocent submissive, the wailing, moaning woman who had begged for his hands and mouth. In her place was the other Angelique. The one who showed no mercy.

Stooping down, she picked up the discarded crop from the floor. 'You, boy. Over there. Now!' she rapped out, using the crop to point at the stack of hay bales in the far corner of the room.

For a split second Jock looked as though he were about to demur and then he turned abruptly and walked across the room.

Angelique sighed loudly. 'Not like that. Face me,' she ordered sternly, 'and take off your clothes.' Walking over to him, she stood boldly in front of him, hands on hips, legs apart. Even totally naked she looked and felt in control. Almost fearsome. And by the wondering expression on Jock's face as he stripped his own clothes off, she certainly felt as though she now had the upper hand.

Clicking her tongue against the roof of her mouth in disapproval, Angelique shook her head slowly from side to side. 'Well, well. You are a pathetic article, aren't you?' she said, waiting for Jock to nod in reply. 'Look at this.' Reaching out with the crop she hooked the tip under his limp penis and considered the broad pink organ. 'Shameful,' she said scathingly. 'Totally useless.' Before her very eyes, his cock began to stir, rising and stiffening until she could no longer support it with the end of the crop.

Angelique nodded her head. 'Better,' she said, 'but not good enough. I want that to really be of some use to me. I want your cock to be ultra hard when it goes inside me. Like a rock. Is that understood?'

Smiling at his fervent nod, she flicked the end of the crop across his upper thighs.

Jock groaned.

Feeling confident now, Angelique told him to turn around once again and to bend forward over the stack of hay bales. She winced as he did so, imagining how scratchy the straw must be and in the next instant remembered how much more unforgiving the wall had been to her delicate flesh. The recollection gave her the impetus to strike him hard several times across the buttocks, before bringing the crop down on his shoulders and upper thighs.

At her instigation his legs were spread wide apart and she delighted in watching his balls jiggle each time she hit him and he flinched. Reaching between his thighs, she took the full globes of his testicles in her hand and squeezed them gently. This time he moaned and thrust his buttocks towards her.

'Please,' he gasped hoarsely, 'please punish me, mistress.'

The plea got to her, sending adrenalin coursing through her body. It was time to up the tempo and this time she meant business. Swapping the crop for a tawse she walked back over to him, pressed one hand firmly against the small of his back and administered six of the best to each buttock.

By this time Jock was panting. To her delight his bottom glowed and his balls looked enormous, as though they were about to burst.

Angelique took a step back. 'Stand up, Jock and turn around,' she ordered sternly.

Eagerly, he obeyed and stood upright in his usual stance. Feet hip-width apart, hands behind his back but this time he bowed his head in submission.

For a moment Angelique afforded him the torment of appraising him. His face was now as flushed as his behind, she noticed with a surge of satisfaction and his torso and even his cock were marked with a pattern of tiny scratches left by the straw. Kneeling down in front of him, she took the hard shaft between her fingers and regarded it thoughtfully. A quick glance up to his face told her how much he was enjoying the shame of her treatment of him and a small droplet of viscous fluid oozing from the tip of his glans confirmed her thoughts.

Making sure that he was watching her first, Angelique licked her full, pouting lips as suggestively as she could and was gratified to hear another heart-wrenching groan.

'That's my, Jock,' she said softly. 'What a good boy you are. Now, how hard are you going to get for me?'

Between her fingers his cock twitched and hardened still further. With the pointed tip of her tongue she licked at the drop of fluid, tasted it as though it was a new wine and nodded approvingly. His cock twitched again and seemed to strain towards her.

So far everything had gone like clockwork, but now she wondered what to do next. For a fleeting moment she wished she had a script of some kind. It was all very well to find out about her dominant tendencies but she was more practically inclined than creative. Suddenly, a stray piece of string that had bound one of the hay bales caught her eye and she picked it up and threaded it through her fingers as she contemplated the situation. She was struck by a flash of inspiration. Taking the string, she tied one end quite loosely around Jock's shaft, held the other end and rose to her feet.

'Come on,' she said, tugging on the string as though it was a leash. 'Come with me.'

To Jock's humiliation, she forced him to bear the indignity of being led along by his cock and to his further shame they ran into several other A-list guests along the various passage-ways. It was obvious that for him it was a gloriously horrendous experience and by the time they reached the door to his suite, his face was almost puce – a shade that matched the colour of his swollen glans exactly.

This time when Angelique and Jock fucked, Angelique was in total control. Having untied his cock she grasped it firmly with one hand and led him over to the bed by it. Once there she pushed him back so that he sprawled awkwardly on the chintz coverlet.

'Don't move,' she said, climbing astride him.

Just as she hovered over him she paused. The experience had made her feel as hot and as ready as she had felt earlier. Perhaps even more so. Which made her wonder, just for a moment, if her body actually had any sexual limits? Slipping a hand between her legs, she felt the proof of her arousal for herself and gasped with astonishment as she realised just how wet and swollen she really was. Her vagina was awash with her own juices and the flesh around it as tender as a ripe peach.

Moving further up Jock's body she straddled his shoulders and ordered him to look at her. 'Can you see how excited I am?' she asked hoarsely, feeling a fresh surge of excitement as he trained his gaze on her swollen sex. 'Look how much I need a man like you. How much I need your strong, hard cock.' The very thought made her stomach clench in excitement.

She groaned with encouragement as she felt Jock's

fingers replace her own, stroking and probing until she was rocking and grinding her pelvis against his hands.

'Yes. Oh, God, yes!' She gasped as she felt the pad of his thumb slick back and forth across her swollen clitoris on a thin film of her own juices. The torment was unbearable and yet she hardly wanted it to stop. It was so exquisite. Gratification for the sake of gratification. If this was to be a regular part of her job at Thornbury Court, she could easily see herself becoming a workaholic.

Chapter Fifteen

'Here we are sir, I hope you enjoyed your stay,' said Christina, tearing off the printout of Jock's receipt, separating the copies and handing him the top one.

'I certainly did enjoy it and I plan to be back again very soon,' he said, smiling at the familiar blonde girl behind the reception desk. 'Although the next time I won't be coming to stay, more's the pity. Just to report on my success or otherwise as an angel of mercy.'

Christina stared at him blankly. 'I don't– ' she began, but he interrupted her with just the gentlest of touches of his hand upon her bare arm.

'I promised Angelique I would try to do something for her,' he said. 'I just hope I am successful.' He paused and glanced around the otherwise deserted reception area. 'That reminds me, is Jordan around? I wouldn't mind having a quick word with him before I go.'

Christina nodded and pointed to the door on her right. 'Yes, I think so. You'll find his office through there. First door on the right.'

'Yes, I know,' Jock assured her. Then, turning on his usual charm full blast, he gave her his most winning smile and added, 'By the way, Christina, did I mention you look particularly lovely today? I must say this place seems to have the monopoly on fine-looking women. The rest of Buckinghamshire is drab in comparison.'

As if to add weight to his blatant flattery, at that precise moment Liz and Polly both sauntered in from outside, looking like a pair of English roses – positively blooming and freshly plucked from the garden. He raised his eyebrows as if to say, 'see what I mean?', making Christina giggle. Flashing an interested look in Christina's and Jock's direction, the other two girls giggled themselves and shared a knowing glance. Although they looked as though they were dying to linger, they continued through reception and into the dining-room.

As soon as they had gone, Jock gave Christina a broad wink and said that he was off to find Jordan, adding that if Angelique should put in an appearance before he left he would be pleased if she would join him for elevenses.

If he could have seen Angelique right at that moment, Jock would have known instantly that there was no way she would be surfacing in time for elevenses, or even lunch for that matter. Thoroughly exhausted from her night with him, she still lay fast asleep snoring gently, her satiated body loosely wrapped in a cream-coloured satin sheet.

When she finally awoke it was with a long, luxurious stretch and a yawn which a moment later turned into a guilty glance at the clock by the bedside. It was almost four o'clock. She had slept the whole day away. Stumbling out of bed and into the shower, she felt the last vestiges of sleepiness ebb away to be replaced by a ravenous hunger of a non-sexual kind. Ignoring the temptation to ring for room-service and go back to bed, and covered only by a towel, she darted down the corridor to her own suite where she quickly pulled on a pair of jeans and a cropped white T-shirt, before going downstairs in search of food.

Having rummaged through the cold produce fridge, she came up with a platter of cold cuts and cheeses, to which she added a generous heap of mixed salad leaves. Then she poured herself a tall glass of iced tea, put the whole lot on a tray and took it out to the terrace where she sat and ate and enjoyed the last rays of the afternoon sun.

She was just reclining in a white, wrought-iron chair, eyes closed and on the point of dozing off, when footsteps sounded behind her and a shadow fell across her face. Opening one eye she saw her visitor was Jordan.

'Hi,' she said softly, a smile lighting up her eyes, 'I was wondering if I would see you today.'

Pulling up a chair, he sat, rested his elbows on the table top and cupped his chin in his hands. 'I thought I might have to come and drag you out of bed,' he teased. 'Lesley said she couldn't make up Jock's suite because you were still in there.'

'Oh, gosh, sorry,' Angelique said, struggling to sit up straight. 'I missed our picnic.'

Jordan smiled and put a comforting hand on her arm. 'Don't apologise. From what Jock told me this morning, a lie-in is the least you deserve.'

Angelique glanced at him warily. 'Was he happy with things?' she asked. To her relief Jordan nodded, and so she added, 'And what about you, are you okay?'

His nonchalant shrug didn't fool her for a minute. 'Why shouldn't I be okay?' he said. 'You did an excellent job which resulted in a very satisfied customer.'

Inhaling deeply, Angelique let out the breath as a long, slow sigh. 'I thought you might regret allowing me to entertain Jock.'

Jordan pursed his lips before speaking. 'I didn't *allow* you, Angelique,' he said. 'You are a free woman. Free to know your own mind and make your own decisions.'

'So it didn't bother you?'

There was a moment's silence. 'I wouldn't say that exactly.'

'So it did bother you. Why didn't you say something?'

Infuriatingly, he shrugged again.

Leaning forward across the table, Angelique took his hands and squeezed them. 'I want you to know that I have decided to stay here, Jordan,' she said, gazing resolutely at him, trapping his attention. 'At least for the foreseeable future. Oh, I know it was only supposed to be a temporary arrangement, while I sorted myself out mentally. But to be honest I like it here. I like the place. I like the people. I like you . . .'

She broke off and tried to force a smile that wouldn't come. Instead, tears sprang to her eyes and she cursed their unwelcome appearance. She was trying to be more adult than she had ever been and yet the stupid, stupid drops trickling down her cheeks were making her look like an idiot.

Leaning forward, Jordan licked the salty drops from her face and Angelique sighed softly.

'I'm glad you have decided to stay,' he murmured, sitting back.

She glanced down at the table top where her hands still held his. Flexing his fingers, Jordan entwined them with hers and pulled her towards him. Their lips touched and instantly Angelique felt all her doubts and fears melt away.

'I do believe you mean that,' she replied softly to his earlier comment when the kiss ended. 'And strangely enough I believe that in your own way you love me.'

Jordan smiled and kissed her again, just lightly. 'I do love you, Angelique. I always have but now it is in a different way to before. Having said that, I don't want to change the way I am, or the way I live my life. Next to you, Thornbury Court is the most important thing in the world to me. I have to feel free to run it the way I always have.'

His words made Angelique's stomach clench, and yet she knew deep down how strongly he felt. And after her experience with Jock the previous night she could hardly claim not to understand how Jordan managed to separate 'work' sex from the other kind. The kind they enjoyed together.

'I don't want to run your life, Jordan,' she said slowly. 'No more than I expect you to run mine. We are two separate people who happen to like each other, respect each other and really enjoy each other's company.'

'And who love to fuck each other,' Jordan added with a lecherous twinkle in his eye. 'Don't forget the most important part of our relationship.'

Excitement sizzled through her as he spoke and the way he looked at her made her insides turn to jelly. 'How could I forget?' she murmured. 'I will never forget the way we fuck as long as I live.'

There followed a long moment when the two of them simply gazed at each other in silence. The minds of each were filled with a maelstrom of conflicting thoughts, their bodies struggling with a range of feelings that made them feel both fearful and excited. At that moment all either of them wanted to do was ravish the other, but then the thread of erotic tension between them was unexpectedly broken by the appearance of Deborah.

Stopping a few yards away, the red-head held her hand up to her ear in a familiar gesture.

'I guess that means I'm wanted on the phone,' Jordan said, leaping to his feet.

Angelique sighed. 'That's the price I have to pay for being in love with a very busy man.' She smiled softly as he seemed to waver. 'Go,' she ordered. 'Get lost before I throw you down on the grass and fuck you right here and now.'

Glancing over his shoulder, Jordan gave her a cheeky

wink. 'Yes, mistress Angelique,' he said. 'Whatever you say.'

For the next few days Angelique found herself too wrapped up in the diverse concerns of everyday life to think about Jock's promise to speak to Sir Anthony, so she was surprised when he called her to say he had arranged a meeting.

'Already?' she gasped into the receiver. Her heart was beating fast and she had to struggle to control her breathing. She felt nauseous and a small hammer started to beat inside her head. Anxiety had well and truly taken hold.

Unaware of the emotion he had stirred up, Jock's voice was deep and smooth. 'The thing is, Angelique,' he said. 'When I told him about you he didn't attempt to deny anything. That can only mean he believes there is a good possibility he is your natural father.'

Angelique shook her head as if trying to clear it. She was amazed by the way things were falling into place. 'God! I don't know what to think. Or what to say,' she said. 'Except that I'm scared shitless.'

A peal of laughter rumbled down the phone. 'You are priceless, Angelique,' Jock said when the laughter ceased. 'For such a beautiful, delicate-looking woman, you have a very dirty mouth.'

Although he couldn't see her expression, Angelique grinned cheekily. 'You should know, Jock,' she said.

He laughed again and she waited until he stopped before asking him when and where the meeting was to take place.

'Here at Westminster,' he said. 'I'd like to invite you and Jordan to be my guests for drinks on the terrace. I shall send a couple of passes over to you by courier and expect to see you this evening at six o'clock.'

Angelique's head whirled and her body went into

overdrive, clenching, trembling and hammering for all it was worth. 'So soon!' she gasped.

In contrast, Jock's voice was clear and calm. 'Yes, it has to be I'm afraid. Sir Anthony is off to the Bahamas tomorrow morning on a fact-finding mission – at least that's what he claims – and then we'll be into summer recess. It's now or never, I'm afraid.'

Thankfully, Angelique managed to find her voice. 'Oh, God, Jock. Don't apologise,' she said earnestly. 'It's absolutely brilliant of you to set this up. Don't worry, Jordan and I will be there.' It was only after she put the phone down that she stopped to wonder why Jordan was invited at all.

Even if she hadn't been about to meet the man who was probably her natural father, Angelique would have found her visit to Westminster an unforgettable experience. Running almost the whole length of the building, the classic elegance of the terrace was reminiscent of the much smaller one at Thornbury Court. She said as much to Jordan, which made him laugh.

'We could barely accommodate one of those little igloo tents on our terrace,' he said, 'let alone all these marquees.'

Angelique followed his glance along the line of the building where a number of huge marquees had been erected to provide covered dining facilities. Then she glanced over to the bar where the well-heeled clientele stood at least three deep. Most of them were men who were vying with each other to attract the attention of the bar staff by waving ten and twenty pound notes in the air.

'I wish our bar was that busy,' she commented. 'Then our money problems would be well and truly over.' She glanced up at Jordan, noticing how his face seemed to cloud over for a moment. 'What is it?' she asked.

Jordan bowed his head and gave her a long searching

253

look. Then, just as it seemed he was about to say something, they were interrupted by the sudden appearance of Jock. Looking as bright and breezy as ever, he was accompanied by a much older gentleman – white-haired and portly, with a thick handlebar moustache.

'Jordan, Angelique, I'd like you to meet Sir Anthony Fordyce,' Jock said.

Angelique thought his smile was a shade too bright and all at once a range of emotions flared up inside her. Clenching her fists and her jaw simultaneously she battled to control her feelings. With a tight smile she nodded at Sir Anthony, and then Jock.

If their host noticed anything amiss he didn't refer to it. Instead, he led them to a table which directly overlooked the Thames and then took their orders for drinks. While Angelique stared blankly ahead at the dark, greasy water, Jordan attempted to make small-talk with Sir Anthony.

Although the others didn't realise it, keeping his own emotions in check right at that moment was the hardest thing Jordan had ever had to do. The day before he had discovered that Sir Anthony Fordyce was on the board of the merchant bank which controlled the Thornbury Court fortunes. It was the smug-looking bastard seated next to him who had been causing all the problems.

Angelique was dying to say something. From the corner of her eye she studied the man who had given her life and yet could see nothing familiar about him at all. In her daydreams she had been expecting a tearful reunion. Not quite the flinging herself into his arms to cries of, 'Daddy, Daddy!' type of reunion, but something no far off. She had at least expected him to say something, to suggest some kind of explanation. Instead, he accepted the offer of a cigar from a passing colleague, cut the end with a pair of clippers, lit it and reclined casually in a haze of acrid smoke.

You bastard! she found herself thinking. You horrible, self-satisfied bastard!

Jock returned with a tray of drinks and successfully shattered both Angelique's and Jordan's similar trains of thought by putting it down on the table with a noisy clatter.

'Sorry chaps,' he said, grinning. 'The bloody place is packed today. I thought we would all die of thirst.'

Despite her negative feelings, Angelique couldn't help smiling at his cheerful exaggeration. Reaching forward she helped herself to a tall, frosted glass of gin and tonic. As she raised it to her lips the ice chinked merrily, reminding her of all the other times she had enjoyed a similar drink, but under different circumstances.

Having made sure that everyone had the drink they ordered, Jock sat in the only vacant chair and glanced from Jordan to Angelique, and then at Sir Anthony. The revered member of the House of Lords was still puffing away on his cigar, apparently oblivious to the tense atmosphere surrounding him.

'Sir Anthony,' Jock began, 'you recall why I invited you here today?'

The other man nodded and gazed across the table at Angelique who – to her frustration and annoyance – blushed deeply.

'You believe you have some sort of paternity claim against me?' he said, his eyes narrowing as he exhaled a cloud of smoke.

For a moment Angelique stared back at him in silence and then she spoke so calmly that she amazed herself. 'I have no claim to make against you, Sir. I believe you are my natural father and all I want is confirmation – to know who I am.'

Sir Anthony nodded gravely. 'Understandable, I suppose,' he said, rather too blithely for her liking. 'But I don't want any of this leaking out. If the press gets wind of a scandal they'll have a field-day.'

Jordan looked up and gave him a sideways glance. 'The threat of a scandal wouldn't have anything to do with your efforts to force the closure of Thornbury Court, would it?'

Both Jock and Angelique looked amazed, especially when Sir Anthony nodded. 'Frankly, yes,' he said. 'I've lived with the threat for too long but I always thought I'd covered my tracks well enough. However, just lately one of the tabloids seems to have been gunning for me and some of their questions have been coming a little too close to the truth for comfort.'

Jordan's stony expression told Angelique that he had been harbouring such suspicions for some time.

Desperate to get everything out in the open at long last, she managed to compose herself and turned to look at her 'father' again. 'You were a guest at the hotel – one of the A-list?' she said, her question sounding more like a statement of fact.

'True,' Sir Anthony replied, picking up the tumbler of whisky in front of him. 'I used to be a regular in the old days and your mother was one of my favourites.' He paused to sip his drink and then frowned. 'Pregnancy was never part of the equation. It was supposed to be all fun and games but I suppose accidents do happen.'

Angelique glared at him. 'And I suppose I was one of those unfortunate accidents?' she said thinly.

Instinctively, Jordan put out his hand and grasped hers for which she flashed him a brief smile of gratitude. All eyes turned back to Sir Anthony.

'I would be lying if I denied it,' he stated, matter-of-factly. 'But the then owners of Thornbury Court had every angle covered. The private nursing home dealt with everything calmly and efficiently and never once did anyone there try to pass judgement, or threaten my request for anonymity. Then Harvey Hemsley, one of the directors of the nursing home, stepped in and suggested that he would make an excellent adoptive father for the baby – that was you, Angelique,' he added needlessly, nodding in her direction.

'So my father – I mean Harvey – was involved with the nursing home,' Angelique mused aloud. 'Well, that makes sense. In fact, that makes sense of a lot of things.'

She could see the whole thing clearly now. Whereas her blood father and mother had not wanted the burden of an illegitimate baby, Harvey and later her adoptive mother, certainly had. Now the realisation that she had been wanted and loved for all the right reasons really struck home and made tears spring to her eyes.

'Are you okay, Angelique?' Jordan said softly, squeezing her hand.

Jock rummaged in his jacket pocket and brought out a clean white handkerchief which he handed to her. Accepting it gratefully, she gave both men a watery smile as she dabbed at her tear-streaked cheeks.

Sir Anthony looked uncomfortable in the midst of so much emotion. Having summoned a stray barman and imperiously ordered another round of drinks, he patted his pockets, longing to find a pack of cigarettes about his person. Finally he unearthed a battered pack of Dunhills and offered them around. To everyone's surprise Angelique took one.

'I know I don't smoke but I just feel as though I need one right at this moment,' she explained to no one in particular. Leaning forward, she allowed Sir Anthony to light the cigarette for her, then she sat back and exhaled a slow stream of smoke. 'That's not bad,' she said, attempting a smile.

For the first time that evening Sir Anthony also smiled. 'Now we have met I don't want you to be a stranger,' he said to Angelique. 'I think I can trust you to be discreet. I daresay you have a few questions you would like to ask?'

'Just a few,' she replied, laughing and coughing at the same time. Glaring at the cigarette, she stubbed it out in the ashtray. 'But I won't bother you with them yet. For now I'm just happy to know who I am and where I come from. And you can rely on my utmost discretion.'

Satisfied with her answer, Sir Anthony turned to Jordan. 'About the hotel,' he began but Jordan interrupted him.

'The problem is already solved,' he said. 'Yesterday I arranged for our account with your bank to be closed and funds to be transferred to our new bank.' Ignoring Angelique's look of surprise he added, 'I could have used the threat of leaking your story to the press as an insurance policy against the hotel's future but I don't do business that way. Nor would I dream of causing Angelique any hurt or embarrassment. I hope you will agree that, under the circumstances, it is better if we kept our financial concerns free of any personal involvement. Particularly as Angelique is about to become an equal partner in Thornbury Court.'

Knowing how astonished Angelique would be by this unexpected revelation, Jordan threw her a casual glance. She looked suitably amazed – eyes wide, mouth wider still. Capturing her gaze with his own, he smiled and nodded slowly.

'That's right,' he said, still staring at her, 'on the day you told me you had decided to stay, I resolved to give you enough of my shares so that from now on we can be equal partners all the way down the line.'

Angelique was still struck dumb. She wanted to say thank you. She wanted to say that she would be more than happy to pay for the shares – or invest the money in the hotel if he wouldn't take it. She wanted to say that this was the happiest day of her life and that she loved him, and Jock, and even Sir Anthony. But all she did was nod and try to swallow the huge lump in her throat.

The sound of Jock clapping his hands together startled everyone out of their own private reverie. 'Well, well, jolly good show all round, I'd say,' he boomed jovially. 'I think this calls for a drop of bubbly.'

Sir Anthony thanked him hastily but said he had a prior engagement. Jordan and Angelique also tried to demur.

'Nonsense, I won't hear of you two leaving yet,' Jock insisted, pushing Jordan back down again when he tried to stand up. 'We'll have one bottle here and then I'll take you on to a little Italian place I know in Soho where they make excellent Kir Royales and serve the most delicious pasta.'

Angelique found her mouth was watering and murmured to Jordan that she'd like to accept Jock's invitation.

As Sir Anthony got up to leave, Jock took him aside for a quick word about a new piece of legislation that was to be voted on the next day. Meanwhile, Jordan pulled Angelique into his arms and, heedless of the interested stares all around them, kissed her very thoroughly. He only stopped when Jock's voice interrupted them.

'I say you two, can't you wait for the pasta? You're nearly eating each other alive.'

Chapter Sixteen

*B*y the time Jordan and Angelique arrived back at Thornbury Court it was well past midnight. Angelique seemed high on a combination of relief and champagne. Even Jordan was slightly more inebriated than usual. Well, it wasn't every day he managed to get his life one hundred per cent right.

'Bed for you, young lady,' he said sternly, smacking Angelique on the bottom as they walked across the darkened reception area.

Giggling, Angelique stumbled and pouted up at him. 'I'm not tired.'

'Do you mean not tired, or not too tired?'

'Not too tired, of course.' She giggled again and then hiccuped. Clapping a hand over her mouth, she stared up at him wide-eyed. 'I know, let's make a film,' she said suddenly. Grabbing his hand she pulled him towards the door that led to the cellar steps.

Jordan looked stunned. 'A film?'

'Yeah,' Angelique slurred as she nodded fervently, her hand fumbling with the door handle. 'One of Fergus' videos. I assume you know how to work the equipment?'

'I know how to work *all* my equipment,' Jordan said

in an ironic tone which increased Angelique's giggles.
'Just, for God's sake shut up a bit or you'll wake the
entire hotel.'

Looking immediately guilty, she put an unsteady
finger to her lips. 'I won't make a sound,' she promised,
rattling the door like a box of old nails as she opened it,
missing the way Jordan winced.

Down in the depths of the cellar everywhere seemed
deserted. Angelique was wearing a floral-patterned sun-
dress which reached her ankles and – being more than a
little drunk – every so often she caught the toe of her
sandal in the hem and nearly tripped up. Each time this
happened she clutched wildly at Jordan and giggled
some more.

'Oh, shit! Sorry, Jordan,' she hissed loudly when it
happened for the fifth time, nearly falling flat on her
face. Only his quick reflexes saved her.

'Are you sure you wouldn't rather go to bed, Angelique?' he said in a patient tone. 'Under the circumstances I think it would be safer.'

It came as no surprise to him that she shook her head
determinedly. 'No way! I want to make a film. I've got
this lovely, luscious bod,' she began immodestly, unbut-
toning the front of her dress as she spoke, 'and I'm damn
well going to have it immortalised on celluloid.'

Jordan stifled a smile. 'Video-tape,' he corrected.

'Oh, yes. Video-tape.'

Angelique smiled up at him at that moment and the
sight made his heart and stomach clench simultaneously.
She looked lovely. Half-cut, but lovely. A heady combination of innocent and whore, virgin and voluptuary.
That, and the way she pouted so prettily at him was
enough to make his cock explode.

As he pushed open the door to the 'film studio', Jordan
was surprised to find the room suffused in a soft rosy
glow. Usually that meant filming was underway and yet
he couldn't recall anyone booking the room for that

evening. As far as he was aware, the only A-list guests staying at the hotel were a couple of Swiss businessmen and their boyfriends. All of whom preferred to keep their activities confined to their own twin-bedroomed suite.

Angelique followed in his wake, still stumbling from time to time and squinting to adjust her blurred vision. 'Hell, I must be drunker than I thought, Jordan,' she gasped in panic. 'I can't see properly.'

He laughed softly. 'Relax. It's only the lighting. Someone hasn't shut things off after them.' He made a mental note to speak to Fergus about it in the morning. If the young gardener hadn't actually been involved in the filming, he would know who had. Dismissing all other thoughts from his mind, he turned to Angelique and gave her a wolfish grin. 'Come here, my lusty little wench,' he said. Reaching out, he pulled her acquiescent body into his arms and started to explore it with his hands and mouth.

Groaning with pleasure, she allowed her head to drop back so that she could accept the trail of butterfly kisses he laid down the length of her throat. As his fingers plucked at the buttons on the front of her dress she arched her back in delight. And as she did so, the material parted and fell away from her body, exposing her near nakedness to his hungry gaze. All she wore underneath was the skimpiest of bras in light blue silk and a matching pair of bikini pants.

The lightest of touches sent the silk skimming across the pliant flesh beneath, her nipples reacting with obvious pleasure to the delightful sensation. As Jordan stroked his fingertips over and around her breasts she strained towards him, her breasts swelling with arousal, the hard buds of her nipples forcing themselves against the fragile fabric.

Going down on bended knee before her, Jordan began to suck at her distended nipples. Soon the silk became wet and dark where his mouth worked her desperate body.

Despite feeling light-headed, Angelique couldn't help her frustration at the fact that he tantalised her so slowly and yet she couldn't deny that the piquancy of his caresses added a further dimension to her enjoyment. When release finally came it would be explosive. She knew it and shivered with anticipation.

By the time she was panting with reined-in desire, Jordan's mouth left her breasts and began to lay a trail of wet, sucking kisses down the length of her torso. His tongue lingered at her navel, the pointed tip swirling around and around the inside, gathering up her nerve endings in a tight bundle and tweaking her sex. Instantly, it blossomed in response and a tell-tale wetness soaked the ineffectual crotch of her silk knickers.

Glancing up at her, the expression of Jordan's face told her that he knew the extent of her arousal. There was a sullen wickedness to the look in his eyes, his pupils dilating with desire to turn the irises a dark navy. And as he tipped his head back slightly, she noticed, with a thrill of lascivious excitement, that his lips were curved in a devilish grin.

'Sit,' he said, pointing to a low, wide divan heaped with satin-covered pillows. 'I need to set up the camera.'

Feeling somewhat disappointed at the interruption, Angelique made a slight pout but didn't try to persuade him otherwise. She had insisted she wanted to make a film. Now it served her right that Jordan invariably indulged her every whim. On trembling legs she crossed the room and paused in front of the divan to remove her dress. Tossing it carelessly on to a nearby chair, she sat and reclined gracefully against the pillows. She parted her legs and bent one knee so that she deliberately offered a tantalising glimpse of her burgeoning sex to Jordan when he returned.

He had gone into an ante-room but reappeared almost

immediately with a camera, lights and tripod. To Angelique's surprise he also had Christina in tow.

'Look who I found fast asleep in the other room,' he said, nodding at the diminutive blonde whose slight form was draped in an outsized robe of oyster satin.

Angelique stared as Christina smiled sleepily and raised a hand. The satin sleeve slipped back down her arm to the crook of her elbow.

'Hi, Angelique,' she said huskily. 'I was taking part in session with a couple of special guests who checked in on the spur of the moment. I guess I must have fallen asleep afterwards.' She glanced from Angelique to Jordan and it was as if she suddenly realised she was intruding. 'Sorry, folks. I didn't mean to interrupt.'

Tightening the belt around her waist, she gathered up the front of the long robe in her hands and turned for the door. To her own surprise Angelique found herself denying the interruption and inviting Christina to sit beside her instead. If Jordan was surprised he said nothing but occupied himself with arranging the lighting and fixing the video camera to the tripod while the two young women spoke in low voices.

It had been almost a week since Angelique last had the chance to talk to Christina properly. The most they had shared was the odd wave, or hello, executed in passing as Angelique dashed through reception on the way to somewhere else. And even then, since the night they had spent together, neither of them had dared to allow their conversation to stray into 'dodgy' territory. There was too much of a risk that the other felt embarrassed about what had happened and didn't want to admit to it. Both women were tough in their own way and yet sensitive creatures. To inadvertently hurt the other was the last thing either of them wanted.

'I take it you and Jordan came in here to make a video?' Christina said, settling back against the soft pillows.

Angelique couldn't help noticing how the front of Christina's robe fell open as she reclined, revealing almost the whole of one luscious pink tipped breast.

'Yes,' she replied, clearing her throat and glancing down at her hands. 'Although it was my idea rather than Jordan's.'

'You surprise me.' Christina raised an eyebrow and Angelique laughed.

'I hardly like to flatter myself but I think he has met his match,' she said.

'Jordan – met his match?' Christina countered. 'I don't think so.'

'Want a bet?' Angelique winked and deliberately made sure that Jordan was looking in their direction before leaning forward and planting a soft kiss on the exposed side of Christina's breast. To her delight Christina sighed softly and shifted slightly beneath her. Somewhere to her left, Angelique thought she detected the sound of a muffled groan.

'Is that video camera set up yet, Jordan?' Angelique asked without looking at him. Instead she moved on to her knees and parted the front of Christina's robe properly, so that both her firm young breasts were exposed. Her touch was all knowing as she cupped the breasts in her hands and began to play with the nipples.

As she bowed her head to take one of the distended nipples in her mouth, Angelique sensed Jordan sit beside them on the divan. In a moment his hands were unfastening the catch on her bra and pulling it away from her body. Hardly liking to be interrupted when Christina was obviously enjoying the attention so much, Angelique manoeuvred herself so that she could shrug the bra away and similarly dispose of her silky knickers.

Still with her lips and fingers arousing Christina's breasts, Angelique felt her own passion flame as Jordan's fingers began to imitate her caresses. Massaging, pinching and pulling at her sensitive teats, Jordan quickly

brought her to a state of panting desperation. She wanted
– no, needed – to feel his fingers between her legs. He
would not have to coax an orgasm from her. She was
already on the brink of complete arousal.

Feeling devilishly daring, she stopped caressing Christina's breasts and instead began to fumble with the tie
belt, loosening the knot until it was undone completely.
As she suspected, Christina wore nothing beneath the
robe, and Angelique's questing fingers dived between
her parted thighs to investigate the moist folds of her
friend's vulva.

She was soaking! Angelique noticed as her fingertips
slid over the glossy flesh. And it was only with a slight
twinge of envy that she saw one of Jordan's hands slide
between Christina's thighs to investigate the phenom-
enon for himself.

As they both masturbated the girl, Angelique glanced
sideways at him and smiled. Their fingers jousted with
each other as they probed deeper, further, inciting an
anguished wail of ecstasy from their partner. Then
Jordan slid his fingers over Angelique's and together
they sank their digits into the hot chasm of Christina's
vagina. Twisting and turning, their fingers stimulated
the sensitive velvety walls, their thumbs simultaneously
seeking the swollen nub of her clitoris.

Christina bucked her hips, hoarse screams emanating
from her as Angelique and Jordan brought her swiftly to
orgasm between them. To quieten her and to add to the
pleasure, Angelique pressed her lips against Christina's
berry-soft mouth and tasted her sweetness as Jordan
removed his fingers and sank them deep into her own
vagina instead.

Now it was Angelique's turn to buck and squirm.
Jordan was a master at stimulation. A master at everything. There was no sensation he couldn't wring from
her greedy body. No excitement too great for him to
arouse. Every lascivious thought she had ever had shot

through her mind at that moment. Every dark, sinful desire coursed through her until she felt the first blinding pleasure-pain of her climax. With total abandon she screamed out, relinquishing Christina's lips so that she could throw back her head, open her mouth wide and give full vent to her passion.

For Angelique, sensation heaped upon sensation at the hands of her two lovers. Holding tight to her nipples were Christina's fingers. The slender tips squeezing the tender flesh hard, then harder still. Further below, between her widespread legs, Jordan's hands were still at work. His fingers guiding her skilfully towards a second earth-shattering climax. Losing all sense of self-consciousness, Angelique arched her back and thrust her body lewdly at both of them.

'Fuck me!' she cried into the sex-laden atmosphere. 'Hurt me. Make me come.'

Within moments she felt the familiar hardness of Jordan's cock nudging the hot, swollen entrance to her body. And in the next instant, Christina squirmed her lithe body around and Angelique felt the first exquisite touch of the other woman's tongue upon her desperate clitoris.

'Oh, God, yes!' Angelique cried out and tried to buck her hips only to find that her body belonged to Jordan and Christina.

Even if she wanted it, there was no escape from the dual onslaught of pleasure. Behind her, Jordan knelt and thrust rhythmically into her vagina, his strong thumbs spreading her buttocks apart as he held her. While Christina had command of her clitoris, her tongue straining upwards to tease the swollen nub of flesh. Hot, lustful waves of orgasmic pleasure swept over Angelique – waves that took a long time to ebb away. And when they did, she struggled to open her eyes and saw that Christina's body squirmed with unsatiated desire.

Taking her weight on her forearms, Angelique bent

her head to nuzzle the soft, blonde fluff that covered Christina's mound. It made her smile that Christina automatically bent her legs and urged her pelvis up, her silent plea deafening. Flicking out her tongue, Angelique insinuated the pointed tip between the puffy folds of her friend's labia and instantly discovered the tiny, cock-like swelling that lay hidden beneath. She swirled her tongue around and around the stem, delighting in the way Christina imitated her, her own clitoris responding as though she was licking herself.

It was the strangest and most wonderful of moments and one Angelique half-hoped would never end. Oh, to spend her days and nights in the grip of such bliss, she thought. To have not only Jordan but Christina with whom to take her pleasure. At Thornbury Court the possibilities for sexual gratification were endless.

Now, more than ever before, she knew her decision to stay had been the right one. She would write to her mother and explain everything. And she would write to François. But she couldn't imagine herself going back to France. At least not for the foreseeable future. Her home, her life was here in England now. Here at Thornbury Court with the people she loved and who, she knew, loved her.

'I am very happy you have decided to stay,' Jordan said the following morning as they lay in her bed, legs lazily entwined in the aftermath of yet another bout of love-making.

She smiled contentedly up at him, her hand stroking a delicate trail back and forth across his chest. 'I don't think anyone could feel happier than I do right at this moment. Or every minute of every day come to that,' she murmured. 'Thornbury Court is where I belong. It always felt like home when Harvey was alive and now it truly is my home.' She paused and frowned slightly as she remembered something.

'What is it, Angelique?' Jordan asked quickly. He didn't like to see the light die in her eyes, not for one moment.

Shaking her head briskly, she assured him it was nothing important. 'I was just remembering your offer to make me a full partner,' she said. 'You know I can't possibly let you give me your shares. I must buy them. Let me put the money into the hotel if you won't take it personally.'

Jordan knew Angelique too well to bother arguing with her. 'That's up to you,' he conceded. 'I don't want the money, but I have been thinking a swimming pool would be a great addition to the hotel's facilities. Just think of it, floating lazily on hot summer days, a good book in one hand and a glass of Pimms in the other.'

Angelique's eyes twinkled wickedly. 'I was thinking more of a cock in one hand and– ' She was forced to break off as Jordan pushed her on to her back and entered her swiftly.

'Never mind a cock in your hand,' he growled with mock ferocity. 'This is where my cock belongs and don't you forget it.' He stroked the rim of her vagina as he spoke and allowed one finger to join his penis inside her.

Immediately, Angelique spread her legs wide and squirmed her pelvis against him. This was the life, she thought. Pleasure, sex, work, money, fun. Everything she had ever wanted now comprised her life and she never wanted it to end.

By the end of the summer season Angelique was convinced that her decision to stay had been the right one. Her relationships with Jordan and Christina had gone from strength to strength and she had even begun to take a more active part in the entertainment side of the hotel's activities – chastising the erstwhile schoolboy 'Bobby' and occasionally joining Moira O'Donnell and her son-in-law were two of her favourite scenarios.

With the benefit of hindsight, she realised the night she spent with Jock had been just a taste of what was to come. And Deborah was a very good teacher. Now Angelique could wield the whip along with the best of them. At her instigation, many men had been reduced to quivering wrecks. All in the pursuit of pleasure, of course. The recollection made her smile.

'I dread to think what's going through your mind right at this moment.'

Angelique jumped guiltily as Jordan's voice broke through her reverie. Blushing furiously she smiled back at him and had just opened her mouth to reply when she noticed he was not alone.

'Martin Wreathe!' she exclaimed, in surprise. 'It's great to see you again. What brings you to our neck of the woods?'

The older man heaved his bulk on to a bar stool beside her and clicked his fingers in the direction of the barman before replying to Angelique's question.

'Two things really,' he said. 'One was to see if that housekeeper of yours is around. I wouldn't mind buying her a drink. And the other is to tell you that I had a surprise communication from your mother.'

'My mother?' Angelique immediately thought he meant her adoptive mother in France, who she now thought of as her proper and only mother again.

He nodded. 'Yes, out of the blue I received a letter from Australia. Apparently she's planning to come back to England and has written to ask me if I could start getting together some furniture for her new house. She sent me a pretty comprehensive list, I can tell you.' He paused to order a pint of lager and then glanced inquiringly at Jordan and Angelique.

'Oh, nothing for me,' Jordan said quickly, 'but I think Angelique could do with a stiff Scotch, judging by the expression on her face.' He glanced at the barman and told him to make the drinks on the house.

'Thanks, you're a gent,' Martin said, raising his glass to Jordan. 'Cheers!'

After Martin left a couple of hours later – obviously slightly disgruntled to discover that Lesley did not want to go out on a date with him – Jordan took Angelique aside and asked her how she felt about possibly meeting her natural mother after all.

'It's strange really,' she said, gazing at him with dry eyes. 'I can't honestly claim to feel anything at all. Not excitement. Not anticipation. Not fear. Nothing at all To me she is just a woman. A name on a piece of paper. Does that make sense?'

Jordan nodded. 'You've finally managed to make your peace with your adoptive mother. Of course you feel ambivalent about this latest development.'

'I will see her though,' Angelique added quickly. 'As long as she wants to see me. And if she doesn't . . .?' She paused and shrugged. 'Well, I don't think I'll be crying myself to sleep over it.'

With a tremor of excitement she noticed a familiar expression take over Jordan's face. 'What?' she asked, knowing full well what he was thinking.

'You know what.'

'I know but I want you to tell me.' Her mouth suddenly dried and she licked her lips. It gave her a thrill to see how Jordan's gaze immediately transferred to her mouth. 'You like my mouth, don't you, Jordan?' she said.

He nodded. 'You know I do. And "like" is not a strong enough word.'

'Care to sample it?' she offered, her expression coquettish.

'What do you think?' Jordan leaned forward across the small table that separated them and traced the outline of her full lips with his fingertip before pressing his mouth to hers. Then he sat back and stared at her.

271

'What?' she asked again.

He shook his head. 'Nothing. I just wanted to look at you for a moment.' Reaching across the table he took her hands and turned them over to trace the lines on her palms. 'You have a long life-line,' he said. 'And a very positive heart-line.'

'Really?' She gazed down at her hands, not knowing one line from the other. 'What does that mean exactly?'

Jordan laughed lightly. 'It means you are going to live a long and happy life. One that is totally fulfilling in every way.'

Tears sprang to her eyes, but her smile was strong and unwavering. 'Harvey always tried to impress on me the importance of seizing happiness and that everyone is entitled to pleasure,' she said. 'Even in the last letter he wrote, he urged me to follow my desires wherever they may lead.' Her voice became husky and she edged closer to Jordan so that her breath caressed his face as she spoke. 'I shall never regret the fact that they led me here to you.'

Her heart hammered, knowing how hard he fought against the threat of commitment. But the look in his eyes and the answering grip on her hands were the only reassurance she needed.

It was true, things did have a way of working out.

Theirs might never be a conventional relationship but now, even given the option, she would not want it any other way. Jordan had shown her a way of loving and living that she intended to embrace whole-heartedly. And the other significant man in her life – Harvey – had left her a legacy far more important than mere money.

In her head she bade him a silent thank you, the memory no longer causing her pain she noticed with an inner sigh of relief. Then in a low, resolute voice, she told Jordan exactly how much she wanted him.

THE HOUSE IN NEW ORLEANS – Fleur Reynolds
ISBN 0 352 32951 3

ELENA'S CONQUEST – Lisette Allen
ISBN 0 352 32950 5

CASSANDRA'S CHATEAU – Fredrica Alleyn
ISBN 0 352 32955 6

WICKED WORK – Pamela Kyle
ISBN 0 352 32958 0

DREAM LOVER – Katrina Vincenzi
ISBN 0 352 32956 4

PATH OF THE TIGER – Cleo Cordell
ISBN 0 352 32959 9

BELLA'S BLADE – Georgia Angelis
ISBN 0 352 32965 3

THE DEVIL AND THE DEEP BLUE SEA – Cheryl
Mildenhall
ISBN 0 352 32966 1

WESTERN STAR – Roxanne Carr
ISBN 0 352 32969 6

A PRIVATE COLLECTION – Sarah Fisher
ISBN 0 352 32970 X

NICOLE'S REVENGE – Lisette Allen
ISBN 0 352 32984 X

UNFINISHED BUSINESS – Sarah Hope-Walker
ISBN 0 352 32983 1

CRIMSON BUCCANEER – Cleo Cordell
ISBN 0 352 32987 4

To be published in December

GOLD FEVER
Louisa Francis

The Australian outback is a harsh place by anyone's judgement. But in
the 1860s, things were especially tough for women. The feisty Ginny
Leigh is caught in a stifling marriage and yearns for fun and adventure.
Dan Berrigan is on the run, accused of a crime he didn't commit. When
they meet up in Wattle Creek, their lust for each other is immediate.
There's gold in the hills and their happiness seems certain. But can
Ginny outwit those determined to ruin her with scandal?

ISBN 0 352 33043 0

EYE OF THE STORM
Georgina Brown

Antonia thought she was in a long-term relationship with a globe-
trotting bachelor. She was not. His wife told her so. Seething with
anger, Toni decides to run away to sea. She gets a job on a yacht but
her new employers turn out to be far from normal. The owner of the
craft is in a constant state of bitter rivalry with his half-brother and the
arrival of their outrageous mother throws everyone into a spin. But the
one thing they all have in common is a love of bizarre sex.

ISBN 0 352 330044 9

Published in January

WHITE ROSE ENSNARED
Juliet Hastings

When the elderly Lionel, Lord de Verney, is killed in battle, his beautiful widow Rosamund finds herself at the mercy of Sir Ralph Aycliffe,
a dark knight, who will stop at nothing to humiliate her and seize her
property. Set against the Wars of the Roses, only the young squire
Geoffrey Lymington will risk all he owns to save the woman he have
loved for a single night. Who will prevail in the struggle for her body?

ISBN 0 352 33052 X

A SENSE OF ENTITLEMENT
Cheryl Mildenhall

When 24-year-old Angelique is summoned to the reading of her late
father's will, there are a few surprises in store for her. Not only was
her late father not her real father, but he's left her a large sum of money
and a half share in a Buckinghamshire hotel. The trouble is, Angelique
is going to have to learn to share the running of this particularly
strange hotel with the enigmatic Jordan; a man who knew her as a
child and now wants to know her as a woman.

ISBN 0 352 33053 8

To be published in February

ARIA APPASSIONATA
Juliet Hastings

Tess Challoner had landed the part of Carmen in a production of the opera which promises to be as raunchy as it is intelligent. But to play Carmen convincingly, she needs to learn a lot more about passion and erotic expression. Tony Varguez, the handsome but jealous tenor, takes on the role of her education. The scene is set for some sizzling performances and life begins to imitate art with dramatic consequences.

ISBN 0 352 33056 2

THE MISTRESS
Vivienne LaFay

It's the beginning of the twentieth century and Emma Longmore is making the most of her role as mistress to the dashing Daniel Forbes. Having returned from the Grand Tour and taken up residence in Daniel's Bloomsbury abode, she is now educating the daughters of forward-thinking people in the art of love. No stranger to fleshly pleasure herself, Emma's fancy soon turns to a young painter whom she is keen to give some very private tuition. Will Daniel accept her wanton behaviour or does he have his own agenda?

ISBN 0 352 33057 0

If you would like a complete list of plot summaries of Black Lace titles, please fill out the questionnaire overleaf or send a stamped addressed envelope to:-

Black Lace
332 Ladbroke Grove
London W10 5AH

WE NEED YOUR HELP . . .
to plan the future of women's erotic fiction –

– and no stamp required!

Yours are the only opinions that matter.

Black Lace is the first series of books devoted to erotic fiction by women for women.

We intend to keep providing the best-written, sexiest books you can buy. And we'd appreciate your help and valued opinion of the books so far. Tell us what you want to read.

THE BLACK LACE QUESTIONNAIRE

SECTION ONE: ABOUT YOU

1.1 Sex (*we presume you are female, but so as not to discriminate*)
Are you?

Male	☐
Female	☐

1.2 Age

under 21	☐	21–30	☐
31–40	☐	41–50	☐
51–60	☐	over 60	☐

1.3 At what age did you leave full-time education?

still in education	☐	16 or younger	☐
17–19	☐	20 or older	☐

1.4 Occupation _____

1.5 Annual household income

    under £10,000 ☐   £10–£20,000 ☐

    £20–£30,000 ☐   £30–£40,000 ☐

    over £40,000 ☐

1.6 We are perfectly happy for you to remain anonymous; but if you would like to receive information on other publications available, please insert your name and address

_____

_____

_____

_____

SECTION TWO: ABOUT BUYING BLACK LACE BOOKS

2.1 How did you acquire this copy of *A Sense of Entitlement*?

    I bought it myself ☐   My partner bought it ☐

    I borrowed/found it ☐

2.2 How did you find out about Black Lace books?

    I saw them in a shop ☐

    I saw them advertised in a magazine ☐

    I saw the London Underground posters ☐

    I read about them in _____

    Other _____

2.3 Please tick the following statements you agree with:

    I would be less embarrassed about buying Black Lace books if the cover pictures were less explicit ☐

    I think that in general the pictures on Black Lace books are about right ☐

    I think Black Lace cover pictures should be as explicit as possible ☐

2.4 Would you read a Black Lace book in a public place – on a train for instance?

    Yes ☐   No ☐

SECTION THREE: ABOUT THIS BLACK LACE BOOK

3.1   Do you think the sex content in this book is:
        Too much ☐ About right ☐
        Not enough ☐

3.2   Do you think the writing style in this book is:
        Too unreal/escapist ☐ About right ☐
        Too down to earth ☐

3.3   Do you think the story in this book is:
        Too complicated ☐ About right ☐
        Too boring/simple ☐

3.4   Do you think the cover of this book is:
        Too explicit ☐ About right ☐
        Not explicit enough ☐

Here's a space for any other comments:

SECTION FOUR: ABOUT OTHER BLACK LACE BOOKS

4.1   How many Black Lace books have you read? ☐

4.2   If more than one, which one did you prefer?

4.3   Why?

SECTION FIVE: ABOUT YOUR IDEAL EROTIC NOVEL

We want to publish the books you want to read – so this is your chance to tell us exactly what your ideal erotic novel would be like.

5.1   Using a scale of 1 to 5 (1 = no interest at all, 5 = your ideal), please rate the following possible settings for an erotic novel:

Medieval/barbarian/sword 'n' sorcery ☐
Renaissance/Elizabethan/Restoration ☐
Victorian/Edwardian ☐
1920s & 1930s – the Jazz Age ☐
Present day ☐
Future/Science Fiction ☐

5.2   Using the same scale of 1 to 5, please rate the following themes you may find in an erotic novel:

Submissive male/dominant female ☐
Submissive female/dominant male ☐
Lesbianism ☐
Bondage/fetishism ☐
Romantic love ☐
Experimental sex e.g. anal/watersports/sex toys ☐
Gay male sex ☐
Group sex ☐

Using the same scale of 1 to 5, please rate the following styles in which an erotic novel could be written:

Realistic, down to earth, set in real life ☐
Escapist fantasy, but just about believable ☐
Completely unreal, impressionistic, dreamlike ☐

5.3   Would you prefer your ideal erotic novel to be written from the viewpoint of the main male characters or the main female characters?

Male ☐   Female ☐
Both ☐

5.4 What would your ideal Black Lace heroine be like? Tick as many as you like:

Dominant	☐	Glamorous	☐
Extroverted	☐	Contemporary	☐
Independent	☐	Bisexual	☐
Adventurous	☐	Naive	☐
Intellectual	☐	Introverted	☐
Professional	☐	Kinky	☐
Submissive	☐	Anything else?	☐
Ordinary	☐	_____	

5.5 What would your ideal male lead character be like? Again, tick as many as you like:

Rugged	☐		
Athletic	☐	Caring	☐
Sophisticated	☐	Cruel	☐
Retiring	☐	Debonair	☐
Outdoor-type	☐	Naive	☐
Executive-type	☐	Intellectual	☐
Ordinary	☐	Professional	☐
Kinky	☐	Romantic	☐
Hunky	☐		
Sexually dominant	☐	Anything else?	☐
Sexually submissive	☐	_____	

5.6 Is there one particular setting or subject matter that your ideal erotic novel would contain?

_____

SECTION SIX: LAST WORDS

6.1 What do you like best about Black Lace books?

_____

6.2 What do you most dislike about Black Lace books?

_____

6.3 In what way, if any, would you like to change Black Lace covers?

_____

6.4   Here's a space for any other comments:

_____

_____

_____

_____

Thank you for completing this questionnaire. Now tear it out of the book – carefully! – put it in an envelope and send it to:

> **Black Lace**
> **FREEPOST**
> **London**
> **W10 5BR**

No stamp is required if you are resident in the U.K.